The Ides of Daisy March

by

Sally Patricia Gardner

Henry May Publications

To Ro, with love and thanks for putting up with me when Daisy took over my life!

And to Tara, my proof reader, to Lin and Sian for their invaluable input, and to my lovely family, Alexander, Ali, James and Pete for their help and enthusiasm.

And once again, my thanks to Shorelink Writers, for your support, encouragement and wonderful friendship.

Contents

February.........1916

May 1919

August...........1922

January...........1926

June............... 1927

May............... 1929

October.......... 1931

April..............1932

August...........1934

February.........1935

July 1937

April.............. 1938

February.........1940

April.............. 1941

August........... 1944

September.......1945

January........... 1947

The Ides of Daisy March

February, 1916

I was five years old when my mother told me that she was not my mother. I had, or rather I thought I had, two older brothers, Alfred and George. Otherwise known as Alfie and Georgie. They were the joy of my life, playing silly games with me, teasing me, always making me laugh. I loved them. I was always a bit puzzled because they called our mother Mum and I always called her MumMarch. But our surname was March, so I thought, if I thought about it at all, that I was allowed to call her by a special name because I was the girl in the family. Privileged.

Talking of privilege, a very Posh Lady used to come and see us sometimes. MumMarch would dress me in my best white lacy frock, and brush my shoes and my hair until they shone. The Posh Lady, as we children called her, would stay in her carriage and MumMarch would take me out to her. The door opened at our approach, as if by magic, and I climbed inside and sat opposite her. The carriage was quite dark and she always wore dark clothes, so she was a shadowy figure to me. Once I was seated, The Posh Lady would tell the driver to go on by banging on the small window behind her seat.

We drove around for what seemed like ages, the carriage swaying gently. To the background music of the horse's hooves she asked me questions about what I had been doing since her last visit, and I would do my best to answer. The highlights of my life were playing with my brothers, when they came home from school, and helping

MumMarch in the kitchen. Young as I was, I didn't think that being allowed to scrape the cake mixture from the bowl and lick the wooden spoon was quite what The Posh Lady wanted to hear. So I rapidly ran out of conversation.

At this point in our meetings, she would invariably ask whether I had learnt to read some of the books she had left for me on her previous visits. I had always read them, because I liked reading. I don't remember learning, I just always did it. I used to read them to my brothers, although I was by far the youngest, because neither of them could read as well as me. I thought that was probably why The Posh Lady took me out and not them. On the day I found out that my mother was not my mother I had just finished reading *The Secret Garden*. At the beginning I felt sorry for Mary because she was an orphan, but by the end I wanted to be her. So I told The Posh Lady that.

When she dropped me back home, she did something she had never done before. She kissed me. On the forehead. In all our meetings she had never touched me before.

Then she said, "I will be seeing you again tomorrow, Daisy. You must make sure you are ready when I come for you."

I nodded and jumped out of the carriage, disappointed that she had not given me another book, but then I thought that if she was coming again tomorrow, she might bring me one then.

When I got indoors, MumMarch was waiting for me. The boys didn't ever start eating their tea till I got home and they were already at the table, waiting. Usually the kitchen would be full of chatter about what they had done at school that day, but today it was unusually quiet.

MumMarch sent me upstairs to change out of my lacy dress and put my pinafore on which I did really quickly because all the buttons were at the front. When I came down, MumMarch had cut up a whole loaf of bread and Alfie was toasting slices in front of the fire.

"Dripping toast, Daisy. Your favourite. Special treat." MumMarch sounded funny, not quite like herself.

Georgie, who was older than Alfie by a whole year and was nearly nine, held out his arms to me. "Come on, shrimp, you can sit on my lap while the toast is doing."

This was a very special treat, usually reserved for when I fell over or was upset about something, so, giggling, I skipped across the room and launched myself onto his lap before he could change his mind. He pretended my weight had knocked him over and fell back in the chair, but he still held on to me tightly, which made me laugh even more.

MumMarch began to put the dripping on the hot slices of toast. "Put her down, Georgie. Time for tea."

I climbed down reluctantly and slid onto my own chair. The warm toast with the rich dripping soaking into it tasted as good as it smelt. For several minutes we all concentrated on munching away. Alfie was constantly replacing the bread on the long toasting fork while eating his own, still squatting by the fire with his face flushed from the heat. Finally the last piece was consumed and MumMarch refilled our mugs with milk. This was the bit of the day I always enjoyed, when the kitchen was warm and cosy and we were all together and comfortably full of food. MumMarch said it was our special 'together time'.

Sometimes one of the boys would sing a song, or recite a poem they had learned at school, so that when I was old enough to go I would know what sort of thing to expect. I would be old enough to go to school with them next term which I was very excited about.

Today, Georgie had learnt a song about a boy called Danny, and he sang it for us. It was quite a mournful tune. MumMarch had her sad face on when he sang it, like those times when she read us a letter from Father, who was at the war. I did not really understand where or what the war was, but Georgie said Father was very brave, and was fighting for us all. He said Father was especially brave, as he hadn't had to go but had volunteered. MumMarch had a slightly cross face on when Georgie said that, and I sometimes thought she would rather that he had stayed at home.

I didn't really remember Father at all, as I was very small when he went away, and the boys said he used to work for The Posh Lady, so he wasn't home much even when he was not at the war. MumMarch says he would have lost his job anyway as all the posh people have been asked to let their servants go to fight in the war.

"When I am old enough, I shall go to the war," said Alfie, and he mimed holding a big gun. "Bang, bang, you're dead," he shouted, aiming his pretend gun at Georgie.

Joining in the fun, Georgie clutched at his arm and pretended to fall over dead.

"That's enough, boys. Calm down. I want to talk to Daisy. If you've finished your tea, go and play outside, you can help clear up later." MumMarch sounded strange, not quite like herself, and I suddenly felt anxious about what she was going to tell me.

She waited until the boys had gone, then she sat in the big chair by the fire. She usually only did that when she was knitting or mending things at night, so I knew this was important.

"Come and sit here, Daisy." She motioned to the footstool at her feet.

I sat down on it, and looked up at her. I was shocked to see she had tears on her cheeks. She brushed them away, and then smiled at me, and bent and stroked my hair.

"Daisy, something terribly exciting is going to happen tomorrow, but it might seem a little bit strange at first, so you are going to have to be very brave and not make a fuss."

I looked up at her indignantly. "I never make a fuss."

She laughed. "No, you don't. You are my very good girl. That is why I am pleased for you, because tomorrow you are going to live with Mrs Gosling, and you will have lots of things, and lots of opportunities, that I cannot give you. You are a lucky girl, who is going to have a lovely life."

I stared up at her, uncomprehending. Mrs Gosling was The Posh Lady. "But you'll be coming too? And Georgie and Alfie?"

"No. Daisy. They will be staying here with me. But I hope you will be able to come back and see us sometimes."

In spite of the warmth of the fire, the horror seeped into my head and body like cold mud. I began to shiver. I could hear my voice coming out all squeaky, like it belonged to someone else. "But I can't go and live anywhere else, MumMarch. That's silly."

She turned her head away and another thought hit me. "Is it because I've been naughty and you don't love me anymore? I know I went back to sleep again this morning and nearly made everyone late, and I spilt milk all down my pinafore yesterday and had to have another one, and I ..."

"No. Stop, Daisy. It is because Mrs Gosling is your real mother. Don't you remember that I told you the story about the little girl who had two mummies, and that I was the one who would have to give her back? I told you that you were that little girl, Daisy, you must remember."

"But it was a story." My voice came out shrill and jerky. "Please, please, don't send me away. I love you."

"Oh, Daisy, I love you too." Her voice was funny as well. "But I have tried to prepare us both for this day. I knew it would be difficult, but ..." her voice broke and I could see she was crying too. "Daisy, for all sorts of reasons, which she will tell you herself one day, Mrs Gosling, your real mother, couldn't keep you. So she asked me, who she knew would love you and look after you, to have you until you could go and live with her. And we have been happy, haven't we?"

I nodded dumbly. "But I want to go on being happy with you. I don't want to go and live with her. She is not my mother, you are. I know you are."

MumMarch bent down and pulled me onto her lap. This was unusual enough in itself for me to suddenly know with certainty that I was leaving her, and I could not control the howl of pain that emerged. She cuddled me closely while sobs racked my body, and when they finally abated as sheer exhaustion took over, she mopped my face with her big hankie. I became aware of the boys' anxious faces peering round the door, but MumMarch must have shaken her head at them as they disappeared and the door clicked shut.

I looked up at her worried face and realised that she was crying too. "I thought you loved me. I am your best girl. You can't send me away," I gulped, the tears welling up again.

She set me down on the floor again, and my legs were so wobbly that I sank to my knees in front of her. I put my head in her lap, still warm from holding my small body, and felt her stroking my hair.

"Daisy, I do love you. I will always love you. But so does Mrs Gosling. And it has been very difficult for her not being able to live with you. She has worked hard to make a home for you both, and she is looking forward to you both being happy together. You are a kind girl and you must not disappoint or upset her. You must play a pretend game of being very pleased to be going to live with her, and then the pretend will start to be real."

I thought about that. I knew about pretend games, we played them all the time. Sometimes I was a pretend princess, which I liked a lot. Though once Alfie was a pretend pirate and had captured me and tied me to a real tree, and then gone off and forgotten me. MumMarch said if Georgie hadn't remembered me I would have caught my death of cold and she was quite cross with my brothers. But I knew I would be rescued and thought it was all very exciting. The memory of it caused a tremulous smile to cross my face, and MumMarch gave a sigh of relief.

"Now, Daisy, we are going to leave the boys to wash up the tea things, and we are going to pack up your things and put them in my carpet bag, which you can take with you."

MumMarch knew that I loved her big carpet bag which was red and covered with pink roses. When I was very tiny, and we were playing hide and seek one Christmas, I hid in it and no-one found me for ages and ages. After that, I would often creep inside it and it became my magic place. Once inside its dark and comfortable embrace, when it was winter I would dream of running in the fields in the sun, and when it was summer, I dreamt of snow and skidding round with the boys on the icy lake. I was much too big to get inside it now, of course, but I knew it still held my dreams.

"Can I really take it with me? And keep it until I can come back and see you?"

"You can keep it forever, Daisy. I am giving it to you."

That wasn't quite the reassuring answer I was hoping for, but I was still excited by the gift, and I hopped up the staircase in front of MumMarch and waited while she fetched it from her bedroom.

"Can I take Percy?" Percy was my cuddly pink rabbit who always came to bed with me. He had lived with me for as long as I could remember, and life without him was unthinkable.

"Of course you can."

"And every time I come home, I will put him and all my things in it." We both heard the wobble in my voice as we started to fold up my clothes and lay them in the bag. It didn't take very long as my wardrobe was adequate but definitely not extravagant. When my clothes were in, I reached into the small bookcase sitting under the window that Father had made for me before he left us.

"Oh, we should have put your books in first. How silly of me." MumMarch had a wobble in her voice too.

We carefully took out my folded clothes and lay them next to Percy and then piled the books into the bottom of

11

the bag. Finally, everything was back again and MumMarch placed the bag, unfastened as Percy would not go in until the morning, by the empty bookcase. I think it was the sight of that looking so bare and forlorn, that brought the reality of the situation back to me.

"Please, please, don't make me go?" It was a question, an entreaty, but I already understood that it would make no difference.

At that moment Georgie's head came round the door. "Are you finished? You must come downstairs, Daisy, Alfie and me have got something for you."

Downstairs, Alfie was standing in front of the fire. He had emptied out the old coal scuttle and stood with it on his head, black smears running down his face. He carried MumMarch's mop in front of him. MumMarch started to say something, but before she could, Georgie plonked MumMarch's peg bag on his head, and picking up a saucepan lid and the rolling pin, went and stood beside Alfie and announced in a loud voice: "The March brothers will now give a farewell concert in honour of Miss Daisy March."

They had pushed the armchair into the middle of the room, and MumMarch sat in it and pulled me onto her lap. Georgie banged the lid loudly, and Alfie began to march round in circles, singing *KKKKaty*, which was one of the popular songs of the time, only he had changed it to *DDDDaisy*, and every time he got to that, both the boys saluted me, which made me giggle. By the time they got to the end, my tummy was hurting with laughing so much.

Both the boys had lovely voices, and next they sang *It's a long way to Tipperary*, and they knew all the words. When they got to the end, they put back down the mop and the rolling pin and came and grasped my hands and swung me off MumMarch's lap. Then round and round the room we went, all singing *Pack Up Your Troubles In Your Old Kit Bag*. When we got to the smiling bit, they tickled me until I had to beg them to stop. And finally they did, and my concert was over. We fell, exhausted, onto the chairs, all laughing and still singing bits of the songs.

"That was lovely," laughed MumMarch. "Thank you, boys."

"Yes," I said between latent attacks of hilarity, "Thank you." And I felt my laughter subside as I looked at them both, and I said solemnly, "I shall never, ever forget my concert."

And I never have.

The following morning I was up early and dressed in my coat and boots, with the carpet bag at my feet. I waited at the gate, holding MumMarch's hand, for the coach to arrive. When it did, I was surprised that it was not Mrs Gosling sitting in it, but a lady that I didn't know. She jumped out came across to me.

"You must be Daisy? I am Emma. Mrs Gosling sent me to bring you home."

I opened my mouth to say that I was home already, but then I caught the slight shake of her head that MumMarch gave me, so I just said, "Thank you."

'Come on, then. Oh, is that your bag? How pretty it is." And without pausing for breath, she picked it up and put it inside the coach. Then she turned and saw that I was clutching MumMarch tightly.

"Oh, Daisy, I am sorry. Do you want me to get back inside the coach while you say goodbye?"

But there was nothing more to say. I squeezed MumMarch's lovely warm, comforting hand and then reached up and kissed her cheek. Then I jumped into the coach and flopped down beside Emma. She banged on the window just like The Posh Lady, and we were off, trotting into another world. I stared out of the window, willing myself not to cry.

"Daisy?"

Her voice was gentle and concerned. I turned to face her. She was not old like The Posh Lady, and for the first time I wondered about her. She seemed to understand the question in my head without me asking.

"I work for Mrs Gosling." She giggled in a way that made her seem much more like Alfie and Georgie than a proper grown up. "I am what they call a 'maid of all work'. That means there is only me, trying to do everything. Well, except the cooking. Mrs Grant does that. That's why I stay there really, because she's teaching me how to do all sorts of stuff, and when I know enough, I'll be off. I might even be able to go and work in America."

I stared at her in awe. I knew America was another country, because Georgie had learnt about it at school. But I suddenly felt I didn't want her to go away.

"But you won't go yet?" I asked.

She laughed again, and bending over, untied my bonnet and laid it on the seat opposite us. "We'll put that back on when we get there. No, I won't go off yet. My young man is at the war, and I'm waiting for when he gets back, and then we'll be married and go together. He's from Ireland, and his Auntie is out there already. He says it's a fine place and we'll get very rich." She paused as if she was not quite sure of this, and then she laughed again, shrugging her shoulders as if to say that she knew it would all turn out well.

I decided she was very pretty, with her reddish brown hair and dark eyes. I had dark eyes, but my hair was very fair, which I thought made me look a bit odd.

She smiled at me. "Now, Daisy, tell me about you. Mrs Gosling told me yesterday I had to go and fetch her daughter, and you could have knocked me down with a feather. So where did you spring from?"

I had no idea how to answer her question any way but truthfully, so I replied, "I don't know." How could I explain that I had even less idea what I was doing, or where I was going, than she did? I felt that I should offer something more, as she had told me so much, so I added, "My mother says I must be very good."

Misunderstanding, Emma laughed, "Well, I suppose that is what she is hoping."

"Oh, no, I meant my real mother, MumMarch, she ..." I caught the look of bewilderment on her face and realised that I had said the wrong thing. I frantically tried to put it right, babbling, "No, sorry, I, um, I mean my other mother, I mean, oh..." It was all too much; I put my face in my hands and was unable to stem my tears.

Emma drew me close and put her arms round me. "You poor little mite. Here, let's dry your tears. Come on." She wiped my face with a soft handkerchief, which she tucked into my coat pocket. "There, that's in case you need it again. But I don't think you will. She's a nice enough lady, Mrs Gosling. You'll be alright. She'll look after you. And, so, Daisy-pops, will I." She began to hum a little tune around my name, which made me laugh through my tears.

"*Daisy, Daisy, give me your answer do, look up and smile – there that will do!* Come along then, join in!"

And I did, tremulously at first, but we sang it more and more lustily, till she changed it to *Little Miss Daisy* and we both tried to think of something to rhyme that was like tuffet, and that made us laugh even more. And then the coach stopped, and Emma looked out of the window, and reached for my bonnet and tied it back on.

"We've arrived, Daisy-pops. Now, big smile. I can't see Mrs Gosling waiting, but she said to take you through to the drawing room as soon as you got here, so that's what we'll do."

"Can I have my carpet bag, please?"

"Don't worry, I've got it."

She opened the door and jumped out, taking my bag with her. Then she waited while I climbed out, a bit stiff from sitting so long. The coach pulled away, and we walked up a short path through a pretty garden with lots of trees. The house in front of us was tall, I could see four lots of windows between the black front door and the roof, but it was not huge. We went past the front of the house and through a door at the back which led into a large kitchen. It felt cosy, not unlike the one at home, only bigger. It was warm but there was no-one working there.

"I'll take your bag up to your room. No – don't look so worried," she held up her hand to stem my embryo protest, "I won't let any harm come to it and I won't open it until you are there. I just don't want you having to drag it around, right?"

I didn't want to be parted with this precious gift, so I hesitated, but her smiling face convinced me. "Right," I agreed.

She led me along a passageway and then up a short flight of stairs. At the top of these was a small room with a chair in it and an umbrella stand. I would later realise that this was the front hall and that the kitchen was in the basement. Emma knocked on a door, and I heard The Posh Lady's voice calling me in. I swallowed hard as Emma gave me a gentle shove which propelled me into the room, before disappearing with my bag.

Mrs Gosling was sitting on a small sofa by a large window, and the thin winter sun was shining on her hair, which I noticed was the same colour as mine. She was wearing a dark red dress with lace at the neck and I realised that I had never seen her without her hat and furry wraps and long coat before. She stood up and came across to me with both arms outstretched. I thought she was going to cuddle me, but she dropped her arms to her sides before she reached me and stood smiling but just out of reach.

"Daisy. How lovely to see you. I have waited a long time for this moment, my dear. Come and sit with me."

She took my hand and led me over to sit beside her. I was trembling with the strangeness of everything and couldn't think of anything to say. Indeed, I was not sure what, if anything, was required of me, so I sat down and looked at the carpet, which was a pretty blue with swirling patterns in darker colours.

"Did you have a nice journey?"

I nodded.

An uncomfortable silence fell between us, broken with, "Shall we take your coat off?"

17

As she bent over me I shrank back and pulled my coat tightly round me. I knew that MumMarch would have said that was rude, but I couldn't stop myself. She moved slightly away from me, and sighed quietly. I carried on clutching my coat and staring at my booted feet.

"Daisy, we have to get to know each other. Look at me, please." Her voice was mild and slightly uncertain. I looked up at her. She put out a hand as if she was going to touch my face, but then withdrew it sharply. I jumped, for a moment thinking she was going to slap me.

"Oh, Daisy, I didn't mean to startle you." Again, she half moved toward me, and this time I thought she was going to embrace me. I didn't know whether I wanted her to or not, but then she rose and crossed to the fireplace and pulled on a rope. A clanging noise rang through the house. Emma appeared almost before it had stopped echoing.

"Emma, will you take Daisy to her room, please, and help her put her things away. Then she will come back here while you make us both some refreshment." She paused, "Daisy, what would you like to drink? Some hot milk, perhaps?"

I nodded.

"I didn't hear that." She repeated the question.

"Yes, please." My voice was shaky.

"That's better. I am sure you have been taught good manners, Daisy, and I expect you to practice them at all times. Now, go with Emma, and I will see you later."

I followed Emma up a long flight of very wide stairs. On the landing there were two doors, and she pointed to one of them.

"That's Mrs Gosling's room. This one is yours."

18

She threw open the door to the prettiest bedroom I had ever seen. Even the ones in my picture books were not as pretty as this. The walls were covered in light blue paper with flowers and leaves so real it looked as if they were actually growing. The bed had a blue canopy over it and four large posts round it and a matching blue cover. Even the carpet was blue with little green flowers. There were two windows with places to sit and look out built under them, and a chest of drawers and a dressing table with a mirror on it. In the far corner was a small table with a large jug and basin on it. I walked over to that, and turned to Emma.

"What is this for?"

"It's a washstand, silly. Every morning I shall fill the jug and bring it up to you so you can have your wash and get dressed before you go downstairs for your breakfast."

I was impressed. At home we washed at the kitchen sink, and there was always competition between me and the boys to get there before the water got cool and scummy. This was an unheard of luxury.

"Come on then, let's unpack this bag of yours." Emma undid it, and I reached in and rescued Percy, who was lying face-up waiting for me. I gave him a quick cuddle and laid him carefully on the bed. We began to take out my clothes. I was wearing my best dress so I thought I had better take it off and put my pinafore on, but Emma stopped me.

"No need to change. Mrs Gosling has had lots of new things made for you. Look." She went to a cupboard in the corner that I had not noticed, and I could see some frocks hanging there. They were all beautiful. A rainbow of pastel colours, and three coats in darker colours at the end of the rail.

I gasped. "Are those all for me?"

"They are, you lucky girl."

I caught a slight envy in Emma's voice, and turned to give her a hug.

"Has she made some for you, too?"

Emma laughed. "No, little one, I am afraid not. But I shall enjoy seeing you in them. And one day I shall be a toff and have some smart clothes to march around in."

"When you are in America?"

"That's right. Now, enough dreaming. Let's get you unpacked and tidied up before we go back downstairs. Can you brush your own hair?"

I took the brush she was holding and said indignantly, "Of course I can. I am five years old, not a baby."

"Ooh, sorry, Ma'am," said Emma, making a mock curtsey, and we both giggled.

As I tidied my hair I thought that perhaps being here with Emma might be alright, after all.

When we got back downstairs Mrs Gosling was sitting by the window again, and as I entered I could see she was knitting.

"Oh, I can knit! MumMarch taught me, and she says I am quite good at it. I have been helping to knit scarves for our soldiers. Can I do some?"

"That is a good idea, Daisy. Here, I will find you some needles and, let me see, how about this wool?"

She rummaged in a knitting bag like MumMarch's and took out some dark grey wool, which seemed quite a good colour for soldiers' scarves, so I started to nod, then I remembered that nodding might not be a good idea, so I said, "I think that will do very nicely," in my most grown up voice, and Mrs Gosling looked up and smiled at me.

20

By the time Emma came in holding a tray with my milk and a cup of tea for Mrs Gosling, we were sitting side by side knitting. I could hear some wood pigeons cooing in the garden, and they formed a background to the clicking of our needles. It was strange to be so quiet and also a bit uncomfortable. MumMarch and I were always chatting or singing, so even when the boys were at school the house was never quiet.

Mrs Gosling certainly didn't talk much, and I remembered how often MumMarch had told me to "cease your prattling, Daisy," when she was busy. But it was always accompanied with a smile and she didn't seem to mind when I carried on anyway. However, perhaps grownups really didn't speak as much as children and I resolved to become used to that.

Emma seemed to be something between a child and a grownup, for she cheerfully broke into the silence as she placed the tray on a small table. "Mrs Grant has just arrived. She says what do you want for dinner tonight, and will you want to eat it earlier so the child can have it with you?"

"Tell her we will have the fish tonight, and that Daisy and I will dine at five-thirty. That is thoughtful of her." Mrs Gosling looked down at me. "Is that the time you usually have dinner, Daisy?"

I was confused, and I looked to see if Emma could help. As if she could read my mind, she jumped in.

"Mrs Gosling wants to know what time you have your tea, Daisy?"

I breathed a sigh of relief and smiled my thanks. "We have it about five o'clock, when the boys are home from school, and we all help to get it ready."

Emma nodded, looking from Mrs Gosling to me. "And when do you have your dinner?"

"Oh, that depends on what MumMarch is doing. On Mondays we have it really late because by the time we have wrung the washing out and put it out on the line, some days it is almost afternoon. But because it is such hard work, we have soup with our bread that day, to keep the cold out, MumMarch says."

Mrs Gosling nodded. "Thank you, Emma." She turned to me. "That is the meal we call lunch. Do you think you can remember that?"

"You mean that dinner is called lunch?"

"Good girl. So, Emma, we will have cold meat and pickles for lunch in," she glanced at a large clock on the mantelpiece, "in about an hour. Perhaps you will tell Mrs Grant that, and also that I am expecting a visitor tomorrow and will she make some of her delicious scones as he will be staying for tea?"

I was really confused now. So 'tea' hadn't vanished but was still somewhere around.

After Emma had disappeared, presumably to talk to Mrs Grant, we got back to our knitting. But eventually I decided that I must endeavour to clarify when we were going to eat what.

I cleared my throat, put my knitting carefully into my lap, and said, in my best polite voice, "Mrs Gosling, when ..." but before I could get any further, she interrupted me.

"Daisy, you mustn't call me that."

My face must have shown that I was becoming more perplexed by the minute.

"But I thought that was your name?" I stammered. "MumMarch said it was, and Emma just called you that."

I could hear the tears welling up behind my voice and, panic-stricken, knew I was about to cry.

She dropped her knitting onto the sofa and took my hand. "Oh, Daisy, don't cry, I don't mean to sound cross. But you see, I want you to call me Mother."

I stared at her, all the events of the last day crowding into my head, and I couldn't any longer stop the tears. "But you are not my mother," I sobbed. "You are The Posh Lady who brings me books. I want to go home. Please let me go home. I don't like it here."

She reached out as if to touch me then withdrew to the far end of the sofa. "Daisy, I am your mother and that is what you will call me. And you will live here, with me, because this is your home. I thought Mrs March had prepared you better for today. Now use your handkerchief and dry your face, child. I have a present for you, but not if you are crying. I was going to give it to you tomorrow when our visitor is here, but I think you should have it today. I do understand how strange all this is for you." This last sentence was spoken in an undertone, almost to herself. "Wait here. No crying, please. I will return in a minute."

She crossed to the door, her long skirt sweeping gracefully round her. I was irresistibly reminded of MumMarch's shorter and stouter figure hitching up her skirts as she bent to the oven. It made me want to cry again, but the thought of the present stopped me. I wondered if it was a new book. I did hope so.

After a few minutes, as I was beginning to fidget, I heard a scuffling sound outside the door. My mother threw it open and I saw her smiling at me and holding something small, and furry and wriggling. She crossed the room and placed it in my lap.

23

"This is Sooty. He is all yours, Daisy. Mrs March told me that you have always wanted a dog, and he has come to live with us today, just like you. In puppy years, he is the same age as you. So you will be his mother, and I shall be yours, and we will all grow used to each other. What do you think?"

I held the squirming bundle close and looked into his lovely, black, face. My tears were still damp on my cheeks, but I brushed them away impatiently. "Thank you, Mother," I whispered.

May 1919

It is such a beautiful morning and there is no school today, so I am playing in the garden with Sooty. He has chewed his favourite yellow ball into lots of small pieces but Emma bought him another one when she came to see us yesterday. Then we pulled one of Mother's chairs out of the drawing room into the garden, and Emma took a photograph of Sooty and me on it with her camera. Emma told me it is a Kodak Black Box Brownie, which I think is a bit of a mouthful. A photograph is like a drawing only more real. She has to do all sorts of things to it before I can see it, but she says she will show it to me when she comes to see us next week.

Emma is going to live with Joe's aunt in America. She is the person who sent her the camera. Emma is excited, but sad, too. She and Joe got married when Joe came home from the war, just like they planned. Mother and I went with Mrs Grant to the wedding, which was lovely. Emma was so happy, and afterwards she gave me her flowers which Mother let me put in my bedroom.

It was the first wedding I had ever been to, and it was in the small church near here so we didn't have far to go. Emma wore a very pretty, creamy coloured, dress, which stopped slightly above her ankles. Mrs Grant said, "Hmm. Very modern," when she saw Emma, and I sort of felt that she didn't like the dress much, but I thought Emma looked beautiful. Mother held my hand very tightly during the ceremony, and at one point I thought she was going to cry. But I knew that was silly. Mother never cries. Emma says she never laughs, either, though that is not really true because she laughs at Sooty sometimes.

It was very lonely when Emma left, though I quite like my school. But I think I am a bit more clever than most of the others, because sometimes we have stuff explained to us that I have known for ages. It is only when we are doing arithmetic that I really feel I am learning things. I like the games we play in the playground, though, and the songs we sing.

When I get home, after tea every day I go down into the kitchen to fetch Sooty and play with him and I try to remember interesting things about school to tell Mrs Grant. Sometimes she lets me help with the cooking. She is very nice, but this is a very quiet house. I wish I still had brothers.

Now that I am able to write quite well, Mother lets me send letters to MumMarch and the boys. I tell them all about Sooty, and about what I am doing at school. Sometimes MumMarch writes back and she says that they are all well and busy. She says Georgie is doing alright at school but he is still not as good as me at writing. That makes me sad, but both the boys put big kisses on the bottom of her letters so I know they have not forgotten me.

Even though I still miss them all, I know I am lucky because I have Mother and Sooty and Mrs Grant, and Emma only has an aunt in America that she has never met. After the wedding, she and Joe went to live in London, and Joe had a job driving one of the new big red buses. That was so they could save up for the fare to America. But Joe got ill, almost straight away. Mrs Grant's newspaper said: 'Flu is sweeping through the capital, killing thousands'. And it killed Joe.

All those years they waited for the war to be over, and then they had barely two months of being married. Emma

went to live with her big sister for a while, as their parents are both dead. She had a job in one of the big London shops, but she didn't enjoy it very much. But then Joe's aunt wrote and asked her to come and live with her, and Emma thought, 'Why not?'

She said to me, "Daisy-pops, there is nothing for me here, except perhaps working in a shop till I die. Even if I thought I might love another man, there's not many left, are there?"

She was right, of course. Mrs Grant went on all the time about all the young men lost in the war. So, Emma was off to America.

"To make my fortune," she said. She was serious. She didn't laugh or giggle much anymore. But she was my friend, and I knew she was going out of my life forever very soon, and the photograph might be all I would have left of her.

Sir is coming to see us this afternoon, so I must be careful not to get muddy. He comes every month and Mrs Grant has to make her special scones because he stays for tea. On the other days that is just a cup of tea (milk for me) and a piece of cake for Mother, which we have when I get home from school. Mother usually asks me then what books I am reading, and she sometimes asks who I have played with. But the big thing is that when Sir comes I am allowed to take Sooty into the drawing room, and he has a biscuit with us. Mostly when I am not home Mrs Grant looks after him downstairs. Though Mother doesn't know that I often sneak downstairs in the night to make sure he is not lonely, as Mrs Grant goes home to Mr Grant after we have had our dinner.

Sir is Mother's best friend. She doesn't have any other friends that visit us, so perhaps he is her only

27

friend. But Mother's sister, Aunty Hannah, comes to see us sometimes. I can tell she doesn't like me, she can hardly bring herself to say hallo before looking away, and Mother always says, "You can go and play now, Daisy," before I even have a chance to put Sooty down.

But Sir is different. I think he likes me. Mother is always different when he comes. Sort of happy and smiley. Sir makes me and Sooty sit beside him and he asks me all sorts of questions, not silly ones like '*What did you do at school today?*' but interesting things, like have I noticed the bluebells are out and why do I think they grow under the trees and in the woods. Then he shows me which of Mother's books in the big bookcase will have the answer, so I can tell him next time. He tells me lots of things about the moon and stars and clouds, all sorts of stuff you think about in your head but don't know how to find out.

The last time he was here he said, "Shall we walk around the garden to see if any birds are nesting there?" Not 'we will do this' but 'shall we?' as if it was important that I wanted to. And, of course, I did. We found two nests, but they were too high up for us to see if there were any eggs, but I promised to keep watch and tell him which birds I saw on them. He thinks Sooty is lovely, and told me all about spaniels and their history. I want to tell him today that I have told Sooty that his ancestors came from Spain and that I found some pictures of them in a book, which was very exciting.

I have managed to keep my dress clean, fortunately it is brown velvet and only the collar is white, so even if I haven't it doesn't really matter. I heard Sir's coach arrive and waited for Mother to call me in. When she did, I went over to Sir and curtsied the way Mother had taught me and said, "Good afternoon, Sir. Did you have a nice journey?"

Sir twinkled down at me. He stood up when I came in and he is very tall, so I have to put my head right back to see him. But I am eight years old now and growing quite tall for my age, so that is not as hard as it used to be. I had Sooty under my arm, but Mother nodded that I could put him down. Then Sir sat down and Sooty sat on his feet. He never does that with anyone else, not even Mrs Grant. I think it might be because Sir sometimes drops crumbs from his scones and Sooty licks them up, but I don't say that.

Sir was sitting on the chaise opposite Mother, and he patted it so I should come and sit with him.

Mother said, "I think Daisy has something important to tell you, Jacob." And she smiled at me.

So I told him about finding the pictures, and telling Sooty. He picked Sooty up and asked him if he spoke Spanish before putting him back on the floor, and we all laughed, even Mother, because Sooty looked as if he was trying to think of something to say to him. Then I told him about Emma taking the photograph of us, and that I might have it to show him next time he came.

"I have some exciting news for you both, as well," he said, looking from me to Mother. "I have bought an automobile! And next time I come, I shall be driving that. And I want to take you out. So, Susan my dear, I shall come early, and Mrs Grant will pack up a picnic for us, and we shall go for an excursion into the country. But you must wear warm clothes, it can get quite cold when we go fast."

My mother gasped. "Jacob, are you sure?"

He laughed. "Not frightened of my driving, are you my dear?"

"No, of course not. Just, well, what if we meet someone ...?" Her hesitancy seemed to amuse him.

"In that unlikely circumstance, we explain that I am merely taking my friend's widow and her daughter for a drive. Come along, Susan. It will be an adventure."

"Can Sooty come too?"

In my excitement, I forgot about not interrupting, but Mother didn't seem to notice and Sir responded with, "Of course he can. How can we have an outing without our Spanish Spaniel?"

I picked up Sooty and did a little dance with him. Life was much more fun when Sir came. And we were going in an automobile! I could hardly wait.

"Can I tell them at school?"

"No!" that was Mother.

"Darling, it will be alright, the child needs some freedom. A friend of the family is taking you for a picnic in an automobile. What is there to be worried about?"

Mother was silent for a minute, and I stopped dancing to watch her. She put her hand up to Sir's face and he kissed it.

Mother said softly, "You are always so confident. But we walk such a fragile path."

"Nonsense. Now, come along, Daisy, let us take Sooty into the garden and throw a ball for him."

Which we did. But Mother's words, tinged as they were with sadness, stayed in my head.

We had such an exciting day! My head was still whirling with it all when we got back, and I rushed downstairs with Sooty to see Mrs Grant. She has never been in an automobile and wanted to know all about it. Her daughter, whose name is Joyce, was there as well. When Emma left to get married Joyce started to come and help Mother in the house. I think she is quite old. I overheard Sir saying that Joyce was 'getting on a bit'. She is very nice but not so much fun as Emma.

"Goodness, don't you look smart?" said Joyce, who was tidying out the larder and wiping down the shelves.

I was wearing a new sailor suit that Sir had given me and it was smart, but more than that, it was soft and loose and light, and let me move easily. But I did not want to talk about my clothes; I wanted to tell them about the automobile and the picnic. Mrs Grant poured a mug of milk for me and they both came to sit at the kitchen table with me and waited expectantly.

I wiped my milk moustache off and tried not to babble. "The automobile goes really fast, it feels as if you are flying through the air. Sir sat in the front, driving, with Mother beside him. I was in the back, with Sooty, on something called a dickey seat. The air whooshed past us," at this point excitement got the better of me and I leapt up and ran around the table miming driving the motorcar, which was what Sir said I should call it. They both laughed, and I knew I must have looked funny, so I added to the mirth by tooting an imaginary horn as I went round.

"And what about the picnic? Where did you go?" asked Mrs Grant.

"We went through the town, and lots of people waved to us. Sir tooted at them until Mother told him to stop. Then we were out of the town and we went along lots of lanes with trees on either side until we came to a field.

31

There was a little cottage there, and it was by a river. We had to walk along a rocky path and Mother said she was really glad she didn't have to wear skirts that dragged on the ground anymore.

"Sir and I carried the picnic basket between us, until a man came out of the cottage and took it from us. Sir called him Fred, so they must have known each other. Fred took the picnic basket right down to the banks of the river. Sir found a nice dry place and we spread out the blanket that Mother was carrying for us to sit on.

"There were lots of yellow plants growing in the field, and Sir said it was wheat, and it would be used for making food when it was ripe. I asked if that was like the potatoes and beans that MumMarch used to grow in our garden at home, and Sir said it was. I started to tell him about the boys and me growing tomatoes there as well, but Mother stood up and walked away and Sir went after her. When they came back he told me about the river being called the Medway, and I forgot all about the tomatoes.

"I had taken my butterfly net, but Sir said why didn't I use it to fish for tiddlers. I thought that was an excellent idea and said so, and both Sir and Mother laughed at that. Mother said, 'She is going to have your brains, Jacob. Such a vocabulary already.'"

I was a bit puzzled as to why Sir wouldn't want his brain anymore, but decided it was a joke. When I told Mrs Grant this bit, she and Joyce gave each other funny looks, but then Mrs Grant said, "Well, go on, then."

I didn't need telling twice as it was all bubbling round inside me, and I felt that if I didn't tell someone about my lovely day, I would burst! So I carried on with my story,

"Mother let me take off my shoes and stockings and roll up my skirt so that I could paddle in the river. It felt so cool and squishy between my toes. Sooty wasn't sure if he liked the water and he ran in and out, shaking the wet everywhere, which made us all laugh. I swished the net backwards and forwards in the river, but mostly seemed to catch flies and weed, though we all got excited when I caught a cork which someone must have thrown in. Sir said, 'Well done, Daisy, keeping the river clean,' and he took it from me and put it in his pocket.

"That made me feel really pleased with myself. I stood in the water for ages, feeling the sun warm on my hair and my feet cool in the river. There was all sorts of buzzing going on from insects, and every now and again Sir would point out a bird, or a tree, by name. He and Mother were lying back on the blanket and talking quietly, with Sooty asleep at their feet. Every now and again they would laugh at something. I thought that I had never seen Mother so happy, I reckon there was something magic about this place. Then Sir called me over and he dried my feet on a towel he must have brought specially and we laid out the picnic."

I turned to Mrs Grant, "Sir said that Mrs Grant made the best picnic in the world and that it was perfect."

Mrs Grant's face assumed a beaming smile, and she turned to Joyce. "Well, as you know, I was determined to do them proud. You and your mummy don't often go out, do you, Daisy?"

I was so confused by the use of the word 'Mummy' it took me a moment to understand, but then I smiled my appreciation.

Mrs Grant continued, as much for her own satisfaction as that of her listeners, to describe the result of her efforts. As I listened, I felt the warmth of the sun on my back once more and enjoyed the tastes of the picnic all over again.

"I did a veal galantine, a lobster salad, some tiny cucumber sandwiches, a dish of ham, some cheese biscuits – I wrapped the butter carefully and put it all in a cool china dish just before you left – and I added in some sweetmeats. I wondered whether to do some sardines, but I thought the lobster was enough."

"It was," I assured her. "Sir said the lobster salad was magnificent."

I thought Mrs Grant was going to explode with pride, but the bell rang just in time to prevent that catastrophe. Joyce jumped up to answer to it.

Coming back down, she said, "Your Mother says you must wash your hands and face and go and say goodbye to Sir Jacob. Leave Sooty here, he is still a bit wet."

I slipped off the chair and ran up to do as I was told. Entering the drawing room, I saw that Mother and Sir were standing by the window, and their silhouettes made them look like one person. Then I saw that Sir had his arm round Mother. They turned and drew apart when they heard me come in.

"Have you had a nice day, Daisy?" Sir was smiling, and he came across and lifted me up so my face was near his. He had never done that before.

"I have had the best day of my whole life, and so has Sooty," I assured him.

To my surprise he planted a kiss on my forehead before putting me down. Since Emma left us, no-one ever kissed me. Mother stood watching us and I was sure she was going to tell us off, but she didn't. She just stood there, with a funny, sad but happy, look on her face. I went and took her hand.

"It was a lovely day, wasn't it, Mother?"

"Wonderful," she agreed. But she was looking at Sir, not me, and soon after, he was gone.

The very next day, Emma came and there was more excitement. Because she had the picture of Sooty and me. It shows Sooty on the chair, and I am holding his biscuit in the air and he is on his hind legs reaching for it. You can only see the back of him, but you can still see how pretty he is with his dark fur and lovely long ears. And you can see that I am laughing and happy. You can tell Sooty is black, but you can't see that my dress is red, because the photograph is all a brown and cream colour and Emma says it is called sepia. Mother says she will buy me a frame for it, and that I can put it in my bedroom. I shall keep it forever and ever!

Emma says she has a copy of it that she will keep to remind her of me when she is in America. I asked her if she could do another one for me to send to MumMarch, but Mother shook her head at Emma, so Emma said no. But I think she could do one, really. Sometimes I just don't understand Mother. The only time I am sure I am pleasing her is when she gets a report from school saying how well I am doing.

My school is very nice, much bigger than the one Georgie and Alfie go to, with more teachers and over two hundred children. It is a Church of England school, even though we don't go to church, and Joyce says that I am very lucky to be going there. There is a little school in our village which would be much nearer, and more like the one the boys go to, but Mother says Sir chose this school for me and that I must 'make the most of it'. I have no idea what she means by that. A man comes in a horse-drawn bus at half-past-eight to pick me up, and there are five other girls and six boys who have already been collected. I am the last one, so I am always ready and waiting. Then, when he brings us home, I am the first one to be dropped off.

Rose is my best friend. You have to have a best friend at school, so you can sit together on the bus and at school and tell each other your secrets. Or we would if we had any, but we don't, so mostly we make up jokes and try to outdo each other seeing who can be the silliest. Sometimes we get told to 'stop messing around,' and to be quiet. But it is nice to be silly and noisy like I used to be at home. Now Emma has left there is no-one who makes jokes in our house.

Mother lets me bring Rose home whenever I like. We always go straight down to the kitchen to fetch Sooty, and then we play with him in the garden. Rose says I am much luckier than her because I have Sooty, which is true. But I love going to her house, she has an older sister and brother and they tease her and make her laugh. I like it when they tease me. Her mummy has a baby, too, and I am allowed to hold him.

Rose lives quite near us, so when it is time to go home, Joyce comes to get me and we walk through the lanes together. I have a skipping rope that Sir gave me and I often skip most of the way. Joyce gets out of breath trying to keep up and she makes me slow down. She asks me all sorts of really strange questions when it is only her and me. The other day she asked me where Sir lives.

I stared at her, perplexed. "I don't know, Joyce. I've never asked him."

She made a sort of clicking noise. I've noticed she often does that when she is a bit cross, so I tried to think of something to say that would please her.

"He is very nice, isn't he? When he came the other day he said how nice Mrs Grant's cherry cake was, and he had two pieces."

Joyce stopped the clicking. I know she likes it when her mother's cooking is praised. And Mrs Grant is a very good cook and he did say that, so it is not a fib.

Mother says fibbing is bad, but I get a bit confused about it. Mother was very cross with me because I told Miss Parsons, our teacher, that Sir brought me lots of presents. I thought Mother would be pleased that Miss Parsons had said he was very generous and that I was a lucky girl. But Miss Parsons asked if he was my uncle, and I said I didn't know and Mother said I shouldn't have said that. But I really don't know, so what else could I have said? Then Mother said if Miss Parsons asked again, I was to say, yes, he was my uncle. I was pleased about that and wondered why she had not told me before.

Next time Sir came (that was the time he brought me my skipping rope, with its lovely shiny red handles), I asked him why he had not told me he was my uncle. He laughed and said because that wasn't quite true. So I think it must be a fib. And I am not supposed to tell fibs. I am very confused. Perhaps I will understand when I am grown up.

August 1922.

Such a wonderful surprise today – Georgie came to see us. He has grown into such a handsome young man now, but I recognised him straight away. Well, I did as soon as he took his helmet off, anyway. I haven't seen him for nearly six years. He came roaring up on a motor cycle, wearing a leather helmet, gloves, and goggles. Mother and Mrs Grant both came rushing out into the drive to see what the noise was, because although we have seen (and heard!) motor cycles in the town, we have never had one visit us before. Later, Georgie told me that his father used this one during the war, and it was badly damaged, but it somehow came home with him and has been sitting in the shed ever since. Georgie got it going again all by himself!

It was almost unbelievable to see him standing there, smiling at me, his dark hair flopping on to his forehead just the way it used to. For a moment, a sort of shyness stood between us, then I just threw myself at him and we had the biggest hug in the world.

We were both laughing and talking and nearly crying all at the same time, then Georgie stepped back and held me at arm's length, and, looking at me, said, "Daisy. My own dear sister. I have missed you so much."

And then we were hugging again, and, stupidly, I was crying with happiness, too.

Mother came up to us and said, "Daisy, you are forgetting your manners. Please introduce me."

So I dried my face, and taking a deep breath, I said very formally, in spite of my shaking voice, "Mother, this is George March, my brother. George, this is my mother, Mrs Gosling."

Mrs Grant had disappeared. I guessed Mother had sent her indoors.

Mother and George shook hands, Georgie grinning from ear to ear but Mother was giving her polite smile. I could tell she was not as delighted as I was with our visitor.

"Daisy, please take," she hesitated, "your brother down to the kitchen. I am sure he will be glad of some refreshment. Then perhaps you could collect Sooty and go for a walk together?"

I stared at her. Take my brother down to the kitchen? Like the butcher or baker? Then get him out of the house? I was eleven years old, nearly twelve, and beginning to be aware of the odd social niceties that Mother employed, but this was my brother. This was Georgie. I felt angry that she was prepared to snub him this way, even though I had a feeling that he would neither know or care. Because, suddenly, I did care. Very much.

"Of course, Mother." I turned to Georgie. "You will be glad to get some of those heavy clothes off, you must be quite hot. We will pop downstairs and Joyce will hang them up for you, and then we will come and join you for tea, Mother."

It was the first time I had ever defied her. Our eyes met, and hers dropped first.

"Very well," she said. "I will ask Mrs Grant to bring up tea for three."

Unaware of the minor drama raging around him, Georgie said, "Come on, then, Sis. Lead the way. We have got so much catching up to do. And I have only got a couple of hours."

Without looking back at Mother, I took his hand and led him downstairs, where he was the object of much interest to Joyce and Mrs Grant.

"Your brother, eh?" said Joyce, shaking his hand. "Didn't know you had a brother, Daisy."

"None of our business, Joyce," said Mrs. Grant sharply, "but Daisy told Emma and me all about you when she first came, Mr Georgie, and it is very nice to meet you at last."

"And you, Mrs Grant," said my brother politely, handing his long coat to Joyce, who hung it behind the scullery door.

We went back upstairs and sat having a rather stilted conversation with Mother, who asked after MumMarch and the family. Georgie assured her that everyone was well, although Father had returned from the war much quieter than Georgie remembered him.

"But Mum says we should just be grateful that he came back in one piece," he added.

That caused us all to pause, conscious that the stories the soldiers had brought back with them were still very vivid in many people's minds. Mrs Grant's husband had been one of the ones who had not returned, and Joyce told me that one of her father's brothers had also been killed. Even I, who had no real memory of the war and was untouched by the aftermath, understood how sad it had been for such a lot of people.

It seemed that neither Mother or Georgie knew how to break the awkward silence that had fallen over us, and I was just beginning to wish I had not insisted on bringing him upstairs when Mother remembered a convenient errand she had to do, and left us alone together. As the door closed behind her, we simultaneously breathed a sigh of relief.

I jumped up. "Come on, Georgie, let's take Sooty into the garden and you can tell me what you've been up to. I thought you were going to work in Snowden?"

Snowden Colliery was the big Kent coalfield that was providing work for most of the local men and MumMarch had said in one of her rare letters that Georgie would be working there. I had asked at school about it and Miss Parsons had said that mining was 'a good, honest living for a working man'.

"I wasn't really very keen," said Georgie. "I didn't really fancy being underground in the dark all day. But Father works at the pit head, and there wasn't really any other work around. However, they've closed the pit, because there has been a strike there. I don't really understand a lot of it, but it made up my mind for me. Guess what, Daisy?"

I shook my head at him, with no idea where this was going.

"I've joined the cadets, and as soon as I am old enough I am going to be a soldier."

I thought of the conversation we had just had and must have looked as disconcerted as I was feeling. Georgie picked up my confusion.

"Oh no, Daisy, I know what you are thinking, but it won't be like that. The war is over, so being a soldier will be all about making sure there is peace everywhere. And I shall be sent all over the world! I'm going to see the world, Daisy! I've already passed all the preliminary exams, and, do you know, Mum says that's because I got interested in books after the time when you used to read to us. When you left, I thought I'd better learn to read

41

properly and one thing led to another, until I was coming out top of the class. You remember Mr Davy, our headmaster?"

I nodded. I never actually met him but Georgie and Alfie talked about him all the time.

"Well, he said I should do something with my life because I was what he called a 'bright spark' and he got me a job last year with the Post Office because they encouraged their boys to become cadets. So I get paid to deliver telegrams while I am learning to be a soldier. And in another two years I shall be able to join the army." He sat back, grinning with excitement and anticipation.

"Oh, my goodness, Georgie, how thrilling. I am so pleased for you! And you really think my reading all that stuff to the two of you helped?"

He nodded, and I felt proud enough to burst.

"Do you deliver your telegrams on that?" I pointed up the drive to where the motorcycle was.

"No, not allowed. Have to use an old bone-shaker bike, even though I tell them this would be a lot quicker. But I don't care, Daisy, it is all a means to an end. Soon, I'll be in a soldier's uniform when I visit you." He took my arm and, to Sooty's delight, we danced round and round the lawn, just as he had done with me when I was small. Sooty ran round us, barking madly, until we collapsed on the garden bench, laughing and gasping for breath.

"And what about Alfie? Is he doing well at school?"

"No, not really. He says he will go down the pit, it is bound to be open again by the time he leaves school. He is not stupid, but he can't be bothered. Mum tells him off and tries to get him to read the books he is supposed to, but to be honest, he is only interested in playing football with his mates. But he is happy enough."

"And how is MumMarch?"

There was an unexpected pause before Georgie answered. "I don't know," he said finally. "She says she is fine, but she has lost an awful lot of weight this last year, and I notice that she gets very short of breath sometimes. I mentioned it to Father, and he said he had tried to persuade her to see the doctor, but she won't go because it is so expensive. Father thinks she is just going through a bad time that he says some women have, and she will soon recover."

"Oh, Georgie, I do hope she is going to be alright." I felt fear clutch at my stomach. Even though I had not seen MumMarch for so long, I could not imagine a world without her. I still touched the carpet bag every night before I went to bed and felt near to her. When I said my prayers I prayed for Mother and Sir, as I had been taught, but I also asked God to look after MumMarch and let me see her again.

"I must be getting back, Daisy. I am delivering the evening telegrams today, we do shifts. Is there any chance you might come and see Mum? She talks about you all the time, and keeps your letters in a special box. She is so proud of you. I know she would be overjoyed to see you."

We started to walk back to the house, arm in arm.

"I keep asking Mother if I can come and see you all, and she always says 'we'll see' but somehow we never do. But I promise you I will try very hard. Perhaps if I tell her that MumMarch is under the weather, she might let me. Joyce's husband has an automobile and runs a taxicab service, and I am sure he would take me."

"She would love that."

We went and fetched Georgie's coat and he said goodbye to Mrs Grant and Joyce, who both said it had been a pleasure to meet him. Then I looked for Mother, but she must have gone for a walk because I couldn't find her.

"Tell her thank you for the tea."

I nodded, suddenly bereft that he was leaving. He grabbed me in a bear hug.

"Take care, little sister."

And he was gone, roaring off down the drive. Sooty and I walked slowly back up the drive, but my mind was galloping. By the time I got back into the house, I was resolved that, whatever the obstacles, I was going to visit MumMarch, and soon.

The following day, Sir came to see us. I was playing outside with Sooty when his motorcar drew up and Sooty rushed over and jumped up at him. Luckily Mother was indoors, or she would have been cross with us both.

But Sir just laughed and said, "It's nice to know he is pleased to see me, but I am glad it is not a muddy day!"

This was because Sooty had once jumped up and covered his trousers in dirt, and Mother had to ask Joyce to get a clothes-brush, and I got a telling off and Sooty was sent to the kitchen in disgrace. To be honest, I think Mother was more upset than Sir, but in the end there was so much fuss we were all upset.

Today, Sir did not seem to be in any hurry to go and find Mother, because he suggested we walk around the garden together. I put Sooty on his lead to make sure he behaved himself and we wandered down to Mother's rose garden, where Sir suggested we sit on one of the stone benches and enjoy the lovely rose smell. I started to chat about my friend Rose, and told him I thought we were meant to be friends because we were both called after flowers.

"You know you are going to have to go to another school soon, Daisy?"

I nodded. I was nearly twelve now and Mother had been talking about where I would go next, but apparently it wasn't decided. I was looking forward to moving on, as, to be honest, I was often quite bored in lessons and it seemed a long time since I had learnt something new. Rose says I am a 'bluestocking'. I told Sir that, and he laughed.

"Not a bad thing to be, Daisy. In fact, I am told she is not far wrong, and that you are far ahead of your contemporaries in your schoolwork."

I didn't quite know how to respond to this. It was true, but if I agreed it would make me look cocky, and Mother had once sent me to my room and made me miss tea because I had said that I was the best at drawing in the class. I was not boasting, but I really was the best, and I thought she would like to know. But I always seemed to get things like that wrong, and was forever incurring Mother's disapproval.

"I can see your mother has taught you to be modest." Sir was smiling at me. "Nevertheless, your aptitude for study has greatly influenced our choice of school for you." He paused, and I waited while he lit a small cigar, then he continued, "There is a new girls' school which opened in Kent last year. I have made enquiries and I think it would suit you well. They are aiming at very high academic standards, and, unusually for girls' schools, expecting the pupils to be accomplished in the sciences as well as the arts. They are already gaining a good reputation." He turned to me. "How does that sound?"

I didn't hesitate. "It sounds wonderful."

"You would have to be a boarder there, and only come back here in the holidays. Would you mind that?"

I had read all of Angela Brazil's school stories; she was one of my favourite writers so I knew all about boarding schools. My emphatic, "No, it would be lovely," obviously convinced Sir, because he smiled and said, "Then we should go and tell your mother."

I jumped down and stopped dead. I had forgotten Sooty! What would become of Sooty without me? I picked him up and cuddled him, looking anxiously at Sir.

He frowned. "Mmm. We had forgotten this chap, hadn't we? He will be alright, you know, Daisy, he will see you in the holidays and be well looked after while you are away."

But I had the germ of an idea which might possibly kill two birds with one stone. I started to tell Sir about Georgie's visit, and he sat back on the bench, motioning me to do the same. I told him how Georgie was worried about MumMarch and how much I wanted to see her, and that it had just occurred to me that if Sooty could stay with them while I was at school, Alfie would play with him, and throw his ball, and take him for walks. All of which would be good because there wouldn't be anyone here who would do that. And we could take Sooty down on a visit and ask them if they would like to look after him. And I could see MumMarch again.

It all came out in a rush, and when I said about MumMarch I was a bit tearful, but Sir sat there and didn't interrupt. When I had finished he sat quietly and I knew he was thinking.

"Do you still miss MumMarch so much?"

"Yes."

"And does your mother know?"

I shook my head. "She doesn't really like me talking about her, or the boys. I don't know why. She doesn't tell me off or anything," I added quickly, "but I sort of just know."

Getting to his feet, Sir said, "Well, it might be quite a good idea, but I'll talk to your mother about it. Will you leave it to me, Daisy?"

I nodded. "Yes, Sir."

"And, if I tell you it is not possible for you to visit the March's, will you accept that?"

I thought about that. "No, Sir." I felt very brave, as I knew this was not the right answer. "I must go and see MumMarch somehow or other, if she is not well. I am sorry."

He tipped my face up and looked into my eyes. It made me think how rarely he touched me, so it felt special.

"I think you are probably right, and a very grown up and caring girl. So I shall do my best, Daisy. Now, I want you to stay out here with Sooty until your mother calls you in for tea. OK?"

That wasn't hard on such a beautiful day. I threw the ball for Sooty and then, when he started to pant a bit and lay in the shade, I fetched my skipping rope from the summerhouse and started to count my skips. Rose got up to three hundred last week and I am determined to beat it.

I was just at two hundred and something when Joyce appeared and said, "Your mother says to come in for your tea," and I caught my foot in the rope and lost count.

But as Sooty and I ran indoors, I had my fingers tightly crossed behind my back.

January, 1926

It is so strange the way sometimes your whole life seems to be turned upside down and there is absolutely nothing you can do about it. Thank heavens for Harding House. It feels like the only place that stays the same – a sort of refuge, I suppose. Coming here was definitely the good part of the 'upside down', if you see what I mean. I am so grateful to Sir for finding it, and arranging for me to be a pupil. When I go back home in the holidays, Mother always says she hopes I know how lucky I am, and I say that I do. Because I really, really do.

I am learning so much here. Not just about things like physics and chem., or books, or maths (though I do learn about all those things, and much more, of course) but about living. About caring for the people you are living with. And all sorts of modern things, like the new fashions and hairstyles and most of all, the wonderful jazz music.

The school has a ball every summer, and we are all allowed to go. When you are seventeen you can invite a male guest, and there is always much guessing and whispering in the dorm about who will invite who. When I am old enough I shall invite Georgie.

Sir arranged for me to go and see MumMarch one Sunday a month, from the time I arrived here, which meant I could see Sooty as well. He loves being with Alfie, and they have so much fun together. It is only a couple of miles away and I use the school taxi. I was shocked the first time I saw MumMarch after so long. Georgie had been right, she was so small. Not just because I was so much bigger, but she was thin, and sort of diminished. She was so pleased to see me she cried, and I cried too, but then she couldn't get her breath and Alfie rushed into the kitchen to find her medicine. They finally persuaded her to go to the doctor, and she thought the medicine he gave her was helping. She said she was a lot better, and felt more like her old self.

Alfie was a bit in awe of me when I first came back. He said that I had become The Posh Lady myself, and that I 'talked funny'. But it didn't take long before we were all nattering away nineteen to the dozen and the years just fell away, and I was their little sister again. And he and Georgie do make me feel little, such a couple of hunky chaps they are. Man mountains, as their mother says.

I felt as if everything in my life was turning out to be quite perfect. In the holidays, Mother sometimes takes me shopping with her and we listen to the radio together, and even though we still don't talk much, we are quite good companions. She even asks my opinion about her frocks nowadays, and I persuaded her to shorten her skirts. And we actually went up to London to the theatre once. We saw *No, No, Nanette* and it was terrific. Sir got us tickets. Mother said it was a lot of effort to see something so frivolous but I know she enjoyed it.

I asked Sir why he didn't come with us, and that was a bit strange. He said he didn't enjoy the theatre, but when he gave us the tickets he talked about it as if he had already seen it.

When I said, "But it would be lovely to all go together," Mother got up and walked out of the room.

Sir said, "Daisy, that is not possible," and then went after Mother, leaving me wondering what I had said wrong. But they came back together some time later and no-one said any more about it. But I must admit, it is sometimes more relaxing at MumMarch's house, where I never feel I have put my foot in it, than it is here, in my own home.

Which brings me back to the thing I have been putting off writing about. MumMarch is dead. She died quite suddenly. I had been with them only the week before. I remember vividly how amused we all were at Sooty's antics that day. He is getting old now, but he is still very active. Alfie dropped a piece of sausage and Sooty picked it up and ran into the corner of the room and ignored our efforts to make him drop it, because he is not allowed to steal. He turned his back on us and chewed like mad, and MumMarch was laughing so hard there were tears in her eyes.

"Daisy," she gasped, between gales of laughter, "You've not brought that dog up properly, he's a right little hooligan."

Not a bad last memory of your mother, I suppose. I tried to keep it in my head as I stood between the boys at the graveside. Dust to dust. The world seems empty without you, MumMarch.

After the funeral, I went back to the house with the boys and their father. He seems stunned and sits silently in his chair by the bare hearth, staring into it as if he is trying to see flames that aren't there. Alfie goes to fetch some coal and sets about building a fire. The house is cold, which somehow feels right, because we are cold, inside and out. But then Alfie manages to get the fire going and the warmth seeps through the rooms and into our bones.

Some of the neighbours who were at the church have come for the wake. Three ladies from the village who I barely know are in the kitchen laying out sandwiches and small cakes. I realise that they must have made them specially, and it makes me think how kind and thoughtful some people are. And that makes me think of MumMarch and I want to cry, but I am not going to, so I busy myself fetching and handing round the refreshments.

I have permission to stay overnight. Mother was reluctant to give it, but Sir persuaded her. The school taxi will come for me at eight in the morning. A few more people, some of the men who were at work earlier, filter into the house and it gradually starts to fill up. People are talking in whispers, until the boys' Uncle Bert comes. He is Father's brother, a large, noisy and jolly man who has a small farm a few miles to the east of the village. I haven't seen him for ages. When I was small, I used to be frightened of him on his occasional visits, and often hid behind MumMarch's chair. But MumMarch always chided me and made me come out and say hallo. Which was what I did now, once Father and the boys had greeted him.

He took my hand, and to my surprise gave me a kiss on the cheek. "She loved you like her own," he said. "And it meant so much to her that you never got too proud, and always remembered her."

"I could never have forgotten her," I said truthfully, "I loved her more than anyone in the world."

He gave me a searching look that made me unexpectedly aware there was much more to him than the bluff farmer I knew.

"Sometimes, Daisy," I never remembered him calling me by name before, "life can come from nowhere and kick you in the stomach. But you have to learn to deal with whatever it sends you, as I think you know already.

But if you ever need a bit of help, well, you know where I am." He smiled, and released my hand. "Down on the farm with my cows – but always happy to see you. Don't forget."

Before I could thank him for his kindness, he moved back across the room and took out his mouth organ. His playing that instrument was my most vibrant memory of him. Under the babble of soft talk and reminiscence came the first few plaintive notes of *Danny Boy*.

Georgie moved over to stand beside me. "Do you remember me singing ...?"

I nodded, choked with tears. "Of course," I whispered, as the music floated over us, "I remember everything." And I did.

Once back at school I tried to put the funeral, though not my love for MumMarch and the boys, behind me. Life at Harding House continued to be enjoyable. We were a totally female society, but as we were mainly taught by interesting and independent women, we were not especially conscious of that. And most of us had brothers or male relations who visited regularly, and there were always the holidays. We were a hard working lot; on the whole aware of how privileged we were to be receiving such an education. Now in our fourth year, we had our eyes set on eventually matriculating well and then a possible place at Oxford University, an ambition almost unheard of by previous generations.

But every summer the famous Harding House Ball became the main topic of conversation for us all and on the night, when the cars swept up to the house, those of us too young to participate gazed enviously from the dorm windows. The lucky seventeen-year-old girls, bedecked in shimmering short-skirted dresses and some even with bobbed hair, were allowed to welcome their escorts out in the drive, and even wander around the grounds in the evening, arm in arm with the men in their lives.

It would have felt quite shocking if it had not been so obviously sedate – and extremely well regulated. I speculated endlessly with my special friend, Jennifer, who had started at the school when I did, about the imagined relationships between some of the couples. But in spite of our wildest imaginings, they usually turned out to be the girl's brother, or uncle, or father.

"Quite disappointing, really," murmured Jennifer, when a very elegant and attentive chap turned out to be the head girl's father. "No-one should have a father as sexy as that."

I gasped and then we both giggled at her daring use of the S word. "He looks a bit like Valentino," I whispered, referring to the great movie heart throb.

Jennifer said she hoped that by the time we could go to the Ball, short skirts would be out of fashion, so she could wear a long, old-fashioned, but gorgeous, gown. "Because," she continued, "I haven't got the legs for those short skirts."

But we both agreed that I probably had, and I loved the new flapper dresses and the freedom they gave you.

"And next year – it will be our turn!" said Jennifer.

June, 1927

The night of the ball was the most wonderful, exciting and splendiferous night of my life. Sometimes, when you have looked forward to something for ages and ages it is a bit disappointing when you get there. As if it couldn't possibly be as good as you had hoped. But it was, it was, it was! Although there was some strange stuff going on at home before the Ball.

I had asked Sir if he would like to be my guest, because that seemed a right and proper thing to do, but I was really hoping that he would say 'no, thank you,' because as much as I love him (and I do) I wanted Georgie to come. And Sir said, very formally, that he was honoured that I had asked him but it would not be possible for him to come. But then he handed me a huge amount of money to spend on my dress!

I was so grateful that I threw my arms round him and kissed him, but when Mother began to remonstrate with me for being so forward, Sir just laughed and gave me a hug.

"I think it is allowed, Susan. Especially as I shall be going away soon, and won't be seeing you both for a long time."

I was a bit taken aback, but I could see from mother's face that she knew what Sir was talking about.

Sir patted the seat beside him. "Come and sit beside me, Daisy. I have been telling your mother that I am being sent away. To India. The other side of the world. His Majesty is doing me a great honour by asking me to be one of his representatives there, so, even if I wanted to, I could not refuse."

Greatly daring, I asked, "But you want to go, don't you?"

His face lit up with a smile. "Yes, Daisy, I do. I shall enjoy new sights and new people and believe I can do this job well. I shall not let His Majesty down. But I shall miss you and your mother."

"But not your family, who will go with you." That was Mother, from the other side of the room where she stood watching us.

Sir turned to her. "Susan, my dear, of course my family will be with me. But I wish you could be, too."

Mother left the room, abruptly. For a moment I thought she was crying, but Mother never cries. I stared at Sir, completely out of my depth. I had no idea that he had a family, and wanted very badly to ask about them, and why we never saw them. But I sort of knew absolutely that I mustn't.

Sir said, "I will be back in a year for a holiday, Daisy, and I will make sure I come and see you. And your mother will write and tell me how you both are, and I would like it if you wrote sometimes, too. Your mother will send on your letters. You must work very hard. I am told you are likely to get a place at Oxford, and if so you will be there by the time I come back to England permanently. But whatever happens, I am trusting you to look after your mother while I am away. Will you promise me that?"

"Of course I will."

"Good girl. Now, I must go and talk to her. I am afraid she has taken my news badly, but I am sure she will be pleased for me when she has got used to the idea."

Never before had Sir discussed Mother with me. On one hand, it made me feel very grown up and in his confidence, but on the other, almost as if I was conspiring against her.

Sir seemed to sense my ambivalence. "Leave me now, and go and write to your brother. I expect he will be delighted to accompany you to the ball, and you will be very proud of him in his smart new uniform." He held out his hand for me to shake. "Goodbye for now, Daisy. And good luck with everything, my dear."

I went to walk round the garden, glorious in its early summer clothes, with Sooty ambling along slowly behind me. But my head was whirling. I realised for the first time that Mother had no other friends; her only visitor was Aunt Hannah who came once in a blue moon, and was always very curt to me and hated Sooty. Mrs Grant was the nearest person Mother had to a friend.

For the first time, I wondered who we were, Mother and I? We didn't seem to have any other family. All I really knew about Sir was that he was not my real uncle.

But then I thought about the money Sir had given me and all miserable thoughts left me. I was going to the ball! I had no time for introspection. I rushed indoors and sat at the writing desk.

Dear Georgie, I wrote, *would you do me the honour of accompanying me to ...*

And, as I wrote, all other thoughts flew from my nearly-seventeen-years-old head.

Georgie came in his soldier's uniform and looked incredibly smart. His hair is cut really short, and he is quite brown from being out of doors all day. He has just been promoted and is a corporal now. I was so proud of him. None of the other girls had a brother as dashing as mine!

Jennifer's brother, Henry, was really, really nice. I have met him before, but he has always visited the school with their parents, so I have never had any chance to chat properly with him. He and Georgie seemed to like each other immediately so the four of us had the most fantastic evening. We danced every dance – actually, Henry is a better dancer than Georgie, but I wouldn't dream of saying so – and we just didn't seem to get tired. I felt as if I was floating all evening. We girls had been practising the dances like mad for weeks, and Henry and I had such fun doing the Charleston that everyone else stopped dancing to watch, and then clapped us at the end!

Of course, we were not allowed alcohol, but the cooks had concocted some lovely fruity drinks which Henry said were just like cocktails. We felt very sophisticated and worldly as we clinked glasses with our escorts. The Ball went on until nearly midnight, but it seemed no time at all until we were dancing the last waltz. Georgie is being sent abroad soon, which would have made me sad except that he is so excited about it. He says he is helping to look after our Empire. But even though life will be odd without either him or Sir around, I refuse to be gloomy. Henry is at Oxford and he says I would love it, and I am going to work even harder so I can go there.

And the Ball was absolutely the best night of my life – ever!

Two days later we were still recovering from that sparkling evening, when a parcel arrived for me. I don't think I had ever had one before, not at school or anywhere else for that matter. But there it was, late that afternoon, sitting on the table in the study Jennifer and I shared.

"Go on, open it then," said Jennifer.

I was turning it over and over trying to imagine who it was from. Then I recognised Mother's writing on the label and realised that there was an envelope attached to the outside. I removed it carefully and read the enclosed short letter.

Dear Daisy,

Sir came to visit today and he brought this for you. He says he hopes you will enjoy using it, and that it will enable him to see what you have been up to while he is away.

His ship sails in two days. He sends his love to you. I hope you appreciate what a lucky girl you are. Please send your 'thank you' letter home, and I will pass it on to him.

Mother.

I unwrapped the parcel carefully, and then gasped with delight. He had sent me a camera. He knew I was fascinated with them, and with the whole idea of taking images, ever since Emma had taken my photograph all those years ago. I picked it up carefully, along with the instructions for using it, and scanning through those I saw how easy it was to use. I opened the case and checked it was loaded with film, and then I ordered Jennifer to stand by the door and smile at me. After several minutes fiddling around to make sure the light wasn't flooding the window, I pressed the button and we both heard the click.

"There," I said, "that's my first ever photograph. When we have taken the whole roll we will have them developed and you will be able to see yourself as others see you."

"Goodness, I hope that's not as scary as it sounds. Henry took one of me once and I looked all scrunched up and strange in it. The worse thing was that Mummy said it looked just like me."

We both laughed and I said, "Let's go and show Miss Turner."

Miss Turner had come to the school to teach science last year, and, unlike some of the other, older, mistresses, was young enough to make her feel accessible. Lessons were over for the day, so we went across to her rooms and knocked tentatively.

"Come in." She was sitting at her desk reading and marking papers. "Hallo, you two. What have you got there, Daisy?"

I showed her. To my surprise she went to a cupboard and retrieved an almost identical one.

"I bought this one a couple of years ago. Yours is a newer version, Daisy, very smart indeed. Have you used it yet?"

I told her about taking Jennifer's picture, and how Emma had taken mine and Sooty's. She reached into a drawer under her desk and brought out a large bundle of photographs.

"These are some I have taken. Have a look."

We thumbed through them. There were loads of her parents, and her sister, and a small cat, which she said was called Charlie. There was also one of a young man in a soldier's uniform, but somehow we knew not to ask about him.

But the majority of the pictures did not have people in them. They were more like paintings. A solitary tree with the wind blowing it sideways, a bird perched on a dry-stone wall, a hat on a hat-stand, which for some reason made us both laugh. I glanced up, hoping we hadn't offended her, but she was smiling.

"It made me laugh too, that's why I took it."

"I hadn't realised that you could do all this kind of thing," I said slowly, still thumbing through the pile of photographs. "The ones of your family are nice, but these are beautiful."

"You can do whatever you like. One or two of mine have been published. Look." She pulled out a pile of magazines and thumbed through until she found what she was looking for: a stunning picture of a punt on a river, with a young man on the prow, and willow tree branches making a natural frame.

I recognised the young man as the soldier in the other picture. She saw me looking and said, "His name was Eric. That was before the war, when we were at Oxford. I took it with his camera, and won a prize with it."

There was a pause, weighed down with unspoken words.

Then I said, "I am sorry."

"Thank you, Daisy. But it was some years ago and, at least, I have the photograph. Now," she stood up, "I must get back to marking, but, if you would like, I can show you how to develop your pictures yourself, Daisy. We have a cupboard in the basement which I use as a dark room."

"I would love to do that, thank you so much." My enthusiasm must have been transparent, as she gave me a huge smile.

"Then, as soon as you have finished that film, come round with it, and we will find the time for an unofficial lesson. Now, go and get used to using it, that's the first step."

Dismissed, we ran into the gardens and walked around looking for interesting things to photograph, but the light was going so we decided to leave it for that day. After supper, I sat down and wrote a long letter to Sir, and enclosed it in a shorter one to Mother. Then I wrote to Georgie and then Alfie. Then I tumbled into bed just before lights out, my head full of images.

May 1929

The Head called me to her office this morning. I thought it must be about Oxford, because I am waiting to hear if I have got a place. But before I could even knock, she opened the door and motioned for me to walk with her.

"Daisy, my dear, you need to pack your bag and go home. Your mother has sent for you. The school taxi will be here almost immediately. If you cannot come back, I will send anything you leave here."

I stared at her. Go home? Not come back? Term still had a whole month to go. "Why, what has happened?"

"Your mother will tell you. Now, off you go. And, Daisy, I will, of course, send on the letter from Oxford when it comes."

She turned and left me in the corridor. Never a woman of many words, her behaviour still seemed unnecessarily abrupt. I went back to my room and threw some things into my beloved carpet bag. Jennifer was at a lecture, so I wrote a quick note saying I had no idea what was going on, but would be back soon. I hoped. Then I ran down to the taxi, which was waiting impatiently in the drive.

It was nearly dark before we arrived home and I was feeling slightly travel sick and also angry that I had not been given any explanation for the day's events. It was as if I had been summarily ejected from Harding House for some misdemeanour that I did not know I had committed.

Mrs Grant came out to greet me. She moved more slowly nowadays, but had the forethought to have brought a tip for my driver. I thanked him for his service and he drove off. She tried to pick up my bag but I stopped her.

"Mrs Grant, I am younger and fitter than you and can carry my own bag. But, what is going on?"

She peered at me as we entered the gas-lit hall. "Oh, Daisy, your mother will tell you. She's a bit upset. Don't rush her. I'll bring you both up a pot of tea. Are you hungry?"

I was a bit, so I nodded my thanks. It had been a tiring journey.

"I made a batch of shortbread yesterday. A piece of that will tide you over till dinner." She patted my arm and went down to the kitchen.

I left my bag in the hall and went along to the drawing room, which was not yet lit. I could just see Mother, silhouetted against the window, in the same place that I had first seen her over a dozen years ago. I crossed to her and touched her shoulder. She turned and for a minute seemed not to know who I was.

Then: "Daisy. You're here. I didn't realise it was so late." She looked round the room "Oh, and it has got dark. Will you light the gas, please?"

I found the taper on the mantelpiece where we always kept it and lit the central mantle from the small fire in the grate. Then I came and sat opposite her.

"Mother, what is going on?"

She handed me a letter. The heading on the notepaper was of a firm of solicitors that I had never heard of, but it was addressed to Dear Susan, and signed Dickie Lambert, the informality at odds with the business-like layout of the letter. The contents were simple to the point of starkness, however.

You need to know that Jacob was assassinated this morning. He was shot and died instantly. It will be in the

64

papers tomorrow. He had intended to set up a trust for you and Daisy but, like so many men who are of no great age, had never got round to it. I am so sorry. The house and everything else will, of course, belong to the family, once the will is read.

I will come and speak with you tomorrow.

I stared at her, the letter still in my hand. Sir was dead? MumMarch gone, and now Sir? Before I could stop myself, a cry erupted from me, and I knelt down beside Mother and cried with my head in her lap. I felt her fingers stroke my hair, but when I finally raised my face she was looking out of the window at the dark night.

"He loved you, you know," she said, as if it was something of a surprise to her. "And now he is gone." She gave a deep sigh, as if her whole body was wracked with pain that had no other outlet. Then she rose and walked to stand in front to the fire, putting distance between us. "We shall have to move, of course. Very soon. I have a little money, and Mr Lambert will help us to find somewhere."

A light tap at the door was followed by Mrs Grant bearing the promised refreshment. We sat in silence while she poured the tea and then left us alone again.

Mother handed me mine and then stood back by the fire. After a moment she broke the silence.

"Daisy, I am so, so sorry. But I will find a way to make it all right again, somehow. I always do. I shall not eat dinner tonight. I am going to bed. I will see you in the morning." Then, head bowed, she left the room.

I wanted to run after her, screaming, 'I don't understand! What are you sorry for? Tell me what is going on!' But I didn't. I just sat by the flickering fire,

65

sipping my tea, and waiting for everything to become clear. As it inevitably would. And, as I now realised, I had been waiting since I was five years old.

Mr Lambert came this morning. I had not spoken to Mother as she did not come down from her room until his arrival, but I was curious to see him, so I got to the front door before Joyce to let him in. He is older than I expected, though I don't know why I thought otherwise. Probably because the name 'Dickie' made him sound young. I showed him into the drawing room, but before I had a chance to call her, Mother was there.

"Thank you, Daisy. Will you ask Joyce to bring us some tea, please?"

So I was not to be part of any conversation. But I lingered outside the door, not exactly eavesdropping but taking my time to move away.

I heard Mr Lambert say, "I am so sorry, Susan. Such a dreadful shock for us all."

And Mother reply, her voice shaking slightly, "What shall I do, Dickie?"

"We must move fast, my dear, to avoid any scandal ..."

At that moment I heard Joyce coming up so I quickly moved away from the door and went to meet her. Like Emma had done all those years ago, she came in early to do the grates and get the breakfast.

"Mother says can you take some tea, up ..." but I stopped abruptly, realising that she had the tray already.

"I guessed it would be needed when your mother said there would be a visitor today. And there's two letters for you."

She handed them to me. It was a lovely spring morning, so I grabbed my coat from the hall-stand and took them into the garden. My heart was beating so loudly I could hear it in my head. I sat on the bench under the tree and, taking a deep breath to steady myself, I opened the first one.

I had been accepted! I was going to Oxford. I had a moment of sheer, unadulterated exhilaration, before the events of the last twenty-four hours made me suddenly have doubts about the future I had worked so hard to achieve. I sat for a minute, the words of the letter mingling in my mind with the word 'scandal'. I simply had to know what was going on. I had to understand why Sir's death, as horrid and unexpected as it was, seemed to be causing so much havoc. After all, he was not part of our daily lives, only visiting us occasionally, and apparently not even a relation. I did not begin to comprehend what was happening.

I glanced at my other letter, which was from Jennifer. I would save that for later. Meanwhile, I would disregard Mother's injunction to leave them alone, and go and tell her my wonderful news. At least, I hoped it was

I knocked at the drawing room door but did not wait for an answer. After all, I reasoned, this was my home and that should give me some rights. My confidence in this theory evaporated rapidly when I saw the look Mother gave me, but I proceeded with my news.

"Forgive me for interrupting," this was addressed to Mr Lambert, "but I have just received some excellent news and I wanted Mother to know straight away."

He smiled at me, and I decided that he had a nice, kind face. "I am sure your mother will be anxious to hear your news, Daisy, and we could all do with hearing something cheerful, couldn't we, Susan?"

Mother gave an almost imperceptible nod. Her eyes were cast down, but I could see the deep black shadows under them. She looked terrible and I was beginning to regret my hasty entrance.

"Mother, I have just heard from Oxford. I have a place at Somerville College, where I hoped to go. I can start in the autumn."

Mr Lambert got to his feet and held out his hand to shake mine. "Well done, Daisy. What a triumph. I am sure you will help to prove how right it is to have women at our universities – even though we never managed to persuade my father, who remained deeply shocked by the idea of women's colleges all his life, I am afraid."

Mother had barely moved, but now she got up and gave me a brief hug, a gesture that was so unusual it made me feel uneasy. Rightly, as it turned out, because as she sat down again, she said, "Daisy, that is wonderful and I know your ..." here she hesitated and then, "I know Sir would have been so proud of you, as am I. But I am afraid it is not to be."

I stood in front of her, the letter dangling from my fingers, suddenly knowing, although not quite believing, what was to come next.

"You will have to write and tell them that your circumstances have changed and you will not be able to take up your place."

"Susan, my dear, that's a bit hard, isn't it? You can't be absolutely sure what is going to happen. Perhaps they would hold the place over for Daisy until things are more settled."

Mother turned on him with an unexpected vigour. "And when will that be, Dickie? Even if I could find the money for her to go, which is hardly likely, there are forms to fill out. Remember them? Jacob would have found a way round them. His patronage would have been enough for them to turn a blind eye. But now we are outcasts. And probably penniless ones at that. Everything we have discussed this morning makes that quite clear."

Abruptly, I sat on the sofa, aware that I was shaking. My world was disintegrating round me, and they were both talking as if I wasn't there. Mother was pacing around the room rubbing her hands together. I had read the phrase 'wringing her hands' but had never known what it meant until now. Before I had the chance to ask any of the questions that were clamouring in my head, Mother turned and spoke to us both.

"I shall write to my sister Hannah today. She has been telling me it would come to this for many years so I imagine she will have some pleasure in giving us shelter until I have decided what to do. Dickie, I will give you my address. I shall write to her within the hour, and, with luck, will hear back today. But I have no doubt of her hospitality; she has a good heart in spite of her sharp tongue. We shall be at this address," she rapidly wrote on notepaper pulled from her writing desk in the corner of the room, "it is in East Kent, near the marshes that Mr Dickens wrote about so eloquently." She stopped and took a deep and steadying breath. "I am babbling. I apologise to you both. Daisy, you must go and start packing your things. The furniture and the ornaments belong with the house, so we shall be travelling lightly. I must go and see Mrs Grant when she arrives, though I imagine she will want to stay, at least for a while."

Mr Lambert nodded. "I will write to the family today and ask them what their wishes are."

Mother turned back to me. "Daisy, I am so sorry about Oxford. I know how much it meant to you. I will do my best to make it up to you."

The realisation, revelation even, that she did understand, and that she did care, tipped the scales and, in that instant, made my grief for her loss greater than that for my own.

"Don't worry, Mother. Whatever happens, I am sure we will come through it." Greatly daring, I gave her light kiss on the cheek, and was conscious for the first time that I was now taller than her. I ran upstairs to begin packing, aware that there had been some kind of shift in our relationship.

Joyce was in my bedroom, wielding the new upright vacuum cleaner that she had persuaded Mother to buy recently, now we were on the national electricity grid. It made a dreadful noise, but I could see that the pattern on all the carpets was much prettier than we had previously thought, so I guessed it must be as good as she insisted. She switched it off as I entered.

"So what's up? My mum said she's come in early today to see if you needed her so she'll be here soon. Are we going to lose our jobs?"

"Joyce, I am sorry but I really don't know. But from what Mr Lambert said I think probably you'll be OK."

"He's the lawyer chap downstairs? Well, I suppose he'll have as good an idea as anyone. I've finished in here, love. I'll go and start organising lunch." She began to gather up her things. "That cleaner's a godsend. I suppose if new people come here they will get the electric wires in everywhere like they should be, but it was good of your dad to have the point for this put in."

She closed the door behind her. My dad?! Was that what this was all about? I remembered the business over the cleaner. Mother saying that she liked the gaslight, it was soft and flattering, and Sir laughing and saying, well then, he would arrange to have electricity put in to make life easier for Joyce, but Mother could keep her gaslight. I wondered why it was up to Sir, but I hadn't thought anymore about it.

I sat down on the bed heavily. Gosh, I had been so blind. I caught a glimpse of myself in the mirror over the washstand. I even looked a bit like him. Sir had been my father! But he had a family. So that must mean that I was – who? Or what? And how come Joyce knew, and not me? This last thought galvanised me. I got off the bed and went downstairs before my courage failed me. Mr Lambert had gone, and Mother was at her desk.

"Why have you never told me that Sir was my father?"

I watched her stiffen, and then she turned round to face me.

"How dare you speak to me like that, Daisy. And I don't know where you got this nonsense from, but, I told you many years ago, your father was killed in a riding accident."

"Are you telling me that Sir was not my father?" My voice was squeaky with the effort of controlling myself. For the first time ever, I did not believe my mother. She had turned away from me and was bending over some papers, but her voice was clear.

"I don't like your tone, Daisy. I am making allowances because you are upset today, as am I. Please

71

put this stupid idea out of your head. There is so much to be done, I do not need further distractions."

Thus dismissed, I stood for a moment glaring at her back, and then I stomped from the room, slamming the door behind me. I half expected Mother to come out and hit me, though she never had, but then this situation was unlike anything that had happened between us before.

Because I knew, and so did she, that she had evaded answering my question. I began to pack up my clothes, but my thoughts were churning. I was an innocent, as were most girls of my time and my age, but I was a well-read innocent.

I recalled Esther's plight in Mr Dickens's novel *Bleak House,* in which her mother gives her away because she is not married to her father. And *Oliver Twist,* who was only able to come into society when it was proved that his mother had married his father. Charles Dickens seemed to know a lot about this subject, I reflected. So was I a foundling, an orphan? Why had I been with MumMarch, and why had I been whisked away? And most of all, why would Mother not tell me the truth?

I threw my things willy-nilly into the carpet bag, and then I saw Percy, my tatty old pink rabbit, peering down at me from the top of the wardrobe, abandoned there when I outgrew his comforting fluffiness. I reached up for him and found myself cuddling him. As I sat down with him on the bed, all the pent up disappointment of the day and all the hurt and anger erupted from me. Placing my head in the pillow to muffle my sobs, I felt my heart break.

Later that evening, having cried myself dry, I washed my face and decided to go down to the kitchen to see if Mrs Grant had cooked some supper. I thought Mother had probably had hers in her room and not bothered to call me. Glancing down, I saw that I had dropped Jennifer's letter on the floor and it had lain there, unopened and forgotten. I reached for it.

Dear Daisy,

The Head says you will not be coming back, surely that can't be right? She wouldn't tell me what was up. Did you get your place? I do hope so – I have been accepted by Somerville, so if you have as well, what fun we shall have! Miss Turner says you are to carry on with the photography, she says you have a natural talent. A compliment indeed.

Do write and let me know that you are OK, and perhaps your mother will let you come and stay with us in the hols? Henry would like that as well, I think! He sends his love.

As does your worried friend, Jennifer. xxx

I folded the letter and put it in my pocket. I'd write to Jennifer tomorrow. With a slight lift of the heart I recalled that her family lived somewhere in Sussex, not a great distance away, so I might indeed be able to go and stay. And then another thought hit me. If I was not to go to Oxford, then what was I going to do with the rest of my life?

October 1931

The mornings are getting colder and colder; today I had to scrape the frost off the inside of the bedroom window with my finger-nails. Winter has definitely arrived, but so early this year. I crept downstairs, being careful not to wake Mother, and washed in nearly freezing water. Thank heavens the pipes aren't frozen yet, that caused so much trouble last year. I must find some sacking and try to lag them before that particular catastrophe strikes.

Back upstairs I found my thickest stockings and put on two pairs and some heavyweight underclothes – I look at the glamorous lingerie advertised in the magazines with a mixture of envy and amusement. Then I added my heavy coat and skirt over the jumper that Alfie's fiancée knitted for me. Patsy is such a little gem, Alfie is lucky to have her. Then, to complete this mundane but practical ensemble, my boots that Mother hates so much, but they are just light enough for me to cycle in. Mother has never understood the sartorial restraints that cycling to school every day imposes on me.

Her constant diatribe on the subject of how teachers should dress comes from another age, I am afraid, and her knowledge of my world is minimal. Which probably suits us both. She has no idea how lucky I was to get this post, up against stiff competition from women older and far better qualified than me. But I have discovered that I enjoy teaching and that I also have some expertise in passing on the joy I find in great literature. And the head, Mrs Green, is talking about putting on a play at Christmas and I shall offer to help with that.

So things are better than I could have hoped, really. The dire experience of living with Aunt Hannah feels like a depressing dream now. Try as I might, she regarded me as the cause of all Mother's troubles, which seems a trifle unfair. No, what am I saying? It is desperately unfair. It is I, who have done nothing wrong, who has to skulk around pretending to be respectable because the truth would put me outside society.

Mother still will not talk about Sir, or her (and my!) past, so we continue the polite fantasy that my father, who incidentally has no name that I am aware of, died in a traffic accident. My request to see my birth certificate called forth a stony silence. I did not pursue it, as at the moment I have no need of it, and I imagine I could easily track it down if I did.

But for all that, we have come to some kind of unspoken alliance. Aunt Hannah, in an unguarded moment, after rebuking me for some minor misdemeanour, added, "I will never understand why Susan worked so hard to have you with her. With her looks she could have put it all behind her; married well and have a proper family now."

It was the most anyone had ever told me about either Mother or myself. But the news that Mother had worked hard to have me with her must surely mean that she loved me. For the first time I began to see her coldness as her way of protecting me. In the past I had seen moments of warmth between her and Sir. Seen them laughing together and caught looks that suggested, well, passion, perhaps? Maybe 'passion' was something to be avoided, I thought.

I was beginning to vaguely understand what it meant. Not just from books, but from my own very limited experience. When I had visited Jennifer the summer before last, Henry made it obvious that he wanted us to get to know each other better.

Jennifer, a true romantic, thought that was wonderful. "You might get married and then we should be sisters," she declared.

I had to tell her, that although I did find her brother attractive, I thought she had been reading too many of the 'romance books' that had become so popular. But when Henry found an excuse to take my hand, I confess that I did feel a frisson of excitement that was new to me.

And, yes, I was definitely enjoying the attention, and also the holiday. They lived in Worthing, a Sussex town boasting both lovely beaches and exhilarating walks across the downs, and the three of us indulged in both the bathing and the hikes. And we talked and talked, of course. I enjoyed hearing about Jennifer's life at Oxford, and though I had to confess to my great disappointment at not being with her, I had become philosophical. I had my beloved camera with me, of course, to record virtually everything that caught my eye. It seemed to be an idyllic break – until that was revealed as an illusion.

Jennifer's parents were pleasant enough to me, but we didn't see much of them. They were a quiet couple, seemingly uninterested in our jaunts. So I was startled, early one morning, to hear them arguing under my bedroom window, and even more startled to catch the end of their conversation.

Her father was saying, "But Jennifer's known Daisy for years. And although Henry obviously likes her, I see no sign that he is besotted. I really don't think there is any need for alarm."

"Perhaps not. But Sir Jacob and the family were our friends for years, and how would they feel if Henry were to propose to his bastard daughter? How would we feel, for that matter?"

I had not intended to listen but I was riveted.

Jennifer's father said, "My dear, that is a little strong. We have no proof that she is his daughter."

"Oh, for heaven's sake, she looks just like him. And everyone who is anyone knows. We have to tell her to leave, before things go any further between her and Henry. I will say that we have decided to go down to the cottage in Norfolk for a week and there is no room for her there. I promise that I'll be tactful."

I was stunned, and hurt and angry, but I did not hesitate. I threw on my clothes and packed my bag. Then I went downstairs where they were just starting breakfast. I was relieved that neither Jennifer nor Henry was up yet. I didn't give their parents a chance to speak.

"Thank you for your hospitality. Will you please tell the others that I had an emergency and had to leave unexpectedly? I could not help overhearing your conversation this morning, and I should hate you to have to go to Norfolk on my account."

With what I hoped was a dignified exit, I walked to the station, fortunately not far away. It was the first time I really understood that I was some kind of social outcast. Educated and civilised, but don't let your daughters or, even more especially, your sons, get too close. They needn't worry. I was never, ever going to let anyone get close to me again. I was beginning to understand Mother.

I had a letter from Miss Turner today. I had sent her some of my photographs taken on the marshes. Between us, Mother and I have been able to rent a small cottage on the edge of Hoo Village. My teaching carries a reasonable salary, and Mother dress-makes quite successfully. I love living here. Georgie visits whenever he is home – he is a sergeant now! – and I insist on him touring the area with me so that I can show him all the things that fascinate me. The marshes look bleak and unattractive but, in fact, are alive with wild-life. And, if I am being honest, I like the isolation. Our nearest neighbours are just in sight, but not near enough to be intrusive, and there is almost no passing traffic as there is nowhere to go.

"Back of beyond," sniffed Aunt Hannah, on her one and only visit to us. She was quite right, but I think that is a virtue, and I think Mother does as well. She was never vibrant, but nowadays it is as if the stuffing has gone out of her. She goes through the essential motions of living, but no more. I try to tell her about my pupils, but she is not interested. The only time she is at all animated is when one of her customers comes to discuss a dress or shirt. I had no idea she was such a clever and inventive seamstress. When I asked her if she had done such work before, she gave me one of her 'looks'.

"How do you think I made enough money to keep you with Mrs March until Jacob returned from abroad?"

Ah! A bit of our history slipping out. But I knew better than to ask any more. I just tucked that snippet away in my expanding memory bank.

But back to Miss Turner's letter, which I read with mounting excitement. I had taken a series of photographs against a very grey and dismal sky, so the marshes appeared to almost rise up and merge with the misty horizon. When I developed them (I had commandeered our tiny cupboard under the stairs for a dark room) I realised that in one of them I had managed to catch the shadow of a large bird. He was no more than a dark, almost malevolent shape, on the edge of the photograph, sitting so still that I had not been aware of him.

Miss Turner was telling me that she had sent it to the new National Trust magazine and they wanted not only to publish it but to pay me for it. I could barely believe it. All day, while I was teaching the children, my excitement kept intruding until I found myself telling them about it.

"Can we see it?"

James was a bright lad, one of the grammar school scholarship boys and a natural leader in the class. We were talking about the place of art in history, and it occurred to me for the first time that photography could be as valid an art form as painting.

"I don't see why not, I will bring it in tomorrow."

The following day I took my own print in and showed the children. I could tell some of them were disappointed by what were, in fact, somewhat gloomy images, so I tucked it back in my desk, promising to bring in the magazine eventually. I was therefore slightly surprised to find James waiting for me at the end of the afternoon.

"Miss, I told my dad about your picture, and he would really like to see it. He said perhaps you could come round to ours for tea, one day?"

I was taken aback and rapidly trying to bring his parents to mind.

My confusion must have communicated itself, because he said, "My dad hasn't been able to come to the speech days because my mum was ill. My gran came to the last one. But my dad takes pictures like you do, and he has got some in a magazine, as well."

I told James that I would love to come to his house for tea, and we agreed a date the following week. I found I was quite looking forward to meeting a fellow 'picture taker', as so far Miss Turner was the only acquaintance I knew who shared my hobby.

More excitement when I got home. A letter from Alfie announcing the date of his and Patsy's wedding. They have been hoping for so long to be able to get married that I think Patsy was beginning to fear it might never happen. The age-old problem of where to live has been the main obstacle. But Father is moving in with Uncle Bert, and Alfie has been able to take over renting the cottage, so wedding bells at last. I sat down and scrawled a letter of congratulation to them both and accepted the invitation for both Mother and myself.

Over supper I told Mother both pieces of news. She had made an especially delicious and warming stew that evening, which filled our kitchen with mouth-watering smells. Mother's cookery skills had been as much of a revelation to me as her dressmaking ones. I sometimes wondered if she had actually been rather bored with her life as a Posh Lady. But that question was definitely out of bounds. And she makes it obvious that she takes no pleasure from her talents, that the exercise of them is a necessary evil.

She was pleased by Miss Turner's news, but uncomprehending as to why anyone would want to publish anybody's photographs, let alone mine. But the wedding invitation required manoeuvring over rockier ground.

"Why do they want me to go?"

"Because you are a sort of relation, Mother. As am I." This was not going to be an easy conversation. I knew I would have my work cut out persuading Mother to go, but I also knew they had asked her to please me.

"But I hardly know any of them. I will be uncomfortable."

"No, you won't. You can make an effort and talk to people, Mother. We both owe Alfie for taking such good care of our Sooty, right up to the end of his long life So please, do this for me. Because I am asking you to."

This was daring. I never asked Mother for anything, and she knew it. There followed a long silence while we ate.

Then: "What shall we wear? Will it be dressy? Should I make something for us both?"

Goodness, I had actually won. We chatted about clothes for weddings as I piled our plates into the sink, and Mother became quite animated. I had a brief glimpse of what our relationship might have been, had things been different.

James's dad was a surprise. Mr Carrington is quite young, not much more than late thirties I would guess. As James and I both use our bicycles to get to school, he led the way to his home along lanes that are already showing signs of the mud tracks they will have become by Christmas. But there are still some leaves on the trees, and the autumnal colours of the fallen ones remain to decorate and cushion the paths. It was a pleasant ride, James calling back over his shoulder at intervals to point out an interesting view or a row of farm cottages in the distance. We stopped to let a farmer move his sheep across the tracks to another field, and laughed together at the incredible, but endearing, noise the animals made.

"I wonder what they are saying?" I said.

"'Leave me alone!' I expect," answered James, waving back at the farmer when our way was finally cleared.

It struck me how enjoyable it was to have the restrictions of school lifted and to be able to see, and chat to, one of my pupils more as an equal. As we cycled along, I mused that I really hardly knew most of my charges and their backgrounds and wondered if there was any way of rectifying that. Food for thought.

Their cottage was similar to ours, though not quite as isolated as there were three or four others nearby. James rang his bicycle bell as we approached, and his father must have been watching for him for the door was thrown open almost immediately. Unexpectedly, I suddenly felt quite shy, then I told myself not to be ridiculous. I resisted jumping off my bicycle and tried to dismount with dignity, remembering that I was a teacher visiting a pupil's parent, not a tomboy still in her early twenties! My attempted decorum was rather undermined with the realisation that I was standing, sinking even, into thick mud.

As I pulled one boot free, the other sank further down and splashed onto my stockings. Seeing my predicament, Mr Carrington called, "Wait there!" and rushed into the house. James was staring down at my sinking feet with such horror that in spite of myself I began to giggle.

"It's alright, James, just mud, not quicksand," I assured him, but even before I had finished speaking, his father was back, bearing a large plank to make a path for me to tread on. With a mock bow, he stretched out his hand and helped me on to it, and did not let go of my hand until my feet found harder ground.

"My heartfelt apologies. Miss March. We had some rain earlier in the afternoon, and I had not realised this quagmire had appeared, or I would have stayed by the gate and warned you both. James, put Miss March's bicycle in the shed in case it rains some more."

"Please don't worry," I said, rubbing my wet stockings with my handkerchief as I spoke, "a bit of mud is not going to kill me, is it?"

"But it will, I am afraid, make you very uncomfortable. Now, please follow me, and let us get you warm."

Once inside the cottage, Mr Carrington disappeared upstairs and to my surprise returned almost immediately with a pair of stockings, similar to my own.

"Allow me. My mother stays here with James while I am away, and I know she would be glad for you to have these." Seeing my hesitation, he added, "Upstairs, the door on the left. Please go and change, and we can dry yours by the fire."

All this was said with such deference, and, as I was indeed feeling rather cold and uncomfortable, I smiled my thanks and did as I was bid. Changing in the bedroom, I tried not to be nosy, but could not help noticing some framed photographs on the walls of a most beautiful woman. I was sure she must be James's mother as I could see a resemblance. I wondered where she was.

Back downstairs we hung my stockings from the mantelpiece.

"It looks just like Christmas," said James.

We all laughed, and I said, "Sorry, James, I shall be putting them back on as soon as they are dry, you have to wait a few more weeks for Father Christmas."

Mr Carrington sat me in a cosy chair while he and James busied themselves in the small kitchen which adjoined the room. They were obviously conjuring up some tea, and, tired by the ride, I felt my eyelids closing. I pulled myself back from the edge of sleep on hearing my name spoken.

"Miss March? Would you like a cup of tea?" James placed it on the small table beside my chair.

Mr Carrington appeared with a plate of sandwiches. "I am sorry they are of the doorstop variety. My wife always said that I could not cut a thin slice of bread to save my life, and I fear she was right. But Mrs Mead down the lane bakes our bread daily and who would want that to be wafer thin?"

Taking my first bite, I could only agree. It was the nicest bread I had ever tasted, spread thickly with butter and just the right amount of fish paste. There was a companionable silence while we munched.

Then, brushing the crumbs off my skirt, I asked, "Did you take those wonderful photographs upstairs?"

Mr Carrington nodded. "They are all of my wife. I took most of them in the months before she died."

"Oh, I am so sorry. How tactless of me. I had no idea."

"James and I talk about Ida all the time, so you have no need to be embarrassed. In fact, I am surprised he had not told you."

James had been looking into the fire. He looked up at me and I saw that his eyes were glistening slightly. "Mother said she did not want us to forget her and we were not to do that silly thing where you mustn't talk about dead people in case you get upset. She said she would be very cross if we didn't get upset for a bit, but then we were to get used to her not being there and get on with our lives."

"Your mother sounds like a very special person," I said softly.

Mr Carrington replied, "She was, Miss March,"

"Please, call me Daisy. And you, James. Though I have to be Miss March at school, I'm afraid."

"Then you must call me Arthur. And now, Miss, er, Daisy, show me what you have in that splendid document you brought in with such care. I am itching to see this photograph that James has described, and perhaps some more of your work?"

"It is more of a hobby than work, but if it was possible to earn a living from it, I would." I was unwrapping the oilcloth from round my thick leather brief case as I spoke. Although I have a splendid, covered, bicycle basket, I am extra careful if I am carrying my camera or my photographs.

I laid out half a dozen of my marsh photos, including the one that had been so admired. Arthur (as I must learn to think of him) was bending over them. He picked up one and moved under the gas light to look at it more carefully. Then he returned it to the table and picked up another and repeated that. So on, until he had examined all of them without comment. I was beginning to feel distinctly nervous. I glanced at James and thought he was also feeling a bit nervous on my behalf. This caused me some slight amusement and I grinned at him.

"Daisy, you may well smile. I think you are an artist. You have a natural gift for composition. Who taught you to use the light as well as that?"

I was blushing with pleasure. "My former science mistress has been my mentor and teacher ever since I was first given the camera. It is she who has sent this one off to the National Trust Magazine, who are going to publish it. Her own work is excellent."

"What does she photograph?"

"Just about anything that catches her eye. It was her pictures that made me realise the possibilities. That you could do so much more than just take formal portraits."

"You can indeed, Daisy."

"Can I see some of your work?"

"You certainly can." He crossed to a large cupboard and extracted, not, to my surprise, photographs, but a large pile of magazines. He put them on the table and beckoned me over to sit beside him. "These are my published pictures, needless to say the ones that I am most proud of."

They were bookmarked so I was able to flip through easily, and I quickly realised that he had every right to be proud of the photographs. They were amazing, even more astonishing than Miss Turner's. He had taken normal, everyday subjects but in such a way that they became extraordinary. An old man sitting on a step, his pipe smoke curling around his head, a dog rootling for food outside a butchers yard watched by a thin cat from the top of a wall, a sparrow flying overhead and the landscape below transformed magically – they were breathtaking, each one a complete narrative. I thumbed through them in silence, and then went back, and back again, picking out my favourites, the ones that could not possibly be categorised.

I looked up to find both Arthur and James watching me. "They are beyond words, quite wonderful, Arthur. I am in awe of what you achieve. But it also makes me understand what a total amateur I am. I feel elated by what is possible, but depressed at my own inability to get anywhere near what you have created here."

"James, go and make us some more tea, please." When James had left us, Arthur asked, "Daisy, forgive me if I ask how old you are?"

"I am nearly twenty-one."

"I thought as much. You see, I had expected 'Miss March' to be much older than that. Not only because you are young to be teaching, and obviously teaching very well from all James tells me, but from what I guessed must be the calibre of your photographs. I know firsthand how hard it is to achieve publication. My first pictures were not published until five years ago when I was nearly thirty-four. And, Daisy, my photographs were nowhere near as good as yours when I was twenty. No, I am not exaggerating," (I had leaned forward to interrupt and express my disbelief.) "I am absolutely not being modest. You have a very real talent, my dear, which you must not neglect."

"Arthur, as we are being frank, may I ask what you do for a living, as I assume you do not yet earn enough from the photographs?"

He laughed. "You are so right, my dear. Though in the last year, since both Vogue and Punch have published my stuff, the money is improving. No, I am a writer. I was a journalist, but when Ida became ill, I needed to be at home, both for her and for James, so I now write articles for both the newspapers and some magazines. Happily I already had a lot of contacts. Since my wife's death I do occasionally accept a commission that takes me away from home, and my mother looks after James. But only when it is very lucrative."

"Do you illustrate your work with your photos?"

"Increasingly. That is good because it gives me focus, but sometimes frustrating because it is limiting. But I daresay that is the difference between photography as a hobby and photography as a job of work."

"Would you help me?" I felt very daring.

"To do what?"

"To get better."

He hesitated, and then a smile lit up his face. "How could I resist such a perfect answer? Of course I will, Daisy. In fact, it is time that I paid more attention to these marshes myself. Shall I meet you and your camera by the church next Sunday afternoon? I expect James would like to come, too."

"Next Sunday is perfect. About two o'clock? And, thank you so much!"

The light was fading fast, so we quickly drank the tea that James had brought us and I took my now-dry stockings back upstairs. As I changed, I touched one of the pictures gently with my finger. Looking into her eyes, I whispered, "I do wish I had known you. But thank you for letting me know your family." I could almost convince myself that her lovely smile was meant for me.

As I cycled back through the twilight, I was conscious of a pleasant sense of anticipation that I had not felt for ages.

Mother was sitting by the fire knitting when I got in. She had lit an oil lamp and it cast a glow on her hair and face. I was holding my briefcase and my camera was slung round my neck. I quickly put the case down, raised the exposed viewer to my eye and snapped. I had no idea if the picture would come out or not, but today Arthur's work had shown me that I could be more relaxed about the technical limitations of my camera. I had learnt that it could be worth taking risks to achieve beautiful shots.

"What are you doing?" Mother put her knitting down.

"Taking a picture of my industrious mother."

"Hmm. As long as you don't show it to anyone, me wearing my house dress and with my hair barely tidy."

But I could see she was actually quite pleased. I snapped another, this one with her looking up at me.

"Enough, Daisy. Go and take your coat off. Do you want something to eat, or did your pupil's family feed you?"

"They did indeed." Taking my coat off, I hung it in the small hallway and came and sat opposite her. "James's father takes the most amazing pictures; he's been published in Vogue!" I knew that would impress her, as I occasionally brought in a copy and knew she devoured it when she thought I wasn't looking. "And he is going to help me take better pictures, Mother."

"How? I thought all you did was point it and push the button."

"Well, sometimes, like just now, that is exactly all I do. But there is so much to learn, especially about how to use the light. But it was such a good afternoon, and Arthur said I had 'a very real talent'."

"I thought the boy's name was James?"

"Yes, it is, but he is only twelve, so would hardly know or care. Arthur is his father, he is the photographer, Mother."

"You are calling him by his Christian name? And what is he calling you?"

I sensed a storm brewing, for no reason that I understood. "He calls me Daisy. It is my name, Mother, as you should know."

Why was she making me feel so defensive? The joy began to drain from the day.

"And are you planning to see this man again?"

"Yes. I am meeting him next Sunday to take some pictures on the marsh."

"No, you are not." Her tone was icy. "I am not having you cavorting on the marshes with some man I do not know and is already becoming familiar with you. I forbid it, Daisy." She rose as if to leave the room, but I moved into the doorway to stop her.

"Mother, I am nearly twenty-one, and I am a teacher. He is the father of one of my pupils and a respected writer. And I am going to meet him on Sunday."

"I repeat, I forbid it."

"What do you think is going to happen?" I cried. "For heaven's sake, Mother, have you such a low opinion of me that you think I am going to throw myself at him like a heroine in a cheap novelette? And," I added as an afterthought, "James will probably be with us anyway, so if you believe I need a chaperone you can be satisfied."

We still stood facing each other in the doorway, like a couple of boxers. Mother's eyes fell first.

"Very well. I will allow you to go. But on one condition, that you arrange for him to come here so that I can meet him first."

I took a deep breath and decided to recognise the olive branch for the sake of peace and quiet. "That is quite unnecessary but I will ask James to convey your wishes to his father."

Mother pushed past me and disappeared upstairs. I sat down heavily in the chair she had just vacated and stared into the fire, clutching the arms of the chair till my knuckles went white. I found I was still shaking with –

90

with what? With anger, yes, and with frustration that Mother still saw me as a child, but something more that I could not identify. I sat watching the fire slowly die, until there was a chill in the air, and still I did not move.

It was resentment. That was the elusive emotion, above all others that I was feeling. Fifteen years on, and I still could not really accept her as my mother. Somewhere in my head, I could still hear my five-year-old sobs and feel my infant pain. What right had she then or now, to control my life? I knew such thoughts were unacceptable. I knew she was my mother. I even understood that in her own way she struggled to do her best for me. I was less sure that she had ever been able to love me.

I finally rose stiffly from my chair and gathered up my things. Tomorrow I would use the rest of the film in my camera and then develop it, including the two shots of Mother. I hoped they would come out. Possibly capturing a rare moment of warmth between us.

April, 1932

There is something very uplifting about seeing two people as happy as Alfie and Patsy were today. It was a simple ceremony, and although they had decided against a formal white wedding Patsy looked so pretty in a cream skirt and coat, holding a spray of spring flowers. We arrived at the house a little bit early and when Mother saw the flowers, to my amazement, she picked up some left-over ones that were sitting on the table and twisted them into a tiara.

When Patsy came downstairs, Mother gave it to her with such a lovely smile I felt quite envious. Then she helped Patsy arrange it in her hair, and asked me for my opinion.

"You look lovely, Patsy," I said truthfully, "and so do you, Mother."

Mother had made us both costumes, mine in a silky, pale green, fabric, and her own in a heavier material of dark purple. I had knitted us both delicate, lacy, jumpers in ivory coloured wool to set them off – and to make sure we were warm! We both wore hats in the same colour as our costumes, but in a deeper shade. We had actually made an excursion to Gravesend to see the milliner who was to make them for us. We took scraps of the fabric to illustrate what we required. When we had finished our business with the hats, we had tea in a nearby hotel – scones with raspberry jam and cream and a pot of Earl Gray. Then we took the train home. It was extremely rare for Mother to initiate any kind of excursion but she appeared to enjoy it, as did I. And there was something that felt very special in just being two women out shopping together.

And so yes, back to our attire, we did both look rather splendid, though I found myself hoping not too much for a village wedding. I had no idea Mother was so interested in fashion, or in her appearance. I had never seen her so energised, but when I thought back, she always spent a long time dressing before Sir came to visit, and she had a large wardrobe of clothes in those days. I supposed most of them would be hopelessly old-fashioned now, which was probably why she had got rid of them.

Georgie had managed to get leave, and just when it was nearly time for the walk to the church, we heard the noise of his motor bike, and there he was. He burst through the door, still the same ebullient brother, and threw his arms round me. Lifting me up in the air, he knocked my hat off, and Mother said, "Oh, do be careful, George," but she was smiling.

He turned to her and laughed, "How nice to see you here, Mrs Gosling. And how beautiful you look."

And Mother blushed! It really was turning out to be a day of surprises. Georgie was Alfie's best man, so he shot off to join him at the church, so as to get there ahead of us. He looks so smart in his uniform. The boys' father came and took Mother's arm, and then beckoned to me to take his other. Then Uncle Bert, who is giving the bride away, led the procession to the church with her, as her own parents are dead. Her father died in a mining accident when she was quite small, and her mother had tuberculosis and died last year. Uncle Bert has been very kind to her and she has been living at the farm with him. He says he doesn't know how he will manage without her, but you can see how pleased he is for her and Alfie.

Happily, it is not a long walk to the church, and it was a bright and sunny day. No need to use the umbrellas that

Mr Clark, the thoughtful vicar, keeps in the church porch for inclement weather on these occasions. The crocodile tailed back through the village, as various friends and relations joined us. We were soon near enough to hear the thunder of the ancient organ, and we all filed past the bride, waiting in the porch, to take our seats in the church.

Georgie was standing beside Alfie at the front, and they both turned to smile at us. Then, after a pause the music began again and there was Patsy, seeming to almost float down the aisle on Uncle Bert's arm to the strains of that wonderful Mendelssohn chorus. The look on Alfie's face when he saw her brought tears to my eyes – in the unlikely event that I should ever be married, I hoped someone would look at me like that. I briefly remembered Henry, and his parents' remarks, but then pushed the memory away. Today was about happiness and I was not going to let anything besmirch that.

After the ceremony, to the joyful accompaniment of the church bells, I made the bridal couple stand still in front of the church, because I had, of course, brought my camera. I took several photographs, but gave up on trying to snap the guests as no-one would stand still.

Then we followed the happy couple to the church hall, where there was a wonderful wedding breakfast already laid out. Mrs Clark, the vicar's conscientious wife, must have been marshalling the villagers for days. Patsy had told us earlier that she had been ordered 'to leave it all to her' but the spread was beyond any expectations. Even Mother was impressed, whispering to me, "They could hardly have bettered this at the Ritz." Which left me wondering about the huge areas of her life which I knew nothing at all about.

Once we had eaten and drunk so many toasts that we were all reeling with a combination of alcohol and good will, Uncle Bert produced his mouth organ, and the dancing began. Alfie led Patsy on to the floor, and Georgie leapt up as soon as they began to dance and offered his hand to me. Soon everyone was on their feet. Two dances later I was amused to see Uncle Bert had been replaced by a lady pianist on the rather out of tune hall instrument and he was now dancing with Mother.

Now that was a sight I had never expected to see. Georgie looked down at me with a grin on his face. "Life is full of surprises, isn't it?"

I could only nod in agreement.

"So," I asked, "is there a girl in your life, Georgie? I never thought Alfie would settle down before you."

"There's been no-one else for him since they were at the village school together. I don't think either of them has ever looked at anyone else. But then, I am a one girl chap, too, and you are the only girl in my life, Daisy," he replied with a grin.

"Sisters don't count. You know perfectly well what I mean."

"Indeed I do." He paused, as if thinking how to answer. "And no, there is no-one. Anyway, I am moving around far too much to ask any woman to take me on yet. But I do love the army, and the life. It was a good choice for me. What about you, sister mine?"

"Well," I could feel myself blushing.

"Oh, so there is, is there? Let's stop this jugging around and go and sit in the sun, and you can tell me about him."

We went and sat on the bench outside. The noise from the hall receded into a pleasant background of music and laughter.

"Well, go on, then. Tell me about this young blade who has obviously captured your heart."

"That's a bit strong, and I'd hardly call him a young blade! Arthur is a widower, and he is probably nearer Mother's age than mine. Also he has a son of nearly thirteen, who is one of my pupils."

"So is that how you met him?"

"Yes. James, his son, said his father wanted to meet me because he is a keen and successful photographer and James told him about my photographs. And, Georgie, his pictures are amazing, and he is showing me how to get the very best from my camera, and what to look for, and how to 'trap the moment' – that's how he describes getting a really good image. I have had three photographs published in magazines now, and I am putting the money toward one of the new cameras that you can do even more with."

"And are you falling in love with him, or his photos?"

"I don't know how to separate them. Mother insisted that he came to meet her before we went out shooting (that's what he calls taking photographs) on the marshes together, and now he comes to the house all the time. Mother doesn't seem to mind at all. He helps me to develop my films, and has given me such a lot of information about the technicalities involved. Miss Turner was so good helping me, but Arthur not only knows more, he is near. You could almost say just down the road. And I like him a lot."

"Not love?"

"Oh, Georgie, how would I know? Apart from you and Alfie I've only ever known one other man that I have had any friendship at all with and that, well, it didn't turn out well. I just know that I enjoy Arthur's company. And perhaps, yes, perhaps I do like it a bit when he puts his arm round me to show me how to hold the camera or something like that. But that's not wrong, is it?"

"No, I am sure it isn't, you goose." Georgie used to call me that when I was little and the recollection made us both smile. "You would know if there was anything not right about it. But who was this other chap? The one you were friends with. Why don't I know about him?"

I hesitated, then decided. After all, Georgie was my brother, and he must have guessed Mother's and my circumstances, even if no-one ever mentioned them. "It was Henry. Jennifer's brother. Do you remember? You met them at the ball at our school."

"Yes. Of course I do. I thought he seemed quite keen on you. He didn't...?"

"No, he didn't." I interrupted him. "Henry always behaved like a perfect gentleman. It was more complicated than that."

"Go on. Whatever it is, you can tell me. And I can see it might be better shared."

"How well you know me."

He waited patiently as I sat quietly for a minute, gathering both my words and my courage. And then, taking a deep breath, I told him about the morning I overheard Henry's parents, and recounted their conversation, word for word. Which was not difficult as it was etched in my mind forever.

"So, you see," I concluded, "I am not likely to recognise love because, since then, I have quite deliberately shunned the possibility of ever being in such a situation again."

Georgie had lit a cigarette while I was speaking, and now he rose and threw it to the ground, stamping on it with considerable force. I understood that it represented Henry's parents, and the tears which I had been determined not to shed while telling him about them miraculously disappeared.

"Oh, Georgie! You have made me feel better already!"

"I should like to go and, and ... oh, I don't know what. Shake them until their teeth rattle!"

This conjured up such an absurd image we both burst out laughing, and a voice called down the path, "What are you two up to, lurking out here? Come inside and join the party."

"Coming, Uncle Bert." Georgie pulled me to my feet and held me close. "If ever any idiot speaks about you like that again, promise you will tell me."

"What could you do, Georgie? After all, they were right."

"They may have been accurate, but they were not right. We had better go back inside. But promise me, Daisy."

I promised. What else could I do? And I loved Georgie even more for wanting to be my knight in shining armour.

August, 1934

I gave in my notice at school today. I was a little bit sad and more than a bit nervous, but in spite of Mother's dire predictions I know I must seize this chance. I have been getting so many commissions and I have had to turn down far too much because of my time strictures, but next month I shall be a free woman.

"Free to starve," muttered Aunt Hannah, charming as ever on one of her mercifully rare visits.

"I don't think that is quite the case," intervened Mother on my behalf, more because Arthur was there than because she believed it, I think.

But I accepted her defence with gratitude. Georgie says I am pathetically grateful for the crumbs of praise that fall from Mother's table, and although I recognise there is some truth in that, I cannot seem to change. However, I do realise that she is completely unaware how huge an accolade this offer of an exhibition by the V&A is, and how overwhelmed I am by it. And thrilled!

Alfie and Patsy were delighted with the photos of their wedding, and they pinned them up in the church for all to see. Then I had a call from the local paper, asking if they could publish them and offering me a respectable amount of money. The next thing I knew, I was inundated with people asking me to take photos of their weddings. After a few months of this, Arthur pointed out that I really needed a car. I had thought about this, but although I had heard that some women did drive, I did not have either the knowledge or the courage to facilitate it myself.

However, Arthur took charge, took me to a garage where he knew the owner, and somehow I ended up the proud owner of a Ford Coupe. Mother was very nervous, as there have been ridiculous amounts of traffic accidents these last few years, but the government have just reintroduced the speed limit in towns, and anyway, as Arthur says, I shall mostly be driving in quiet country lanes. The actual bit of learning to drive was very simple, I could not help thinking it is shrouded in male mystique to frighten women and keep it as something only men do.

"A bit like photography," said Arthur, when I told him this.

Apparently, they are about to introduce a test for drivers, which I think will be a good thing. But Arthur is such a good teacher I am sure I would have no trouble passing it. He is already teaching James to drive their car. He thinks one day everyone will have cars, and no-one will need buses or trains anymore.

I laughed at him when he said that. "Where is everyone going to keep all these cars?" I asked.

"They'll find a way," he says, and pulls his: 'I am older than you and know everything', face.

Having the car made it possible for me to go further afield and I began to notice some of the beautiful buildings in our part of Kent. Until now, apart from the weddings, I had mostly photographed aspects of the marshes, and travelling through the towns was a revelation to me. I spent quite a bit of time snapping some of the churches and historic buildings, and I was fascinated by the way the river Medway snaked through the middle of some of the towns. I took so many views I was sometimes in danger of not cataloguing them properly, but Mother became used to our dining table being covered with my pages of notes.

Arthur suggested that I send some of my pictures to the relevant local papers, with a potted history of each. I began with some of Rochester, and to my great surprise they were all accepted and published, so I followed with the ones of Chatham. Then the newspapers in Gillingham and Tonbridge asked me to do their towns and I hurriedly added to my stock, thanking heaven I had my little car.

The idea became so popular that, within the year, I had done pictorial representations of all the major Kent towns and I had enough money to buy the new 35mm Leica, which I had been coveting ever since Arthur let me handle his. And then came the letter from the V&A.

"However did they know about my photos?" I asked Mother as I showed her the letter.

"I think you might find that Arthur contacted them. He is a very generous man, and a great admirer of your pictures, Daisy."

I could not think of an answer to that, as I was very conscious that so much of my expertise was down to Arthur's mentoring. The exhibition was to be in six months time, so I was already wondering about the gallery and the prospective light there. I could see I had a busy two months ahead of me. But the first thing was to let Arthur know. Always in the forefront of technology he had a telephone installed recently, so I drove down to the post office to put a call through to him.

He brushed aside my thanks, but had some important advice. "This is the chance of a lifetime, Daisy. You can't prepare your portfolio in odd moments. It has got to be your proper, full time job. Which is what you wanted, isn't it?"

I confessed that it was indeed what I had dreamed about, but never really expected it to happen.

"Well, it has happened. And you are going to have to tell the school you won't be back next term. I am sure, if you explain why, they will be sympathetic."

Which turned out to be true. Mrs Green expressed regret but not great surprise. So here I was, twenty-four years old, preparing to exhibit in the most prestigious place in London. And, as Mother said, 'with no proper job'.

Arthur has promised to help me. That is a huge comfort. If I stop to think about all this I do feel a bit out of my depth, but his belief in my capabilities buoys me up. We are going up to London together tomorrow to view the gallery and talk to the director.

February 1935

'*Glorious Kent, a Photographic Exhibition by Daisy March',* opened last night with a private viewing. I was incredibly nervous, and half-expected that folk would come in, walk round, and go 'what a waste of time' on their way out. The museum had invited the press and 'dignitaries', which turned out to mean mostly politicians and posh people, but there were some people from the theatre, which I thought was very exciting.

Gertrude Lawrence and Noel Coward came and wanted to be introduced to me. I was stupidly tense and almost intimidated by their fame and sophistication; they are so glamorous and looked like people from another, more exotic, world. Mother was standing beside me, and I introduced her and they shook hands with us both. Mr Coward said, "You have a very talented daughter, Mrs Gosling, you must be so proud of her."

And Mother replied, "I certainly am." When they had moved off, she turned to me and said, "Wait until I tell Hannah that!"

I would have liked to have introduced them to Arthur, but by the time I spotted him they had gone. Then I realised he was chatting to the director so would not have wanted to be interrupted, anyway. Not even for the theatre's two biggest stars!

The museum had arranged for us to stay at the Savoy that night, which was very grand indeed. Mother was quite at home there, but I don't know if I could ever get used to all those people running round after me. They even turned down the sheets on our beds.

"Do they think we are helpless?" I asked Mother, which she thought was highly amusing.

"It is the practice in all good hotels, Daisy. The little touches which make you relax."

They had the opposite effect on me. I felt uncomfortable and like a fish out of water. As if I was pretending to be something that I wasn't.

"You have worked so hard for this, Daisy. Enjoy it," said Mother, as she wafted off to lay in the porcelain bath that came with our suite. That was definitely an improvement on our cumbersome tin bath in the wash house in our cottage; I had to admit that when we moved there, I missed having a proper bathroom more than anything else. Though I knew it was a luxury that none of MumMarch's family even imagined.

I was relieved that Mother was enjoying it all so much. I had not told her until a couple of days ago that I had reverted to my original name of March, and then I merely said that the museum felt that Daisy Gosling did not have the same ring to it. I didn't say that I had never felt it was really my name, and had leapt at the chance to be called March again. I had thought she might protest, but she barely seemed to notice.

Arthur did, though, and was curious. "I've never asked why you call that soldier chap your brother? His name is March, isn't it? Did Susan adopt you?"

I managed to brush it aside with, "Sort of. It was all a bit complicated." And we were so busy walking around Canterbury Cathedral at the time and working out the best angles, he appeared to forget all about it. Arthur wants me to go up to Scotland with him next month. He is doing some articles on the people and culture, and he wants me to supply the photographs. I like the idea, but I am reluctant to commit to it yet. We should be gone for four weeks, which is not a problem, but I am not altogether comfortable about the project. The thing is, I think I might be in love with him.

I miss him when he is not there. I love discussing our work together, his and mine, and sometimes he stays so late when we are chatting that Mother says he may as well sleep on the sofa. James is off at university now, and doing really well, so Arthur has no need to dash back for him. Sometimes, when he leans over me to guide an angle, or point out a figure on the horizon, I want him to hold me tightly. I want him to kiss me. There. I have admitted it. So it must be true. I am in love. I have read the Brontes and Jane Austen and all the modern novelists, so I know that this is what being in love must be like.

I expected it to be more overwhelming. More, sort of, well, all-consuming. But that is probably just in books. The thing is, if I were to take the lead, perhaps to give him a gentle kiss, would he think that was very forward? And, even worse, how would I tell him the truth about my, well, about my being a bastard. Though obviously I would have to find a more delicate way of putting it. Mother would be shocked that I even know the word. But would he want to marry a bastard? For if he could not overcome his disgust at that then there would be no way forward for us.

All these thoughts whirled round my head as I lay in bed every night. I pictured myself married to Arthur, stepmother to James, and even though I was nearer James' age than his, it seemed a right and inevitable progression of our relationship. Because, the more I examined my own feelings, the more certain I became of his. His constant presence at our cottage, and sometimes on the flimsiest of excuses. And often bearing gifts, of flowers or sweets, always pretending he just happened to pick them up from wherever he had been the previous day, and saying he thought we would enjoy them. Surely these were the marks of courtship? I was more and more persuaded that my feelings were reciprocated. In fact, possibly with more passion than my own, but that seemed to me a pleasant, and not unusual balance, which would be rectified with more open intimacy.

Greatly daring, I resolved to make a move. When the next opportunity presented itself, I would touch his face, or place a light kiss on his cheek. I practiced in front of the mirror until I made myself giggle. Perhaps I should just tell him that I loved him? No, that really was too forward. But could I tell him I was fond of him, would that be enough to allow him to go further? I thought it might. Tomorrow would be the day, I told myself.

I woke early the next day, and was immediately distracted by the sight of the grass in the garden sparkling with early dew. I threw on some clothes and rushed outside with my camera, and caught the rainbow images. I had heard rumours that one day soon we would have colour films for our cameras, but I wondered if anything could be more spectacular than this sharp morning light reflected on black and white films.

Arthur was due to come early that morning to discuss the trip to Scotland, but I was determined to be in my tiny dark room working so that he could not see my face when I made my declaration. I was in there, pegging up some prints on my makeshift line, when I heard his car arrive. Mother and he had quite a long conversation, so long that I thought he must have gone into the garden with her, but then I heard the click of the sitting room door and realised they must have been sitting chatting. So much for starting work early, I thought. I had delayed developing some prints, so as to remain where I was.

Finally, he tapped gently on the dark room door, and I called for him to inch in without letting the light flood my still-damp pictures. We were old hands at that manoeuvre. I deliberately kept my back to him, while he made amusing comments about being stuck behind the horse-drawn milk float in one of the lanes. My laughter at his description of the frustration caused by the ambling horse and the pipe-smoking driver made my projected pronouncement easier than I had anticipated.

"Oh, Arthur, you have made me laugh so much this morning. How much I owe you for all your help. You must be aware of how fond I am of you." There. It was done. The reaction was instant and gratifying.

"Oh, Daisy, how splendid of you to say that. And at just the right moment. Now, young lady, finish those immediately and come into the light. I have something to ask you."

Well. I had not expected everything to happen so quickly, but I supposed we had had a courtship of sorts and, after all, I had made up my mind that I should like to marry him, so I imagined he also thought that there was no point in prevarication.

I went into the kitchen to wash my hands and straighten my hair, glancing quickly at my reflection on the back of the frying pan, the nearest thing to a mirror there. I thought I looked alright. Good enough for a marriage proposal. Arthur was in the sitting room, standing in front of the fire. Mother was standing next to him. She looked so animated that I guessed Arthur had told her of his intentions.

"Sit down, Daisy." I did, my stomach curling with pleasant anticipation. "Daisy, I was so pleased to hear your words this morning, they meant so much to me, because, you see," he paused, "your mother has made me the happiest of men, and agreed to be my wife. We have not known how you would feel about me becoming your father, but this morning we had decided it was time to tell you. I hope you will be happy for us, my dear."

I was stunned, but hoped it didn't show. I kissed them both (there, I finally kissed you, Arthur) and gave them my blessing. How could I have not noticed? Arthur wasn't courting me, he was courting my mother. I was just his pupil, his work mate. I made excuses to leave them on their own, and, picking up my camera, I walked into the garden and gazed across my beloved marshes. In a flash, I knew my heart was not broken. Almost the opposite was true. I felt a sense of relief, of a lightening of heart. I wanted to laugh at my naivety, and raising my camera, I snapped two doves that had just settled on the hedgerow and stood listening to their amorous calls.

Then, out of hearing and sight of the house, I began to laugh out loud. I laughed at my idiotic, unperceptive self and resolved to read less romantic fiction in future.

July, 1937

The Photographic Journal has asked me to go to Germany in the autumn. They are proposing to send me with Kurt Klein, a very well-known and respected travel correspondent, and I am to illustrate his articles. I am going to say yes, of course, (how could I possibly turn it down?!) even though I have a feeling that Mother is not going to be too happy about it. But although I don't like upsetting her, mercifully we have Arthur as the unofficial adjudicator between us nowadays.

He and Mother got married a couple of weeks before he and I left to do the Scotland job. It was a quiet affair, in a registry office with just James and me as witnesses. James is very tickled by the whole business. I wondered if he would mind his dad getting married again, but not a bit of that.

"I was worried about leaving him on his own when I went off to Oxford," he confessed. "It has been a huge weight off my mind. Though for a time I thought it was you he was mooning over, Daisy!"

We both had a good laugh at this and I thought: 'little do you know, my lad!' I am fond of James, and pleased that we are sort of related. I suppose I can say that I have three brothers now, which is very gratifying. Sometimes I feel a bit sort of marooned, not totally part of anyone's family. But Georgie is never out of touch, and I manage to see him quite often, and Alfie and Patsy and their two boys always seem pleased to see me. I am an honorary aunt now which I enjoy very much. Nevertheless I am always conscious of the casual lie in my background. My father is indeed dead, but the only history I can ever refer to, when asked, is fabricated, a lie, and I am caught in its web. Arthur knows the truth, in fact he probably knows more about my background than I do, but the subject is still taboo.

Our excursion to Scotland was a roaring success. Now, here I have a confession. Arthur came home to see Mother in the middle of our four weeks, ostensibly to sort out their living arrangements, though I suspected they seized the opportunity for some canoodling while I was away. I could not quite see how him moving in with us required all this planning. After all, he was practically living with us anyway.

But back to my confession. I have collected a beau. A tall, red-haired Scotsman by the name of Keith. A wee bit (to use his own terminology) older than me, but not by much. He was to be our guide for the trip, and we met up with him in Edinburgh, our first port of call. There was rapport between us almost immediately. He has a very subtle humour, and kept making me laugh out loud, although Arthur was sometimes a trifle bemused by our mirth. Keith actually plays the bagpipes; I thought he was teasing me when he told me that. But then, one cold but bright morning, there he was, underneath my window, and the air was filled with wonderful, haunting music.

I thought he would be hauled off by the police or by the rather fierce hotel commissionaire, as it was only about seven in the morning, but nobody turned a hair. Edinburgh is much more cosmopolitan than I was expecting; very busy, lots of shops filled with smartly dressed people, and trams whirling around all the time. There was a vase of roses in my room, and, getting into the spirit of the moment, I plucked one and threw it down to him. And then greatly daring, when he picked it up, I blew him a kiss. There was a cheer from the small crowd who had gathered to listen to the bagpipes, and I withdrew quickly behind the window!

Keith is the reason I stayed in Scotland while Arthur went back home. We didn't talk about it, but as he was packing to leave on the Friday evening, he said, "I'll tell your mother you have a lot of work to do, then?" and spoiled it rather by giving me a huge wink. Arthur has always treated me like a grown-up who knows her own mind, which is especially a relief now he is my step-father.

Keith and I had a wonderful weekend together. We didn't do the historic sites, because, after all, that was our work, and this was time off. He enjoyed country walking as much as I do, so we donned our walking boots and made for the Pentland Hills. Such a lovely, lovely day. The sun shone, the hotel did a picnic lunch for us to take, and Keith had a flask of whisky, which I had never tried before. I only had a sip, and didn't like it much, but I pretended I did. The whole joyful day sped past, and I enjoyed a kind of singular camaraderie with him, which was quite a new experience for me.

He teased me about taking photographs all the time, even when I was not working, but I couldn't resist the temptation. We met another couple, and they took a photo of us together, Keith with his arm over my shoulders and us both laughing. We had supper together at my hotel, and arranged to go on a coastal walk the following day.

We left quite early the following day and drove to the Firth of Forth. Walking the coastal paths was quite a different experience, more reminiscent of my marshland home, and I found myself telling Keith a lot about our life, Mother's and mine.

There is something about walking with a sympathetic listener, and I suppose I must have revealed more than I intended, because Keith suddenly said, in his soft Scottish burr, "So this visiting toff turned out to be your dad, did he?"

I stopped mid-stride and turned to face him. I expected to confront a look of horror, or condemnation, but there was nothing but mild curiosity, so I nodded and looked away, not knowing how to answer.

He took my arm, and turning me round to face him, said, "Daisy, I get the feeling this is very important to you, and perhaps not often discussed?"

Again, I nodded an affirmative.

"Well," he continued, still holding arm close, "you should'na fret over it. In the village where I was bred, half the bairns aren't too sure who their da is."

And then he roared with laughter, and after a moment, so did I. And somehow felt everything shift, as if my perspective had been irrevocably changed for the better.

That evening, tired from our two days of walking, we had a quick supper in a cafe in the town before returning to my hotel. As I said goodnight to Keith and thanked him for our weekend, he bent and kissed me. Startled, I lifted my face, and he kissed me again. And this time I kissed him back.

I floated up to bed. My very first proper kiss!

Arthur returned the following morning, and it was back to work for the three of us. On our last night in Scotland, Keith took me dancing. We Lindy Hopped and swung until after midnight, then we walked back to the hotel with our arms entwined.

Back there, standing in the foyer, I promised to send him 'our' photos, and Keith said, "With or without the photographs, I shall remember you and these four weeks forever, Daisy March."

And I knew that I would, as well. Lots of fun, sparkling company, enough romance to add that extra feeling, and most of all, no secrets – it had been the best four weeks of my life.

And now, look out Germany, here I come!

I am not sure I would have ever got over here without Georgie's help. He is a huge tower of strength, advising me on everything from how to get my passport to the best way to travel. He is such a seasoned traveller nowadays, having been all over the world in his soldiering career. Neither of us are especially interested in politics, I just about know that Mr Chamberlain is our Prime Minister, but then it would be hard not to know that as he was only elected in May this year and there has been loads in the papers about him. Almost as much as about our new King.

So I was surprised when Georgie said, "Be careful over there, Daisy, I hear that Germany is a bit weird at the moment."

I thought about that remark on the boat going over. Arthur had told me all about the Treaty of Versailles, ratified after the war, and how angry it had made the Germans. Arthur had said that they had caused the war in 1914, but making them pay more money than the country actually had to their former enemies, might not have been the best way of ensuring future peace. But Germany is picking up again now, so perhaps that is rather a gloomy outlook. I hoped so.

In fact, the reason I have got this job is largely because the country is starting to 'hold its head up again',

113

as the magazine editor said, and they want photographs of some of the big events that Germany is staging. But I am also tasked with trying to get pictures of some of the girls who have signed up to the 'Hitler Youth Brigade', which I guessed was like a sort of Scout movement. So – public pictures and personal ones as well, just my cup of tea!

There is to be a huge rally at Nuremberg in September, and the American reporters have been banned from going there. Apparently this was because they had been instrumental in bringing about the hated Versailles treaty. But it means that any pictures I manage to get will be all the more important, so I am very, very excited. I might even manage to get close to Mr Hitler, the Chancellor.

Kurt, who the magazine has teamed me up with, is a very nice, and very Anglicised, German, and fortunately for us both he speaks perfect English, as I have virtually no German. We met up in London, and discussed how we wanted to tackle the job. He lives in Berlin, and I am to stay with him and his family for most of the time I am here. Kurt says it is good that I am not very political, as I will be able to judge everything with a neutral eye. I thought 'judge' was a strange word to use, and I told him that photographers are neutral by definition. He gave me what I have come to think of as 'one of his looks' and merely grunted. He is quite old, at least fifty, I should think, and we don't talk a lot. But I find that quite restful as some reporters seem to talk non-stop.

We have drawn up our itinerary, and we both expect the rally to be the climax. This is supposed to be the biggest one Germany has staged yet, so there should be loads of interesting opportunities for me. I might stay on as the Duke and Duchess of Windsor are planning to come and see Mr Hitler. Oh – just remembered that Kurt says I must say Herr Hitler now I am here. If I could get some pictures of the three of them together I think a lot of newspapers would be interested in those. I can still hardly believe my luck in being offered this job.

Anyway, tomorrow we have an interview with Jutta Rüdiger, who has just been appointed head of the League of German Girls. I wrote to tell Mother; she always likes to know when I am meeting important people. The League is the only organisation in Germany for young women, and it has recently become compulsory to join it, and they have to stay in until they are eighteen, so I am particularly interested to hear more about it.

Well, interesting hardly begins to describe the interview with Frau Rüdiger, this morning. I think I have a lot to learn about Germany and the Nazi culture. I am beginning to understand why Georgie warned me to be careful. We were ushered into a dark, wood-panelled, office in the grounds of the university, where I understand the Frau worked until recently. I was disconcerted when she leapt up on our entrance and, giving the now familiar salute, exclaimed, "*Heil Hitler*".

I was unsettled but determined not to show it, so I answered her with "Good morning," and when she ignored my out-stretched hand I merely looked down and undid my camera case. Kurt gave a somewhat half-hearted return of the salute, and then she motioned us both to sit down. The only seats were two wooden chairs in front of her desk, so it was a bit like being interviewed by one's head-mistress. However, Kurt produced his notebook and a pen, and I raised my camera to my eye to judge the light, which was absolutely no good at all.

115

Before I could explain this, Frau Rüdiger, got to her feet and began to pace round us. She and Kurt started jabbering away in German, but I caught the word Fuhrer several times so guessed she was talking about the Chancellor.

After a few minutes of this, I interrupted them, and said in my best teacher's voice, "Can you speak English, please?"

The lady was obviously not used to being stopped, because she turned and fixed me with a very cold look. "Do you not speak German?"

"I am afraid I do not."

"You are Engländerin?

"I am indeed."

A silence. I glanced at Kurt, who then said something to her in German. I only had a tiny smattering but, because of the similarity in the nouns, I understood that he was telling her that I was one of the country's leading photographers. It was something of a (large!) exaggeration but it did the trick. She looked me up and down, nodded for us to follow her, and then led the way out into the grounds. There she began to speak in halting but adequate English, addressing us both.

"Herr Hitler believes that while we women are obviously inferior in strength of mind and body to our men folk, it is essential that we are trained to be perfect Aryan wives. Our health is important, and at least once every week, our girls, who are between fourteen and eighteen years old, will be led by their group leaders in physical education to strengthen their bodies for childbirth. They are also expected to have learnt some basic medical knowledge, and acquire cookery and sewing skills. We are the female side of the Hitler Youth

116

Movement, and our members are extremely proud to be part of our glorious National Socialist Party. Many of the girls come to us having already had some training in the junior branch of the League, which takes the girls at ten years old."

Kurt was scribbling rapidly. I asked if I could take some photographs to which the Frau graciously concurred, though she treated my camera to some very severe looks. But that seemed right in view of her general demeanour. I doubted she smiled much. I then asked if we could attend a meeting, and I could snap some of the girls in their uniforms. After some hesitation she agreed, and we arranged to meet the following day at a school just outside the town.

"You did well, there," said Kurt, as we climbed back into his car. "Mein Gott, she was fierce, wasn't she? I thought she was going to refuse to co-operate."

"What was she saying to you earlier?"

"Basically, that she did not have time for frivolities such as interviews. But I reminded her that the Fuhrer recently said that the Nazi message needed to be spread across the world, and then I exaggerated the importance of The National Photographic Magazine."

We both laughed at this. Then I said, "Kurt, what is the difference between him being Chancellor and being Fuhrer? Everyone seems to call him that here, while at home they just say 'Herr Hitler'?"

"It is a big difference, Daisy. When he took the title, he became Supreme Leader, which is what it means. No democracy in Germany anymore. The Fuhrer has complete and absolute power. No elections, no discussions. His word is law."

"Gosh," I said.

"Yes," he answered, "'Gosh,' indeed."

The following day we met Frau Rüdiger, and stood at the edge of a large playing field watching about one hundred girls performing some very sophisticated gymnastics. They did cartwheels and with a dozen or so girls managing to synchronise them in a long line, the effect was rather like one of those wonderful Busby Berkeley musical films. Then, in smaller groups dotted around the field, they ran races, or played ball games. I wandered among them, snapping away for all I was worth. They had abandoned their usual uniform of long blue skirts and white blouses for dark blue shorts and white singlets.

After about three hours of activity, their final act was to form a large column, five girls across and twenty deep, each line with girls of approximately the same height. Then they marched up and down the field in formation with no-one putting a step out of place. Finally, their leader, whose name I had not caught, brought them to a halt, said something to them in German, and they all, quite simultaneously, made the Hitler salute.

Then they were dismissed, but they did not run off laughing as they would have done at home, but cleared the field of their equipment methodically and went quietly back into school. I have to admit I felt some unease. Impressive though it had all been, there was something un-childlike and unnatural about everything we had witnessed, though in all honesty I could not say why I felt that. The girls were all good-looking and obviously healthy, and although there was no laughter or horse-play, there was also no hint that they were not enjoying themselves.

We thanked the leader, and I took her photograph. She was a pretty woman, I would guess in her early twenties, and unlike Frau Rüdiger, smiled into the camera for me. Then we bade them all goodbye and Kurt drove us back to his home, where they had given me the facilities to develop my film in a basement scullery. I checked I had all the rolls in my bag, while asking Kurt, "What was that she said to them? Before the final salute?"

"She said. 'We are one Reich, one people, Aryan and strong. You must despise the degenerates who are not Aryan as we are. God will bless our Fuhrer and the Fatherland forever'," he replied.

"I don't understand. What does she mean by degenerates? Who is she talking about?"

He stared straight ahead, his hands gripping the steering wheel. "She means the Jews, Daisy. She is talking about people like me."

I stared at him in disbelief.

Back at the house, I went straight down to the basement to develop my films. But as I worked in the half-light, my mind was whirling, trying to make sense of it all. I sort of knew that Kurt's family was Jewish, but so many German families were, that I had not given it a second thought. And, although Mother had insisted we went to church when I was younger, I knew hardly more about religion that I did about politics. Our religious education at school had largely been stories from the Old Testament which seemed to have no relevance at all to anything in our lives.

I was beginning to feel like the most ignorant person ever, one way or another. But I resolved to ask Kurt to elaborate when we were next alone. All my instincts told me not to say too much in front of his parents. I knew Kurt was a widower, but apart from that, I realised I knew next to nothing about either him or his family.

Later that evening, after supper, I helped Mrs Klein to clear the dishes and wash up. She was a dumpy little woman with a smiley face who had made me feel very welcome in their house. Her husband was very quiet, a ghost-like presence who sat in same armchair every day, reading the newspapers. I hardly ever heard him speak. Kurt said that he had once been a lecturer at the university. I had been a bit worried about imposing on them, as I knew they must be struggling, like everybody else, with all the food shortages. But Kurt had assured me that the magazine was paying well.

"The money for your board is crucial, Daisy. My parents are helping to support my sister and her family, as none of them are allowed to work under the Nazi regime."

I stared at him, perplexed. "But I thought Hitler had brought about full employment? I read about his 'economic miracle' in the papers."

Kurt laughed cynically. "It is all smoke and mirrors, Daisy. There is so-called full employment because we Jews are no longer allowed to work in the new Germany. And neither are women, as Hitler believes their only role is to be wives and mothers. Our young men are conscripted into the army, and anyone refusing to work is sent to the concentration camps. Jewish academics, doctors, lawyers, in fact any professional person, they are all reduced to doing menial jobs such as street cleaning. And the concentration camps are where I would be sent if they could hear me now. But, because I am employed by a foreign magazine, I have some protection at the moment. But remind me to show you my passport, Daisy. It is stamped with the letter 'J'. Just in case I should forget my status."

I fell silent, trying to digest all this. "Kurt, are you saying that Germany is a police state?"

"Ah, so the little middle-class Englander knows some history! Yes, Daisy, that is exactly what I am telling you. And I am telling you because perhaps, with our work here, we can make others aware of what is happening."

My paltry German was still slightly more than Mrs Klein's English, so conversation between us was almost nil, but we worked together in easy silence. We had eaten a kind of fish stew; I knew that meat, especially, was getting harder and harder to buy, and that everyone was being encouraged to eat fish instead. Mrs Klein was an excellent cook, but it was the third time in as many days that we had had fish, and, inevitably, the whole house was beginning to smell of it. She suddenly held her nose and said, "Fisch," pulling a face and we both laughed. So at least we had managed some communication, I thought, and I was unexpectedly cheered by the little bit of by-play.

When we had finished clearing up, I asked Kurt to come and see my developing pictures, and help me choose which ones to send back to our editor. Very often he would write his article on the basis of what I had photographed, so it was essential we made such decisions together. He spent a long time looking at them.

He finally said, "You are very good, Daisy. You have captured the vigour of these sessions, but emphasised discreetly and truthfully the discrimination that places all those matching blonde young girls so prominently. No non-Aryan misfits there! Also you have managed to reflect something more, a trace of fanaticism, perhaps, in the faces of the girls. How cleverly you have managed to cast the shadows, my dear. And your depiction of Frau Rüdiger, well, let me just say that I am impressed."

"I was just snapping what I saw."

"And what you felt, I think?"

I nodded. "Kurt, I was suddenly very frightened when you told me what she had said to all those marching children. Was I right to be?"

"Oh, yes, Daisy. Very right. And now, my little middle-class English girl, on to Nuremburg we go."

I should probably have been indignant at being so patronised, but I knew he was using a kind of humour, and possibly affection, to warn me. Even though I was still not quite sure of what I was being warned about. I was becoming aware by the hour that my ignorance was unforgivable. There had been a lot in the papers about the trouble in Germany, and even after I accepted this commission, I had been too lazy to read up on it all. I vowed I would never be in this position again. Kurt was right. Along, I suspected, with most of my compatriots I had been too smug and too cosy to take an interest in the rest of the world. Given what I had seen and heard today, that seemed foolish in the extreme. I wondered what Nuremberg would hold.

We were in the car, caught up in a line of traffic that we could see neither the beginning or the end of. Kurt, rarely garrulous, had obviously decided to use the situation to give me some badly needed background knowledge.

"Don't worry," he gestured to the traffic congestion. "It is always like this at the rallies nowadays. When they began, soon after the war, they were much smaller affairs. A sort of jolly party to raise the poor German people's spirits. I remember going to the first one with my wife Ilsa, and we certainly were in need of some cheering up.

"Like many soldiers, I had not long been home from the Western Front before I realised what a parlous state my country was in. Yes, we had behaved badly, though we were not alone in that, but now we were being treated very badly indeed by the rest of the world. As if piling on more wrongs could make everything right – it was truly bizarre.

"I could not find work and was doing anything I could lay my hands on in order to support my family, mainly labouring jobs. It was during those years that Ilsa first became ill with the sickness that would eventually take her. Sadly, that was an all too usual occurrence, so you can see, we did need our spirits raised. And some kind of faith restored to us. The first rally was in Munich, and that was the first time I saw Hitler. The Nazi Party was a small right-wing affair that no-one was taking seriously. Hitler got himself into some kind of trouble that day; I am still not sure precisely what happened. But I think he tried to stage some sort of takeover. Anyway, he ended up in prison. He used his time there to start writing his ideological treatise, *Mein Kampf*. Do you know about that, Daisy?"

Of course I didn't. I shook my head regretfully.

He continued, "In it our Fuhrer outlines his personal history and how he came to understand that all the troubles of the world could be eliminated if Judaism and Communism were exterminated forever. And, of course, if he and the National Socialists were to be permanently in power."

During the time he had been talking, men in the Nazi uniform had appeared and were controlling the traffic and we had been siphoned off down a separate road into a lesser stream of cars. As we drove on, I meditated on what Kurt had just told me. I wondered if the inevitable privations after the war, which he obviously felt had contributed to his wife's death, had coloured his feelings about the Nazi regime. I thought his use of the word extermination must certainly be an exaggeration. I decided that I would be in a better position to judge for myself after the rally.

I had no idea that the rally would be as awe-inspiring as this, though Kurt muttered 'that is the idea' when I confided as much to him. The Zeppelin field was surrounded by over a hundred searchlights, which are like enormous spotlights throwing beams of light into the sky, and they were positioned to make a sort of cathedral of light over our heads in the evenings. Over the two days, we witnessed marching soldiers, some of them Hitler's famous SS men, parades of tanks, processions of naval personnel, aircraft flying overhead, tanks streaming by, mock battles with bombs dropping – I am not sure whether they were real or not, but they were very frightening.

All this war stuff, which was very daunting and upsetting, though the crowd seemed to love it, was constantly interspersed with people calling out praise to Hitler and doing the Nazi salute. There were some scuffles in the crowd but these were quickly dealt with by the guards, and then the military atmosphere changed slightly and the arena was filled with young people doing gymnastics, just like the ones we had witnessed at the school, only even more spectacular. I think these were probably more members of the German Girls League, but due to my lack of German I had a job keeping up with it all.

Then there was another march past the Fuhrer, which seemed to go on forever, by the Hitler Youth Movement. Hundreds and hundreds of fair-haired, well-built young men, who, rather frighteningly and like the girls at the school, all looked very similar. It was as if the youth of the country had been swallowed up and spat out having all been stamped with the same blond image. Then the tempo changed again and the arena was filled with people dancing to traditional music. At least, I think it must have been traditional because everyone seemed to know the dances.

The two days ended with a torchlight procession, and those who did not have torches, mainly women, carried flowers, many of which they threw at Hitler's feet as they passed. I could not understand Hitler's speech, of course, but Kurt said he was 'on about colonisation again'. When I questioned what this meant, he said that Hitler is always banging on about Germany needing more living space. I did not really feel any the wiser, to be honest.

But my big bonus was that one of the SS men saw me taking photographs and moved a path through to the very front of the crowd and stayed with us, making sure that I had an uninterrupted view of the activities. Apparently the Fuhrer is very keen on people taking photographs and giving him publicity abroad. He certainly doesn't need it here, without doubt the German people love him, idolise him, even. I managed to have a conversation with two ladies who spoke English, and they sang his praises loudly. My impression is that he is almost God-like to many of them, and can do no wrong. The ultimate in hero-worship.

There is to be another floodlit demonstration in Berlin in a couple of weeks, so Kurt and I are going to that. I expect it will be a bit of an anti-climax after the rally. I have developed the films I took in Nuremberg and am very pleased with them. Kurt used some of them as inspiration for his articles rather than the other way round, and then let me read and comment on what he had written. We have wired them back and the magazine has said that they are very pleased with both the article and the photographs. This has been a major experience for me in all sorts of ways. Not least what I am learning from working with Kurt.

And so here I am, loading films into my bag once more and off to Berlin. I am still not sure what to make of Herr Hitler. Sometimes he seems so charming, when he is amongst the people, talking to the children and their mothers and accepting bouquets of flowers with a smile. But other times I watch the displays of power and the men guarding him and I wonder if Kurt is right. That he is a monster.

I have never felt so completely and utterly overwhelmed in my entire life, even at Nuremberg. We finally found our way into the huge field where last year's Olympics had been staged. The light was just beginning to go when the massive Olympic Bell began to toll and the whole arena was floodlit with scores of searchlights playing over us all. The Rally to welcome Mussolini to Germany had begun. There must have been a million people there, and for a brief moment there was complete silence, then everyone began cheering and shouting, including me! It was magical, and had the effect of making the entire crowd unite in awe.

After a while the searchlights found the balcony and came to rest on the Fuhrer and another man in uniform, who Kurt shouted into my ear, was Il Duce, the Italian leader, who I knew as Mussolini. On the balcony behind them were many soldiers, and very many representations of the swastika, on the seat, on the arm bands, even on the rope that bounded the balcony. And everywhere you looked there were guards in the uniform of the SS, Hitler's special force. But they appeared to be largely unnecessary. The noise of the crowd was deafening, until Hitler raised his hand for quiet, and then a hush immediately settled on his audience.

The speeches were heartening. Both Hitler and Mussolini declared that they had no wish to further divide an already divided Europe, and Hitler pledged to defend Belgium. I was at a great disadvantage, as Kurt was trying to translate and sum up both speeches for me in a whisper, but I could see from the approbation of the crowd, the nodding and murmurs of assent, that there was great approval.

"What do you think?" I asked Kurt when we were finally back in the car and had left the crowds behind. "They seemed to both be saying that they didn't want any more wars, didn't they?"

Kurt gave a tight little smile. "Yes. Exactly as I translated for you. They went to some trouble to show how peace-loving they both are."

"You don't believe it, do you?"

127

At that moment a young boy, he could not have been more than seventeen, wearing the uniform of the Hitler Youth movement, jumped in front of our car and made Kurt slam on the breaks. I felt his whole body stiffen, and saw the perspiration break out on his forehead. But it was not us the boy was interested in. Along with three of his colleagues, he was dragging a man out of a car that had been stopped some yards ahead of us. The man was shouting at them in anger. I sat, frozen, watching and wondering what the man had done.

Then one of boys hit him hard across the face, so he lost his balance and fell, while another kicked him in the stomach as he lay on the ground. The young men were shouting insults at him and laughing and kicking him again and again. He was bleeding profusely from the head and I went to get out of the car to stop them, but Kurt's hand on my arm was like steel.

"No. Stay still. Don't meet their eyes, look down," he hissed.

His urgency was compelling. I sat and gazed at the dashboard. After a few more minutes of sickening noises which surely meant they were inflicting more violence on the man, all went quiet. Then I heard the familiar 'Hiel Hitler' and raised my eyes in time to see these thugs making the salute over their victim's prostrate body, before driving his car away.

As soon as they had disappeared, with a curt 'Stay!' to me, Kurt was out of the car. He lifted the man up, and loosened his collar. I saw he was quite well-dressed. I got out of the car and ran to help, and this time Kurt did not rebuff me. We lifted the man into the back of our car, and quickly jumped in and Kurt drove off. The man had passed out, but was coming to. I turned to look at him, and realised he was trying to say something. Kurt glanced back and then pulled the car into a side road.

He leant back as the man whispered something to him that sounded like an address. Kurt glanced at me, and then nodded to him. We pulled out and turned back the way we had come, passing the place where we had found him. Eventually, Kurt stopped at a small terraced house.

"Go and knock, Daisy," he ordered.

A small woman of about my age came to the door. Glancing across to the car, her hand flew to her mouth and she ran to help Kurt, who was lending an arm to the injured man. Kurt helped him inside the house, and I heard the woman saying thank you in German, before she quickly closed the door. Kurt got back in the car without a word and we began to drive again.

"I don't understand," I burst out. "What had he done? Why did they attack him? How will he get his car back?"

"It is a game to them, Daisy. He has done nothing. It is what he is that counts. He is a Jew. They noticed him driving his own car, and decided he should not still have it. They are the law. He is lucky that they didn't kill him."

"But won't they be punished?"

He laughed bitterly. "No, they will be praised. They have done their duty. They will boast to their superior tonight of what they did and they will be congratulated."

I was shivering with cold, but also with shock. Kurt kept his eyes on the road.

His voice was gentle, "Welcome to the Fatherland, Daisy."

The Magazine has asked us to stay on and 'continue to record for them our view of events in modern

Germany'. It is an enormous compliment of course, and the letter, which was from the editor himself, says our reports are arousing great interest at home. But I do need to let Mother know. I have been out here for nearly four months already, and this will mean at least another three. But I can't possibly turn it down. I shall write to her this evening.

I have had letters from both Arthur and Georgie, who saw the piece about those thugs beating up the Jewish man, urging me to take care. Though I am not quite sure what it is they think I should be doing. Kurt says to tell them he is looking after me, and although I think I am perfectly capable of looking after myself, I appreciated that. I confess he does me make me feel more safe than perhaps I would on my own.

You would have to be very stupid not to recognise Berlin is a very strange and quite unsettling place to be at the moment. But it is also exciting, and the place I want to be. I never expected my love of photography would lead me down this path, and I am going to make the most of every minute. Though I am pleased to hear that Arthur is quietly censoring the articles that Mother reads, so she has very little idea about what is going on here.

But I think she will be interested in my next assignment. We are to record the visit of the Duke and Duchess of Windsor for the magazine. We had thought we might do that, anyway, and sell our stuff to the newspapers, but it is reassuring to know in advance that we will be paid.

We have a couple of weeks before the royal visit– or should that be ex-royal? – I am not sure of the protocol. Mother was very angry about the King's behaviour. She kept reading the paper and then throwing it down, while saying things like, 'He can't possibly marry that awful American woman!' It was almost personal for her in an odd sort of way. When he abdicated she was delighted, and has become a fervent admirer of the new King and Queen. But she has always been something of a snob, and will like the thought that I might be touching shoulders with even the despised ex-royals.

Kurt has invited me go with him to visit his sister Lotte and her husband and daughter. They live on the outskirts of Berlin and Kurt had already confided in me that he and his parents are supporting them financially. I think he is a bit worried about them which is partly why he wants to go and see them today. We went on the tram, as Kurt said it would be better than driving into the district, because that might draw too much attention to us. I did not fully understand why until we arrived. We walked past many shops that were closed, or had broken windows, and the aura of poverty was everywhere. Kurt explained that many of the city's Jews had lived and worked here, but as they were now forbidden to work at all, many of them were literally starving.

We turned down the side streets and walked until we came to a small house, one of a terrace of dilapidated buildings. We did not see many people. The whole area was hushed, as if all human sound had been prohibited. The paint on the door was peeling so badly it was hard to see what the original colour had been. Kurt tapped lightly with the knocker, and the noise reverberated in the silence almost as if we had struck a gong. The door was opened almost immediately by a child of about six years old..

"Onkel Kurt!" her face was suffused in smiles, and she launched herself at him with obvious joy.

Then, from the woman who appeared behind the little girl, just visible in the dark hall, came a torrent of words that I could not understand, but were all quite obviously expressing pleasure. In spite of the dimness, I could see that she was so like Kurt, she had to be his sister. She pulled him inside, motioning me to follow them, and shut the door quickly behind us. Then she led us through to a small scullery, where she and her daughter proceeded to hug Kurt fiercely. After a moment, she drew back and smiled at me.

"Daisy?" she asked.

I nodded and smiled.

She held out her hand. "Welcome. I am Lotte. I have some English. Not as good as my brother, but enough, I hope. We have heard so much about you."

I took her hand with warmth. I had not realised that Kurt had told her that I would be coming with him. Or told her anything at all about me, for that matter.

Kurt disentangled himself from the little girl. "Daisy, this is my niece, Hannah. Hannah, shake hands with Daisy."

The girl dropped me a curtsy and, holding out her hand to me, said, "How do you do, Daisy?"

I was so staggered at her command of English that I nearly forgot to answer her. "Very well, thank you, Hannah," I answered formally. "Do you know, I have an aunt with the same name as you! Though she is not as pretty." Hannah blushed and giggled. "But how did you learn my language so well?"

Lotte answered for her daughter. "My husband was a lecturer in literature in the university. He speaks several languages, and Kurt and I both learned English at school, which has been good for us, so it seemed sensible for

Hannah to learn. We have always spoken both tongues at home since she began to talk."

Lotte took us through into what appeared to be the only other downstairs room as she was speaking. It was very dark, and I realised the windows were boarded up. In the corner of the room was a bed, and on the pillows lay a sleeping baby. Lotte crossed to the baby and picked her up. The joy had drained from her face as she looked at her brother.

"Oh, Kurt, I am so glad you have come." She sounded near to tears.

"Lotte? Who is this?" Kurt was obviously taken aback as he gazed from the tiny infant, swaddled in a ragged blanket, to his sister.

"Oh, no, of course she is not mine, Kurt. The young woman who was living upstairs has disappeared, but this is her baby, who was left behind. The Gestapo came yesterday. Hannah and I hid in the outhouse. We were very frightened. I heard Myrna, the baby's mother, shouting at them. There was a lot of commotion and noise going on. I think they hit her. Many times. They were calling her names and she was crying. I think they did not notice the baby. I did not see Myrna go, but I heard her screaming, and then the car started, and then there was quiet again. Later I heard the baby crying and I went up and found her. I brought her down here. What else could I do?"

I stared at her in disbelief. "Her mother has just – gone? Where? Why? I don't understand."

Kurt looked at me. "Daisy, you have seen what can happen to Jews in Germany with your own eyes." He turned back to look at the baby. "What do you want us to do, Lotte?"

133

"I want you take the baby and Hannah home with you. I have not seen Franz for three weeks. He has not been home and I do not know where he is. I must stay here for when he returns. But I need to know that Hannah is safe, and she will be better with you and our parents, Kurt. And our mother will take care of the baby until we can think what to do."

"Of course we will take them both home with us. But you must come too, Lotte. You know how I have always hated you living here anyway, but when you had Franz to look after you, it was different. But now you must come as well. Franz will know where you are when he returns. He will find you. Come with us, Lotte."

"It is asking so much of our parents to manage all of us and the baby. I should stay here and wait for Franz to come back."

But I could see she was wavering. I wondered what had happened to her husband, and whether she would ever see him again, and then realised with shock that I was actually getting used to the barbarism of this cruel regime.

Kurt continued to speak to Lotte in reassuringly measured tones, which were having the desired effect of calming her. "If you come with us, you and Hannah can help look after the baby. Lotte, I cannot bear to leave you here alone. It becomes more dangerous daily. Please come, Lotte. You know it is what our parents would want."

There was a long silence, broken by Hannah's small voice, "Please come, Mummy."

We all waited for Lotte to answer. She stood looking down at the threadbare carpet, then looked up at us, her eyes bright with tears.

"You are right, of course. Hannah, help me." She pulled a small suitcase out from under the bed, and began to throw in the clothes that were hanging on a rail in the corner. The movement disturbed the baby, who began to snuffle. Hannah went into the scullery and came back with a baby's bottle. She picked the child up and began to offer it the milk.

Lotte watched her as she picked up some photographs that were standing on a small table and packed them. "We went upstairs this morning and found some of her things. Her name is Ruth. She is only about six weeks old. I know she was only days old when Myrna moved in with her."

"Do you know where her father is?"

Lotte shrugged. Ruth had dozed off, and Hannah passed her to me. I settled her on my shoulder, relieved to feel that she was warm inside her thin covering. Hannah picked up a rag doll from the bed and held it tightly to her chest.

My eyes filled with tears as I suddenly remembered another child clutching Percy, her pink rabbit. Another child jealously guarding the familiar in a life that was being ripped apart.

"What is her name?" I asked, gesturing to the doll.

"Helga," Hannah replied, placing a kiss on the doll's head.

She reached for her mother's hand and clutched it tightly. We were ready to leave. We must have looked like quite an ordinary family as we waited for the tram to take us back home. Kurt with the suitcase, Lotte and Hannah holding hands, me with the baby. On the tram, a woman made a clucking noise at Ruth, and she opened her eyes and cooed.

As she rested on my lap, I looked at her properly for the first time. She had fairish curly hair, an unusual amount for a baby, and she was now looking at me with piercing blue eyes. The lady said something that I did not understand, but I guessed at its meaning.

"Ja," I agreed, smiling, as I dropped a kiss on the baby's head.

October at last and we are preparing for the visit of the Duke and Duchess. Hannah is so excited that her uncle and I are going to meet 'a real king'. All my attempts at a truer definition of his position have fallen on deaf ears, to Kurt's amusement.

"To her, meeting a king is like a fairy tale. Leave her with her illusions, Daisy, she has little enough enjoyment."

He was right, of course. The family are more and more nervous about going out nowadays. Jewish children are not allowed to go to the state schools any more, and groups from the Hitler Youth stand outside the Jewish schools, as they do the synagogues, ready to beat up anyone going in or out. Kurt's father, Mr Klein, is teaching Hannah himself, which has probably been good for both of them, but she has almost no contact with anyone her own age.

Lotte and I try to devise games to play with her, but all this must feel like being in prison for such an active, and very bright, six year old. It is hard to see where this will end. Common sense tells me that Germany will have to come to her senses soon and integrate the Jews back into their society again. Surely this madness cannot go on for much longer?

Well, I imagine the Duke of Windsor must have been very pleased with himself today. Obviously a lot of Germans agree with Hannah, for he was most certainly treated like a visiting king. And she was treated like a queen, which I found even more galling. They arrived at the Military Station in Berlin to be greeted by large crowds of cheering people, some of them calling out, Hiel Edward, which was appalling and actually quite nauseating. The Duchess was presented with a bouquet of pink and yellow flowers, which she passed to a 'lady-in-waiting'. She really does think she is the Queen! But then, he quite obviously still believes he is the King.

Hitler's people were there in force, fawning on them. And they also had a large phalanx of English running around after them, presumably civil servants. I found myself wondering who was paying for all this. Theoretically, so we are told, their trip is to 'study social conditions and housing problems'. I should have liked to have taken them to the place Lotte has just fled from.

Kurt had managed to get us in the front rank of journalists again, largely because Hitler is anxious for his meeting with Britain's ex-king to be well publicised both here and abroad. The Fuhrer is a genius at propaganda, if nothing else. I took a lot of photographs, and was just inserting my third roll of film into my favourite camera when two SS men appeared, and, one on either side, they took my arms and marched me over to one of the waiting limousines. Kurt saw what was happening and followed, trying to ask them what they were up to, but the noise of the crowd was so loud no-one could hear what anyone else was saying.

I was more angry than frightened, because I had been getting some very good shots. As they ushered me into

137

the car I recognised the man sitting inside. I could not place him, but seconds later the door opened for Kurt to enter, and he immediately acknowledged the seated figure.

"This is a surprise. What are you doing here?" He turned to me. "Daisy, have you met Dominic Hargreaves?"

I had not. But I knew who he was. His picture appeared every month in The National Photographic and he was their foreign correspondent. We shook hands, and I waited for him to speak. I was still feeling a bit cross at having been virtually man-handled.

"I must apologise. I asked the soldiers to escort you over here, not to frog-march you, Miss March. I am afraid some of Herr Hitler's men lack finesse."

It was hard not to smile at his deliberate understatement, spoken in the upper-class English drawl of the moneyed public school boy. But he was exuding charm, and I could not help noticing that he also had the shiny, polished good looks of his class. But he sensed he had not totally obliterated my resentment, and, turning down the charm a fraction, put on what I assumed to be his business voice.

"Seeing you and Kurt here today is a piece of huge good luck for me as it enables me to cut corners. The Duke and Duchess are attending a state function tonight, which I imagine you will be covering?"

We both murmured assent. It was on our schedule.

"I have managed to get you a ticket for the reception after, and the Royal couple have agreed to be interviewed for the magazine."

138

I swallowed my distaste at the description of the Windsors as 'Royal', as I understood immediately that this was a huge coup, both for us and the magazine.

Kurt said, "Dominic, do you mean both of us?"

Dominic shook his head. "Sorry, Kurt, there is no way I could get you in. But you guessed that."

Kurt nodded ruefully.

"But Kurt and I work together. I can't do interviews."

"I suspect you could, Daisy. But you won't have to. On this occasion, you will be working with me."

I looked at Kurt, feeling for the first time the real humiliation inherent in anti-semitism, but he smiled at me and shrugged his shoulders.

"You will be in good hands, Daisy. Now, I shall leave you both to plan, and you can find me in the refreshment room when you are done." He touched me gently on the shoulder before leaving the car.

I stared after him, momentarily feeling deflated. But Dominic gave me no time to ponder. And I knew, as did all three of us, that the magazine was calling the tunes.

"So," he said, relaxing back into the limousine's well-padded seats, "you are Jacob's girl are you? I have been looking forward to meeting you."

I was dumbfounded. I felt as if he had punched me in the stomach. How did he know more about me than I knew for sure myself? He saw my consternation, and his tone changed, and became conciliatory.

"Oh, dear, I must apologise again. I have upset you. It was not my intention. Daisy – may I call you that? We are sort of related, you know."

"No. No, I don't know. Who are you, that you think you can speak to me with such, such," I struggled for words, and then spat out, "ungentlemanly discourtesy," as I attempted to open the car door and get out.

"Oh, please don't." He seemed genuinely distressed, so I hesitated. "Jacob was my father's cousin. I think that makes us sort of second cousins or something similar. But I thought you knew. I know Jacob visited you and your mother all the time, we all knew about you. You were a sort of open secret in the family. Never mentioned, but always there."

I collapsed back onto the seat. To suddenly find out so much about my origins, while in Berlin and about to interview the Windsors, would have been funny if it hadn't been so distressing. I took a deep, long breath, and, to give him his due, he sat while I gathered my thoughts.

Finally, I said, with hardly a tremor in my voice, "If we are to work together, and it seems we are, then I wish for you never to talk about this again. I am a professional photographer on a very important assignment, and I will not let you, or anyone else distract me from that. Is that quite clear?"

To my relief, he nodded, and I read new-found respect in his eyes. Not for nothing had I been a teacher for several years. In my best classroom voice, I said, "Then let us work out how we will tackle this interview." And, as an afterthought, I added, "You may call me Daisy, though I should prefer Miss March when we are working."

Half an hour later I found Kurt drinking tea in the station refreshment room. I collapsed into the seat opposite him.

"Did it go alright? You look a bit shaken." His face was concerned.

"It was fine," I assured him. "My main problem now is that we have to get back home and iron my one and only evening dress."

Which is what we did.

Dominic certainly knows what he is doing. I am forced to admit that I do not think Kurt could have handled the interview so well. Of course, Dominic has the advantage of his birth and the innate confidence that goes with it. Kurt says that his father is an earl or something aristocratic.

I suspected his opinion of the Duchess was on a par with my own, but not for an instant did that show. He bowed and kissed her hand with the grace that presumably he would have awarded a queen, and I managed the curtsey he made me practice while we waited in the anteroom for our audience.

The Duke is intent on them both being treated as if he were still King and she, his Queen. That much quickly became obvious. I suppose they can manage that pretence abroad, if not in Britain. It is difficult to understand what he sees in the Duchess. She is not beautiful. But she does have a very strong personality. As they answered Dominic's questions, it seemed to me that against all my expectations, she was in charge, rather than the Duke. I asked if I could take photographs informally, during the interview, rather than posed after it, and the Duke started to demur, but she cut in and said that I could. Then he just nodded and smiled. He takes her hand all the time, like a small boy in need of reassurance.

141

Dominic asked what they had come to Germany for, and the Duke talked at length about how he was an ambassador for peace, and how he saw his role as an international mediator. He went on in this vein for some time, and the Duchess began to look bored and fidget with her handbag and twiddle the enormous rings she was wearing. But she is astute. She interrupted a couple of times and steered him away from what might have been intended to be remarks showing some resentment of his brother, our real King.

She certainly sat up and took notice when Dominic asked about their meeting with Hitler. Before the Duke had a chance to say anything, she gushed about how charming the Fuhrer was, and what a great and inspiring man. And then she fixed us both with a somewhat unnerving stare and said, "I hope your articles will reflect the truth of the miracle he has worked in this great country. I think England could learn a lot from him."

Before we could digest this, the Duke jumped in and said, "The Duchess means, of course, that Britain could learn much from the Fuhrer, and I can only agree with her judgement."

After that, I sensed he was becoming a trifle uneasy with all this forthrightness and beginning to clam up. He must surely realise some of the stuff that is going on over here, even if she doesn't. Anyway, he rose to his feet, and she followed, and we bowed and curtsied again and the interview was over.

Back in the limousine, Dominic asked, "Did you get some good shots?"

"I think so." And I did think so. I believed I had managed to get one or two of her obviously not concentrating as he expounded how he saw his part on the world stage, bringing peace and prosperity to all.

"How did you feel about them?"

I thought for a minute before answering. "I thought he was sad, and to be honest, a bit pathetic with his big ideas."

"And her?"

"I thought she was self-centred, controlling, and actually, not very bright."

He laughed. "I think I agree on all counts, Daisy. Will you bring the pictures to show me tomorrow at this hotel?"

He passed me the address. I glanced and saw it was the grandest hotel in Berlin. Of course.

"Yes, I'll be round about three o'clock. I shall need the morning to develop them all."

"That will be wonderful. I shall look forward to seeing you again."

And he held my hand just a fraction longer than was necessary as we said goodbye.

April 1938

I think I have been in Germany quite long enough. I wired the magazine today to say that I did not wish to have my contract extended again, and that I would be coming home at the end of this month. The politics here are more and more frightening. Hitler annexed Austria last month. A supposedly peaceful adventure, we are told, and certainly the crowds turned out in their thousands to line the streets of Vienna as the tanks drove through.

Hitler infiltrated the Austrian government, aided and abetted by their own chancellor, until the Austrian cabinet was full of Nazi supporters. Dominic says that even the cheering people in the street were a fraud, imported by the Nazi's from countries as far away as Czechoslovakia.

He said it was a tribute to Nazi organisation. And then added, "And their single-minded brutality."

I have been working more with Dominic than I have with Kurt these last few weeks. It is getting harder and harder for Kurt to work at all. He says he managed to 'slip through the Nazi net' for a long time, but that they have finally caught up with him.

It will be good to get back to England, though I have become very fond of all Kurt's family, and quite ridiculously attached to the baby. I think the feeling is mutual, as when she is tired, or hungry, or just plain miserable, the minute I appear, a smile suffuses her little face, like sunshine coming through a grey sky. Lotte says she thinks I am her mummy!

Lotte has grown old before my eyes. We have heard nothing of Franz, and I hear her crying every night. Fortunately, Mrs Klein has taken Hannah into their room, which is on the middle floor, to sleep, so although the child is sad, she does not have to hear her mother's grief as well. I sometimes take Ruth up into my attic room and into bed with me to give Mrs Klein a break from all this child-care that has been thrust upon her.

Dominic is going to stay over here for a while longer. But, of course, that is his job. As he says, a foreign correspondent has to be somewhere foreign to do his job. But it will be hard leaving him. We have been constant companions since Christmas, when he took me to visit some German friends of his who live in the mountains. We stayed in their incredibly luxurious house for ten days and were spoilt as I have never been spoilt before. An excess of everything, especially food and drink, but the very best thing was wallowing in a hot bath every day. The Kleins have neither a bath nor hot water, so that felt unimaginably good. And no-one mentioned Hitler, or not in my hearing, anyway.

Dominic told me to go and spend some of my salary on some decent clothes (his words!) before we went, and somewhat reluctantly, I did. I must say I was glad to have been so advised, as I should have felt even more of a country bumpkin, if I had not done so. I did feel a bit of a fish out of water amongst all these sophisticates, but I know I covered that well enough. Not for the first time, I was grateful for Sir's insistence on my 'posh' education. I should have hated to have embarrassed Dominic.

My relationship with Dominic is ambiguous. We are good friends, and we work together well. But almost inevitably there is a frisson of something more. One of his German pals (who had been, of course, at the same school as him in England) flirted outrageously with me over Christmas, and Dominic became very possessive, as if he had rights over me. However, although we have had the occasional kiss, I keep my distance. I am reassured that at least he does know about my parents, knows who I am, but I will never, ever, again risk the humiliation visited on me by Henry's parents. Ironically, I think he finds my reserve attractive. Life is very strange.

Kurt's family have been so lovely to me, that I would like to give them some kind of thank you present, but I cannot think of what to give them. Money is what they need most, but that would be crass. And anyway it is impossible to buy extra food; they have to queue for the increasingly meagre amounts that are available. I decided to confide in Kurt.

I seized the opportunity one pleasant evening when spring was just beginning to make itself felt. From my bedroom window I saw Kurt standing in the tiny, paved back garden, and went down to join him. He has told me that he is not coming back to England with me and I understand that he feels the need to stay here to protect his family. He was carefully rolling a cigarette. I tease him because he rolls them so thinly, but I know he is eking out the little tobacco he has. I think it is almost his only indulgence. I have grown so fond of him.

"Kurt?"

"Yes, Daisy?"

"What can I get to let your parents see how much I have appreciated all the hospitality they have given me ?

"They know already, Daisy. They have loved having you."

"But it is important to me to show them how I feel. I anticipated just being a boarder in this house, but they have shown me such warmth, they are almost like my own family now. I feel a real sadness to be leaving, not Germany, but all of you."

Kurt was silent for a minute, drawing on his cigarette. I knew him well enough not to hurry him. I could see he was thinking hard.

"Daisy. There is something you could do for us. But it is not a small thing. It is a very large thing, and if you say 'no' no-one else will ever know that I have asked you."

He was looking at me so earnestly that I was suddenly apprehensive.

"Go on. Whatever it is, ask me. After all, I can refuse."

It came out of the blue. The last thing I was expecting. But even as I gasped in surprise, I knew that I would do it.

"Will you take Ruth back with you? Will you say that she is yours, and get her to safety?"

Dominic was a tower of strength. He arranged everything, somehow cut through all the red tape, and almost before I knew it, we were on our way. Mrs March and her daughter, Ruth. That wasn't official, of course, but it was easier on the boat to let people assume it. My daughter was angelic. I worried about how I would manage a small child on the journey, but Mrs Klein's wisdom gave me strength.

"How will I cope? I have no experience of babies at all."

She put her hands on her hips and looked at me, as I sat in her kitchen with Ruth contently on my lap. She is about six months old now, and we have just started to give her a little solid food. I am tenderly wiping a smudge

147

of scrambled egg off her face and she smiles up at me and gurgles with pleasure.

"So," says Mrs Klein, "How much do you think most of us know when we have our first child? Do you think childbirth teaches you how to feed, them or change them, or calm them down? Hmmm, that would certainly be most useful. But we learn as we go along, and," she gave me a big smile, "you have learnt very fast, Daisy. She loves you much, I think."

"I love her much, "I answered, smiling back at her.

"What will you do with her? When you get back home? Will the authorities find her new parents?"

I had no idea, but I wasn't about to say that. Already the thought of giving her up seemed alien. But as Mrs Klein and I had just managed our longest ever conversation, I just shrugged my shoulders and left the question hanging in midair.

Dominic was more forthcoming, however. "I think you are all kinds of a brick, my girl, but you must give some thought to her future. And yours. You are a very talented photographer, and I think you are going to be in demand. And, in any case, you can't live on air, you'll need to work. I've been in touch with a couple of chaps I know at the Foreign Office, here are their details if you need help getting her settled."

And I had taken the envelope he handed me, and slipped it into my bag. And given him a 'thank you' peck on the cheek. And then forgotten about it. Deliberately.

But my confidence was waning slightly now. My journey home had been unexpectedly smooth, but as the taxi took me on the last lap, I mentally girded myself for Mother's welcome. Or otherwise. I had lacked the courage to tell that I was bringing Ruth, in case she tried to forbid me. The fact that I was nearly twenty-seven had not made her any less dictatorial where I was concerned. But, as I regarded the sleeping child in my lap, that was beginning to feel like a mistake.

It was dark before I arrived back, and I needed the lights from the taxi to find my way up the path, carefully holding my precious bundle. Mother's greeting was a wail of horror that I could not possibly have anticipated. She opened the door to me herself, and without giving me a chance to explain, after one look at the baby I was carrying, she screamed, "No! No! You stupid, stupid girl! Have you learnt nothing? Go away!"

And then she tried to slam the door on me in true Victorian melodrama fashion. I was so taken aback I just stood on the doorstep with my mouth open, clutching Ruth, who, woken by the commotion, began to cry. Fortunately, Arthur appeared behind Mother, and taking in the situation at a glance he drew her into his arms where she continued to sob her heart out. Over her head, he motioned me through to the sitting room. To my great relief, James emerged from there, and I quickly asked him to help the taxi driver with my bags, and gave him my purse so he could pay the man. Then I sank, exhausted even more by the two minutes with Mother, than by the whole long journey.

By the time I had calmed Ruth down, James and Arthur had both joined us, Arthur pouring me a glass of something warming from the bottle on the sideboard, and James on his knees beside me, playing peek-a-boo with the baby and making her laugh uproariously, even though there were still tear marks on her cheeks. After a moment, he lifted her up, and to my surprise, sat opposite me with her on his lap, both obviously content with this situation.

"Goodness, James, I am so pleased you are home! I wondered if you would still be here."

"Got another week before I have to go back to college. Time to get to know this one, I reckon." And he jiggled her up and down on his knee.

Arthur came and sat down opposite me, and I said, "Mother has it all wrong, Arthur. She is not mine. Her own mother was taken by the Gestapo, and Lotte Klein rescued her. They asked me to bring her here because she would not be safe in Germany."

Arthur nodded. I could see he did not doubt that I was telling him the truth and I felt a surge of affection for both these men, my stepfather and my stepbrother.

"I am not sure whether it is helpful or otherwise that she looks like you, Daisy," said Arthur.

Startled, I looked across at Ruth, and realised he was right. Of course. I knew that I looked like Sir, who for the first time I realised was, of course, a Jew. As was Ruth. We both had the same slightly sallow skin colouring and her eyes, still blue when I first saw her, were now dark like mine. And, more unusually, we both had fair hair. How strange that I had not noticed this before. But then, until recently I had no consciousness of who was a Jew and who wasn't. Why would I have done?

"She is lovely," said my stepfather, stroking her hair gently. "Now all we have to do is get your mother to listen to the truth. Will you leave that to me?"

"Happily," I said.

It's been over a week now, and I don't think Mother will ever believe me. But I don't care anymore. Her

150

remark today was the last straw. She has crossed an invisible line and I do not think I can ever forgive her.

Arthur and James had brought home a high chair for Ruth, and we set it up in the dining room. When Mother saw it, she said. "It is bad enough having to share my home with one bastard, but I will not countenance eating with another." And disappeared, slamming the door behind her.

For a moment I wanted to cry. Largely because Arthur came and cuddled me and sympathy can make hurt worse sometimes. But my anger outweighed my hurt a hundred-fold. For the first time, I really hated my own mother, I did not care how wicked that was. How dare she? If I was a bastard then whose fault was that? And we knew nothing of Ruth's background except the horror of her desertion. I had always known Mother was a cold fish, but this was beyond anything. I could see that Arthur was almost as shocked as I was.

"She didn't mean it, Daisy," he said. "She loves you dearly. She will be so sorry for what she said in the heat of the moment."

"But she can't ever undo it, Arthur. And she needn't worry. Ruth and I are leaving. I won't stay under the same roof as someone who thinks we are both vile."

"Where can you go?"

"I shall go to the person who once offered me sanctuary if ever I needed it."

I fed Ruth and cleaned her up and then got us both ready. I didn't need to pack much, as most of what we had was still not unpacked from our arrival the week before. I threw our luggage into my small car, grateful for the care Arthur had lavished on it while I was in Germany. I kissed Arthur and hugged James, and then

151

put Ruth, wrapped warmly up in her Moses basket, on the back seat.

"Have you any message for Susan?"

"No," I replied, "none at all."

Happily, Uncle Bert was delighted to see us. But I had been confident that he would be. Over the years, he had occasionally reinforced the offer he made me at MumMarch's funeral all those years ago. Almost as if he knew that I might need a 'safe haven' one day. He knew about Ruth, as I had corresponded with my 'other' family with comparative regularity.

When we arrived, to my delight Alfie was there. He took Ruth from me and, with the confidence of the family man he now was, proceeded to give her the bottle I produced.

As she sucked happily, her eyes searching his face, he remarked, "Well, Daisy, this one's a little cracker. Wait till my Patsy sees her. She's always fancied having a girl, but I tell her our two hooligans are more than enough."

Uncle Bert was busy taking blankets upstairs to make the bed up in his spare room, so I called to him to leave it to me. Alfie put his fingers to his lips to stop me. He has been working on the farm with Uncle Bert ever since his father died, the previous year.

"He's as pleased as Punch you've come, Daisy. He doesn't do so much on the farm nowadays, he leaves a lot of it to me, so he'll be glad to be employed looking after you both. I'm moving the family in next month anyway, as he says he is fed up with rattling round here on his own. So we'll be quite a crowd."

"But I don't want to be a burden to him."

"Hush, girl and listen to your brother. He's in his element. Let him be."

I nodded, and sat back and watched him burping her with an expertise far beyond anything I could yet manage.

"So. Is she yours? You know I won't care either way, I'm just curious."

"No." I told all I knew about Ruth's background, and how she came to be with me. His face clouded as he looked down at her.

"My God, Daisy, there's some terrible stuff going on in the world at the minute. You've been out there, seen this Hitler chap. Is there going to be another war?"

It was the first time I had seriously looked at the question; I had been so busy with my own small life. Now I thought about the Fuhrer, the rally, the tanks, the marching children, the Hitler Youth movement. Lotte's husband Franz, and Ruth, my darling motherless Ruth.

"Yes," I answered. "Yes, Alfie, there is going to be another war, I think."

February, 1940

I thought it would break my heart to leave Ruth, but she is so happy with Patsy and her two scallywag sons I am going with a lighter heart than I would have thought possible. After 'Mummy' (yes, that's me. It just sort of happened) her first two words were Tom and Bobby, and she bosses the boys about all over the place, for all she is not quite two yet. But they love her, and are quite wonderful with her. Every day I am reminded of how good Georgie and Alfie were with me.

Georgie is somewhere in France. We are trying hard not to worry. Alfie is a full-time farmer now, so he is in a reserved occupation, and I shall have the comfort of knowing Ruth has both him and Uncle Bert to keep them all safe. Though I pity any Nazi who tried to take on Patsy, who is a real mother hen and can be much fiercer than she looks.

I had expected to join the Women's Land Army, so I could be near to home, as I knew that I would be called up sooner or later as an unmarried woman with no responsibilities. Theoretically. After the war, I shall adopt Ruth, but with everything going on at the moment, we are all agreed it can wait. It is a mere formality, but as she is still virtually invisible we will need to legitimise her existence eventually. Dominic has promised to help. He is back in England, doing something mysterious.

I think he must have been behind me being noticed by the War Office. I can't think who else could have prompted them to get in touch with me. I was staggered when the letter came, asking me to go up to London and meet Colonel Black. I thought it was probably a mistake first of all, but Uncle Bert said I must go, so I went.

And it was not a mistake. They had seen some of my work for the magazine and have asked me to become a 'war photographer'. I was a bit overwhelmed at first, and then I was excited. They want me to go to France almost straight away, because the Colonel says that is where the action will be next. I am to stay a civilian, even though I am being employed by the War Office, as he says I will be safer that way. I have to go to Pinewood Studios first for a quick course in battle photography, and then I am considered to be qualified.

"We want a record of what their chaps are up to and what the natives are doing out there. Go where you like, speak to who you like. Give us a visual taste of what is happening."

I asked if I would have a journalist with me, and he nodded.

"Yes, American woman. Bit older than you. We want the women's point of view. Her name's O'Leary. She'll meet you in Paris. All arranged. Now, Captain Prescott will talk to you about finances, and he will make sure that you have all the equipment that you need. Off you go."

As I reached the door, he said gruffly, "Miss March."

I stopped and turned to him.

"We are grateful. Your country is grateful. Take care." And he turned back to the mound of paper on his desk.

Back home, I think they were as stunned as me, but there wasn't much time. I had forty- eight hours to get ready. Not much time to think, or to regret. Not that there was any real choice anyway. And if I was honest, I was excited and flattered. I would have enjoyed being a Land Army woman, but this was better. Much, much, better.

And it gets even better! I arrived in Paris yesterday and guess who Mrs O'Leary is? Emma! My lovely Emma, who was my first real friend. My goodness, we have some catching up to do.

It was a rough old crossing. Even I, who have never been sea-sick in my life, was a bit queasy. I think, as well, we were all remembering Churchill's experience last week, when, on his way back from the conference in Paris, he spotted a floating mine. He suggested to the destroyer's captain that they blow it up, and so they fetched guns and did just that. Apparently they were all very pleased with themselves and all, including Churchill, cheered madly when it exploded. However, hearing about this was rather scary for us lesser mortals on, presumably, less well armed boats.

Discussing this event with me during our own arduous crossing, a lady with whom I had struck up a brief friendship, said, "Sometimes, I can't help feeling it's just a bit of jolly fun to a lot of them."

And I knew exactly what she meant.

Emma has changed, of course. Well, so have I! It has been nearly twenty years since we last met. But it only took seconds for us to recognise each other and fall into a huge embrace that chased the years away. We met at a small cafe in the shadow of the Eiffel Tower, and after the joy of our reunion, a quiet fell between us. Then:

"You go first," Emma said.

And I did. I told her everything I could remember that was important to me in the last two decades, from school through to Sir's death, the teaching, the photography, Germany. I told her about Georgie being somewhere in France, I told her about Ruth, and I told her about

Mother's betrayal. For that was how it seemed to me. I even told her about Henry's parents, and also about my idiotic misunderstanding of Arthur's intentions, which made her throw back her head and laugh, that wonderful 'Emma laugh' that I had loved as a child.

"Oh, Daisy. You haven't had time to be bored, have you? And look at you now – a famous photographer! No, don't argue, I actually saw some of your stuff in The National Photographic on the boat coming over. I was very proud and I wondered if that photo I took of you and Sooty had anything to do with getting you interested in the first place. I've still got my copy of it. And you look, well, you look terrific. Is there a man in your life?"

"No. A couple of flirtations, but, Emma, you know how difficult it could be for me. I am not going to risk any more snubs."

To her credit, she didn't demur, just nodded her understanding.

"So, that's me accounted for. And now, what about you? Are you really an American now? You certainly sound like one!"

"I hardly know which question to answer first, so I'll start with the last one. Yes, I took American citizenship a couple of years ago. I didn't think I was ever coming back, and the States have been very good to me. But this war changes everything, doesn't it? I had to see if I could help in any way, and it occurred to me that if I could make some of the Americans understand that it was their war as well, then I would be doing my bit. So here I am."

"Not nearly good enough. Too many blanks. Now, start at the beginning and tell me what happened when you arrived in the States."

"If I can remember it all, you mean." When she smiled she still looked like the Emma of twenty years ago. "Well, Joe's aunt was wonderful. I hadn't realised that she more or less brought Joe up, so his death in that dreadful flu epidemic was terrible for her, as well. To survive that awful war and then succumb to that was unbelievably tragic for us both. So I think, being with her helped me to grieve properly for Joe at last. To let all the angst, the resentment, the loneliness, out. We sort of held each other up. Does that make sense?"

I nodded. It did indeed. I had firsthand experience of how bottling things up, because you could not talk about them, was isolating.

She continued, "But life really does go on, doesn't it? Gradually, the pain got less and I woke up one morning and Jo was not the first thing I thought of. I began to think about what I wanted to do with my life. I had been working in a hotel as a cook, but I wasn't very good at it and I wasn't enjoying it much. I had always liked the idea of doing some writing, and I had fallen deeply in love with the movies. So I wrote a piece about the effect of talking pictures, both on the industry and the public. I was very young and cheeky in those days, and I sent it to the offices of the Albany Evening News, which were not far from where we lived in New York. The next thing I knew, I was offered a job as their movie critic, and, as they say, I never looked back."

"And is there a man in your life?"

"Off and on. I wouldn't really want to get married again, and I am certainly too old to think about kids now, but Harve and I have been knocking about together for some years now. So, sort of, I suppose. But no heavy commitment on either side."

158

We finished our delicious coffee and, armed with a street map, decided to walk to our *pension* which was on the outskirts of Montmartre. The map proved to be illusive and we were both wearing shoes that were certainly not made for walking far. After about thirty minutes or so of not even being quite sure we were going in the right direction, we finally hailed a cab (as Emma insisted on calling the taxi).

Arriving at our destination we were delighted to find a spruce little apartment house (Emma again!) on three floors, and a *concierge* who speaks English. Madame Bisset is a pleasant woman in her early forties. Our room is charming, light and airy with twin beds, and a writing desk for Emma. Downstairs there is a small study where I am to develop my photos. We are both impressed with the efficiency of our employer.

We have decided to go out again for supper, so we freshen up quickly and make for the cafe that Madame recommended, nearby. Paris is certainly not obviously suffering from any shortages, and though we have to guess at half the things on the menu, everything is delicious. The chef has heard that there are two American women in, and comes out to speak to us. I am too tired to correct his mistake and, anyway, Emma does all the talking. She seems to be already able to communicate better than me. He suddenly realises that the bag hanging from my chair is a camera, and, straightening his tall white hat, mimes posing for me.

I laugh, and take out my camera. After all, this is what I am here for. I snap him, and then he rushes off into the kitchen and comes back with a girl we learn is his daughter. Before I have gauged the rapidly fading light, another lady appears, who is his wife, and then we are joined by his father! Cheered on by the other customers in the small cafe, I herd them all outside and take several pictures. I promise to bring them in as soon as they are developed.

As we leave, Emma says. "I hope they are good pictures. Then we should be able to eat there free for the rest of our stay."

"Miser!" I tease her, as we link arms and wend our way back to our apartment, through a Paris which feels so secure and carefree I cannot imagine it ever being touched by war.

We have been here nearly three months now and gradually the horizon grows darker and the Parisians more anxious. In the cafe now only the chef and his wife are left. He has sent the rest of his family to stay with relations in the country. This is a familiar tale and who can blame them? His son has already been conscripted. We went to the station with his parents to see him off on the military train, and wired our report and pictures back home that evening. I am learning that I must not get too emotional, that I must be able to photograph tears without shedding them myself.

And there are very many tears in Paris now. Along with the rest of the population, we have been given gas masks, and know where our nearest place to shelter is if Paris is bombed. There are sandbags piled up all over the place, and shop windows protected with coverings of tape and wood. And yet the women continue to look extraordinarily smart, with their high heels and fashionable clothes, the ice cream sellers still ring their bells and there is laughing and joking everywhere. I am growing to love the French, with their defiance and resolve.

We went to see 'The Little Sparrow', Edith Piaf, at the Pigalle last night. We had heard so much about her, with her rather controversial private life all over the newspapers even in England, that we were determined to get to her concert if we could. She really is enormously talented. It is not that her voice is so fantastic, though it is very good, but somehow she manages to show her heart and soul in her songs. I have never heard anyone quite like her.

Even though we did not understand the lyrics, we knew precisely what she was telling us. At the end she led us in the Marseillaise and Emma and I sang as lustily as everyone else. At least we have learned the words to that. We walked most of the way back in silence, a bit overwhelmed by Edith herself, and the fervent patriotism inherent in the performance. It was all very moving, and quite unforgettable.

Today is the tenth of May, and we heard that Belgium and Holland have fallen to the Reich, and the battle for Norway is virtually lost. We are pinning our hopes, along with the whole of France, on the British Expeditionary Force which has been waiting on the Belgian border. Surely they will be able to protect France? I am doubly anxious. Anxious for France and anxious because Georgie's regiment is with them. I wish I believed in a God, I would like to be able to pray to someone to keep him safe. Instead, I am crossing my fingers when I think no-one is looking. A sort of nod to the God of superstition, I suppose.

We have just heard that the British Expeditionary Force, after waiting so long on the Belgian border, is being beaten back. I can barely believe it. We were sure it would save Belgium and France, and today we heard that the invaded countries have officially surrendered to Hitler. So our troops are routed, surrounded and fighting their way back to the coast, where they will be marooned – cut off by the sea. But what else can they do? Outnumbered and out-manoeuvred.

Madame Bisset has joined the exodus to the country. Her brother came to get her and she is going to live with his family 'until it is all over, *mes chers jeunes filles'*. She has given us permission to use her little car, so Emma and I have packed it up and are on our way to Calais, where some of our soldiers are already arriving. If nothing else, we can try to ensure that as many as possible can send messages home before they are captured. The streets of Paris are deserted as we drive through them. But we can hear the bombs. Emma is driving the first part and I will take over when she needs a rest. It is nearly two hundred miles away, and the roads are awful, so we have packed food, along with all the medical supplies we could lay our hands on. I doubt we shall be able to return here, but we both feel that just to sit and wait for the Nazis to arrive is unthinkable. We were told to 'record the war' and that is our intention.

It has taken us nearly three days to get here, not to Calais, as was our original intention, but further along the coast to Dunkirk. We have been held up over and over again, not only by our exhaustion, but because every time we have stopped to refuel, whole villages have come out to ask us what is happening. We have had to point out that they have radios, while we have none, and that we were hoping that they would be able to tell us what is happening.

And that is how we got news that Calais and Boulogne have both fallen to the Germans. The troops are being diverted to Dunkirk in the hope that some of them can be picked up before that succumbs as well.

In the last few hours we have come across several small groups of soldiers straggling to the coast. They had become separated from their units in the chaos. One young officer, on a motorcycle, stopped to speak to us and told us that he had shot a German soldier and commandeered his vehicle. We congratulated him on his bravery. But, oh, how cheap life has become when killing is normal. The only way to survive.

The noise has been getting louder and louder as we approached. But there is nothing that can prepare you for this hellish picture. There are bombs falling everywhere and unearthly screams from wounded men. The smoke from the fires which are leaping up all over the beaches is turning the June sky black.

I wanted to stand and cry. But instead I pulled out my camera and slung it round my neck. Then, pushing my steel hat firmly down on my head, I crawled between some of the sand dunes. There I found three soldiers, leaning back with their cigarettes as if they were on a picnic in Hyde Park. They were so covered in smoke and grime I had no idea of their age, but as I reached them, one of them looked up and a wide grin broke through the dirt.

"Well," he said, with a lilting Welsh voice, "Look, lads – it's the bloody angel of Mons, all over again!"

I collapsed beside them, and aimed my camera and pressed the shutter before attempting to answer them. Only the Brits, I though, would make jokes while bombs fell round them and death waited round the corner. But before I could open my mouth, Emma came hurtling behind me into the sandy shelter.

"There are boats!" she yelled, "out there! Look! For God's sake, look!"

And we all followed her pointing finger. Sure enough, on the horizon, just visible through the smoke, small boats were appearing. Dozens of them. For a brief moment we all watched in silence, then the soldier turned back to me.

"Said you were a bloody angel, didn't I?"

We left our new friends crawling down the beach to queue for the boats. We had been told about the seven French destroyers that had been sunk previously by the shells and bombs that fell constantly on all sides. So their chances of getting off the beach seemed slim, at best. We found our way to the casualty station, where I snapped some of the medical staff, tired, distraught and covered in blood and other body substances. The makeshift hospital was packed full of the wounded and the dying.

I hesitated over a soldier whose legs were a bloody mess, but he peered up at me and croaked, "Take the pictures, love. Show them what the bastards did to me." And then he died. Just like that. I had never seen a dead person before, and I called to the nurse who was nearest me. She felt his pulse and then closed his eyes, touched my shoulder briefly in a gesture of comfort and moved on.

I stumbled out of the tent into the hell outside, feeling sick. I took some deep breaths and choked on the smoke. Then Emma was behind me.

"No time to feel sorry for ourselves, Daisy. Come on. We have a job to do."

She was right. We went back into the tent. After an hour or so, someone shouted, "They've begun evacuating. And it looks like every bloody pleasure boat in England has found its way over here; bless their little seaworthy hulls!"

We staggered out to see, and he was right. There were even more boats, of all shapes and sizes, bobbing on the water and pulling soldiers aboard. The queues for them did not seem to diminish, however, as the long lines of men stood in the water, patiently waiting for their turn to be hauled aboard.

"Thank God the sea is so calm," said a voice behind me, and I turned to see one of the doctors pulling on a cigarette. His face was deathly white where he had run his hand over it, dislodging the grime. "And we are supposed to be civilised," he said, surveying the beach. "I'm sorry, I don't know your name, but make sure you photograph all this," and he motioned at the decaying bodies, the battered vehicles, the abandoned weapons, "because it is almost beyond belief. The world needs to understand and, who knows," he gave a bitter laugh, "perhaps even learn a bit. Use your camera, my dear. In the end, it might turn out to be the most effective weapon here." He ground out the stub of his cigarette, straightened up, and pushed his way back inside without glancing at me again.

"He's right," said Emma. "We need for the people in the States to see all this. Come on, Daisy."

165

At that moment a Junkers screamed overhead, strafing the beach. We threw ourselves on the ground as it went over. I sat up when it had passed us and checked my camera.

"Seems to be OK," I said to Emma. "I am frightened of getting sand in it, never mind getting blown up!"

I expected one of Emma's chirpy replies about losing a sense of proportion, and when there was none I went to haul her to her feet. As I bent over her to grab her hand, I knew. But I couldn't believe it. She was untouched. Beautiful Emma, my friend, lying in the sand. The doctor who had been talking to us reappeared.

"Gosh, that was nasty. Just checking you are both ... Oh, God," and he was on his knees beside her, listening to her heart, feeling her pulse, but we both knew. He lifted her gently and I saw for the first time that the back of her head was a bloody mess.

"I am so sorry," he said, laying her back down.

"Thank you," I said stiffly, keeping my voice firm, trying to embody her resolution. "I need to work now." And I raised my camera and took the picture of my dear, dead friend that might help to show her country what was happening here.

Horror is piling on horror. There are bodies everywhere. I have reluctantly agreed to leave on one of the small boats that are ferrying men on to the destroyers that stand waiting further out at sea. Only the knowledge that my photographs might be important, might make some small difference especially in America, is driving me away. Some of the doctors in the Casualty Station are staying behind to treat the wounded even though they know it means they will be almost certainly be captured.

166

Or worse. Not all of them are British, some of them are French, and others are Belgian.

"Where else would I go?" asked one of the Belgian medics, with his thick accent, "when your people are saying they will stay."

They told me about the brave British soldiers who are fighting a rearguard action, which is what was enabling so many others to get off the beaches. I confess to them that I had not realised that was happening.

"Yes, indeed. And they will certainly be captured if they are not killed. There will be no way out for them."

He mentioned a couple of the regiments that he had recognised among those that were sacrificing their own hope of freedom and safety on behalf of their fellow soldiers. A cold hand clutched at my heart. One of those regiments was Georgie's.

I wanted to scream and let some of the fear, and anger and frustration out. But I didn't. I took a couple more shots of the beach, half wishing they were in colour and half pleased they were not. I thought the blood that was staining everything from clothes to sand would be obvious even in monotone. I could not reproduce the noise, or the awful metallic smell that blood carries with it, but perhaps I could begin to record the despair and futility of what had happened. Of what was still happening here.

Then I ran down the beach, and began the journey home.

Dunkirk, it seems was a triumph. Or so the British public are being led to believe. It was no such thing, of course. It was an awful, desperate defeat. But a huge proportion of the soldiers who managed to get to the beaches were evacuated. Many rescued by civilians in small boats. And that was indeed a miracle, meaning that we had enough soldiers left to gather strength again to go on fighting the German monster.

My Georgie, my dear brother, was one of the forty thousand soldiers who fought off the Germans, and kept them out of Dunkirk. One of those who made it all possible. And if he is still alive, and that is a very big if, he will have no idea that this rearguard action has saved our nation. His captors will not tell him, will they? And no-one else mentions it either. Not in the papers, not anywhere. It is as if their bravery, their probable deaths have been erased. As if they don't count.

Alfie received a telegram telling him that Georgie is 'missing, believed killed in action'. My dear, courageous brother, who deserves a sackful of medals, please, please, come home to us. I saw enough to know they cannot possibly be sure of anything, and I shall continue to believe he has survived.

The War Office is delighted with my piece on Dunkirk. I wrote it as well as taking the photographs, and the photograph of Emma, an American, laying dead on the sand, has been in most of their papers. She is front page news, and has achieved more than she would have thought possible. The Americans are finally sitting up and taking notice of the war, and there are murmurings from a section of the public that they should be involved. So, my darling friend, your death has not been in vain.

I am being given a month off, and then I have to report to Colonel Black again. In the meantime, I seem to have made the newspaper pages myself and am embarrassed to see a description of 'the angel of the beaches'. If I ever find that soldier, I shall have something to say to him! But the flurry of interest soon died down, and it did give me a chance to tell the reporter who came round about Georgie and his comrades in arms. But he didn't think the rearguard action was worth mentioning in his article. It is as if these forty thousand men are to be consigned to historic invisibility.

To my relief, Ruth has not forgotten me. She greeted me with cries of 'Mama', and even though I suspected Patsy of coaching her I felt tears of relief and joy at being back with her fall on my cheeks.

"Mama sad?" asked my precocious daughter.

"No," I assured her, "Mama very happy."

Patsy says she is very bright, with a large vocabulary already.

"Much more advanced than my two," but Patsy is completely at ease with this.

Uncle Bert has taken on a new sheep dog, as old Shep, the one he seems to have had forever, is not up to looking after the sheep anymore. Ruth is besotted with the puppy, as are Tom and Bobby. Uncle Bert insists on having him in the field to train during the day, but from about 4 o'clock he is home with the children, and follows them everywhere. It gives me so much joy to see Ruth growing up in this normal family, coming, as she does, from such an abnormal world. I shall always be grateful to my adopted family.

And that brings me to my other news. The other day, Patsy was out milking and Alfie was down with Uncle Bert, when I heard a car roll up. Looking out of the kitchen window, I saw Arthur and Mother getting out.

My first thought was that I did not want to see them. But the children were already out through the door, the boys admiring the rather splendid car, and Ruth looking at Mother who was wearing a long green coat, obviously bought before the war, with a matching hat. Ruth was obviously something between awestruck and fascinated. Dungarees were what Patsy and I wore all the time. I watched as my daughter put out her chubby hand and touched the fabric. I waited for Mother to step around her. But no, she bent down and spoke to her. Smiling! Mother was smiling at Ruth?

Arthur looked toward the window and saw me. He waved, and leaving Mother talking to Ruth, came into the house. He gave me a big hug, which I returned warmly and before I had a chance to ask what was going on, he said, "Give her a chance, Daisy, for all our sakes."

I held his concerned eyes for a moment, then I nodded. And waited where I was. Several minutes later Mother was led in by Ruth, who was pulling her hand. They were escorted on either side by my grinning nephews, who chorused, "Someone to see you, Aunty Daisy."

I waited. Mother, still holding Ruth's hand, crossed and kissed my cheek. "Hallo, Daisy."

"Hallo, Mother," I replied. "Ruth, come here."

Ruth dropped Mother's hand, and came to lean against me, sucking her thumb and looking up at us. The boys had fallen quiet.

Arthur said, "Come along, lads, let me show you over my new car." They followed him out with whoops of approval.

I waited in silence, all sorts of emotions bubbling away inside me. Why was she here? What did she want? To insult me? To try to take Ruth away from me?

Into the silence, Mother said the one thing I had not anticipated or ever expected to hear. "Daisy, I am so sorry. And so very proud of you. Will you, can you, forgive me?"

Her eyes were full of tears. And so were mine as I reached and embraced her.

"I have missed you so much," she said.

"And I, you," I answered truthfully.

I felt an immediate sense of relief at our reunion, followed by amazement as Mother picked up Ruth and let her knock her hat off. They sat together in the big armchair, and as Arthur and I made tea in the kitchen, I could hear Ruth embarking on her catalogue of nursery rhymes, to the encouragement and seeming enjoyment of Mother. Wonders would never cease.

Arthur smiled at me. "Thank you, Daisy."

As instructed, I visited Colonel Black again today. In his somewhat peremptory way, he expressed his condolences for Emma's death, and I told him that I had written to her aunt in America, expressing my own sorrow, and emphasising Emma's complete commitment to what she and I were doing at Dunkirk. He told me the War Office had done this as well. Then, he congratulated me on my work in France. I was relieved that he did not want to discuss any of that further, as I felt there was nothing I could have said that my photographs had not done already.

I was a bit apprehensive of what my next mission would be, but as it turned out, I need not have worried. I am not being sent abroad, at least for the time being. In fact, I am to see a great deal of this country. Apparently, I am to work my way round as many of the evacuated children as I can, and photograph them with their temporary families. He handed me a long list that read like a peacetime tour of the British Isles.

"We want pictures of happy, smiling children. It will be immensely reassuring to their families at home, and to the public at large."

"But what about the ones who are not happy and smiling? There must be some who hate being sent away, and, also people who hate having to look after them?"

My goodness, I was getting brave, I would never have spoken to him like that a year ago.

"Just do the job, Miss March. Photograph what you see, and we will choose the ones that will be used. You know the drill by now."

"So, let me get this straight. What you really want are propaganda pictures. And do you want me to write about them as well?"

"Just where and who they are. Our Captain Hargreaves will write the article round your photographs if you just supply the basic information. Names, places, etc."

"Dominic Hargreaves?"

"Yes, indeed. You know him?"

I confirmed I did indeed know him and asked for my best wishes to be conveyed to him. Then decided to ask the question that had been bothering me.

"Why can't I join the army? Surely if I turned up in an official capacity, wearing a uniform, it would make it easier all round. Otherwise some of these families will think I am just snooping around for the newspapers."

"Actually, Miss March, I think you are right. ATS? Lieutenant? Right? My secretary will get you fitted out. You will continue to work independently and report back to me, of course."

"How will I travel? I have my own car. Can I have a petrol allowance for that? And where will I stay?"

"My secretary will sort all the necessary paperwork and finances with you. Now, forgive me, but I have important work to do."

Dismissed – he had obviously had enough of talking to small fry like me – I was taken off by his charming and very efficient secretary, who did indeed sort out everything. She even managed to find me a uniform that fitted quite well, something of an achievement, as I knew the nearly always baggy or too tight jackets and skirts drove some of the new women recruits mad.

So, to the amusement of my family, I returned home to say my farewells to them, not only in uniform, but as a commissioned officer. Lieutenant March, no less. I don't know who was more impressed, them or me. This certainly was a very strange world we were living in.

Before I left, I drove over to see Mother and Arthur to let them know what was happening, and Mother was indeed gratified by my smart uniform. Arthur is very quiet, as James is now a fully trained pilot in the RAF, not a very safe place to be at the minute. And becoming more unsafe by the day. Someone else to worry about. Georgie and James, and thousands of others we don't even know. Since Dunkirk, I sometimes feel we are all walking hand in hand with sudden death.

However, this morning, as I was all packed up and ready to leave, and had said my goodbyes to everyone, and then hugged and hugged my little Ruth all over again and made her promise to do everything that her Aunty Patsy told her, there was a knock at the door.

We all froze. Alfie went and took the telegram from the boy outside. We watched as he stood by his bicycle, waiting to see if there was any answer.

Alfie's hands were trembling as he tore it open. Then, his voice breaking, he turned to us, "He's safe! He's alive. A prisoner, but alive!"

Georgie alive! An inexpressible tide of relief swept over us all, and we were suddenly all laughing and kissing and crying at the same time. Ruth joined in this with great gusto, before suddenly sitting on the floor and demanding, "Who dis Georgie?" which made us all laugh even more.

I swept her up in my arms, and pressing my tear-damp face close to hers, I whispered, "He's the best man in the world, Ruthie, and you are going to get to know him after all."

She chuckled and pushed her fingers into my mouth, "Mama happy! Ruth go down now."

And she extricated herself from my hug and padded off with her 'brothers', Tom and Bobby, to play outside. No wonder I so often had a sense of *déjà vu*!

April 1941

This has been such a strange few months. Colonel Black's list sent me to Wales first of all. I had no idea the country was so lovely. Or indeed so magical. There is something awe- inspiring and otherworldly about those towering coal slopes and the rows of tiny cottages in their shadow. Wales has been hit badly by the German bombs, especially Cardiff and Swansea, but up here in North Wales, we only hear the planes in the distance. Sometimes it feels like a sort of Garden of Eden, removed from all the evil in the world.

And that, inevitably, turned out to be an illusion. But not immediately. My first visit was to a large house, by far the biggest for some miles around, standing in its own grounds with a gated drive. When I rang the bell, two children ran down and pulled open the gates and beckoned me in. I drove through and then opened my window and called, "Hop in the back, I'll give you a lift up to the house."

They did as they were bid, and driving very slowly so as to avoid the three dogs of indeterminate breed that loped along beside us, I asked their names. I already knew they were my evacuees as there were no other children in this family. Marlene and Gary were Liverpudlians and were obviously having the time of their young lives. When I pulled up, they leapt from the car and dashed up the steps to the front door, calling, "She's here!" by which I gathered the War Office had informed them of my visit. I had a sneaking suspicion that Colonel Black had hand-picked my destinations in order to show some rather Utopian situations.

This theory was somewhat borne out by the charming, early middle-aged, couple who greeted me. They showed me the letter they had received heralding my visit, and told me they were distant relations of Colonel Black and knew him quite well. They were about to send Marlene and Gary off to change into more formal clothes for the photographs. I stopped them and explained that I wished to snap them informally, at play, or just doing what they did all day.

The children were still in the Easter holidays, but they volunteered to take me to see their school. I had some walking boots in the car, so suitably clad; we walked down to the village. There I met several of the other evacuees that I had on my list, and was very pleased to see how well they all looked and how happy they appeared to be. The resident Welsh children seemed to have taken them to their hearts. I began to feel rather like the Pied Piper as we walked through the village collecting children. An elderly man came out of the school house as we approached it and stood waiting for us.

"I am Mr Price, the headmaster, and you must be Lieutenant March," he greeted me, "would you care to see our school?"

I felt it would be ungracious to refuse. As he showed me over the small school, I asked how he knew my name, and was unsurprised when he also produced the letter from the War Office. They were determined I should not catch anyone unawares, I thought rather grimly.

I took a great many photographs, aware the sun was shining brightly and all the children were sparkling clean and looking as if they had just stepped out of a picture book. Only one small child, Peter, younger than the others, with a runny nose and a graze on his knee, grabbed my hand and said, "Is my mummy coming to see me soon?" I crossed my fingers and assured him that she was. He ran off cheerfully to play with the rest.

After I had said farewell to the children I drove to the inn a few miles away where I was booked for the night. I was very thoughtful. Aware that the War Office wanted pictures showing how contented the evacuees were, I now realised they had, to all intents, set the scenes that I would find. I wondered how much research it had taken to send me to the places that they were only receiving good reports about. I was not as naive as they believed. I would do the places on the Colonel's list, but I was going to seek out some others on my own behalf.

The following day, I decided to delay going to the next place on my list, which I saw was another village with the two evacuees again placed in a rather grand house. I picked the brains of the landlady at the inn. I asked her what happened when the children had arrived here, and she told me, in her lovely, almost musical, Welsh voice, how they had stood in the church hall and waited for someone to choose them.

"You mean, they were not allocated to certain households?"

She shook her head. "No, dear. Not in this village. The farmer from over the hill came first, and he took the three biggest and strongest lads. He wanted help on his farm. One of the little girls was in a terrible state because she wanted to go with her brother and she cried and cried when they took them off. The vicar and his wife took her in at the end. They also took another little girl who was upset at being parted from her sister. They are very good people, chapel, you know. I see Mrs Vicar in the shop

177

sometimes with the two little girls. If you want to know about the children why don't you have a word with her?"

I would indeed. And I intended to have a word with that farmer. I was under the impression that siblings should stay together. And I was beginning to think that that the War Office was using me to divert people from the truth of some of what was happening here in Wales.

I've sent the first lot of photos off, wondering if the Colonel has any idea how difficult it is to develop them in a tiny bathroom with no shutters on the window. No, of course he has not. But anyway, these pictures of smiling, happy and healthy children playing in the sunlit countryside are exactly what he is looking for, I think. And I am now going to talk to 'Mrs Vicar'. She is not on my list, so will have no idea I am coming, and hopefully will talk freely to me.

'Mrs Vicar' turned out to be a charming young woman of about my age. Her name is Elaine, and we achieved Christian name terms almost immediately. She tells me her husband is torn between continuing his work here, which seems even more important now, or joining up and ministering to the troops.

"I confess I want him to stay here," she says in her mesmerising Welsh lilt, "but I don't tell him, because he has to do what he thinks is right, doesn't he?"

I could only agree. We were both aware of the irony of the perception that North Wales was the safest place in Britain for evacuees was a bit of an illusion. The Luftwaffe had begun to drop off their bombs on the way back from attacking Liverpool, and consequently the noise of the sirens strikes immediate fear into Welsh hearts. They had quickly learnt, as had so many others all over the country, to gather up their loved ones and rush to the comparative safety of the shelters. So while it was hardly like the London blitz, it was all quite scary enough, and there was considerable bomb damage to be seen especially in places along the coast. I had driven through Bangor on the way up here, and was very shocked at the extent of the devastation.

I had no need to ask about 'Mrs Vicar's' two little girls, as they were present the whole time we were talking. Pulling at Elaine's hand, jumping on her lap, teasing the poor, obviously long-suffering cat that was trying to sleep in a pool of sunshine, and constantly interrupting us –behaving, in fact, just as normal, well-adjusted children do. Gently rebuking them for waking the cat, she sent them into the garden to play.

"You are doing a fantastic job there," I commented

"It is not difficult, they are charming girls. But they should not have been separated from their siblings. That is not what is supposed to happen. And I seem to be powerless to reunite them. I have even offered to have the two other children here, but the woman who is supposed to be in charge of it all is invisible and un-get-at-able; I have even tried writing to the War Office and have had no answer."

"Now, why doesn't that surprise me?" I murmured, as much to myself as to her. I pulled out my notebook. "I need your help. Can you give me the addresses of where their siblings are? As long as you are sure about having them yourself, I will try and sort this out."

Elaine assured me that she was, and I gave the little girls a quick goodbye hug before going on my way. The farm was my next port of call. The War Office was paying seven shillings and sixpence toward the keep of each evacuee, and also encouraging parents who could afford it to send more money to their children's carers. I had spoken to some of those parents before I left, and many of them, especially the women, were going short of food themselves, in order to send money to the host families.

Therefore, I reasoned, three strong boys doing free farm work, and bringing the farmer at least twenty-two shillings and sixpence a week, were quite desirable. I hoped that I would find he was showing appreciation for his good fortune and looking after them properly.

I left early next morning. I had instructions on how to find the farm, and knew the farmer's name was Rees, and that he lived there with his wife. As far as anyone knew they had no children, but Elaine told me that no-one knew them very well. "They come to the chapel very occasionally, but although my husband has been up to the farm to see them, he told me that they made it very clear that they didn't want visitors. I think they must have been quite rude to him, because he only went the one time."

Armed with this somewhat disconcerting information, I was not looking forward to this visit. Especially as I suspected that Colonel Black would not be amused to know that his list was screwed up in my bag and Mr Rees was definitely not on it. But something did not feel right here, and I was determined to see these boys, for my own peace of mind, if nothing else.

The entrance to the farm was down a very rutted track, and I hoped my little car was not going to let me down. I could see the farmhouse several fields away. I stopped twice to push open gates, and then close them behind me. There were sheep in the first two fields looking at me with, well, sheep's eyes, I suppose. I

180

suppressed a grin at that thought, and the momentary silliness cheered me up.

The fields directly behind the farmhouse appeared to be empty, but as I approached I saw some figures hard at work digging out furrows. I left the car and walked across the muddy ruts until I could see that they were three lads of about thirteen years. Definitely the boys I was looking for. As I grew nearer, one of them looked up and saw me, and wiping a muddy hand across his forehead, nudged one of his companions. They stood upright and looked at me. They were all holding spades that seemed much too large and heavy for them.

"Hallo there, I am Lieutenant March, and I think you may be the gentlemen I have called to see."

They smiled at the 'gentlemen' but then shifted from one foot to the other, looking at each other, not speaking. I noticed that their clothes were very poor. Thin, torn shirts several sizes too large and cut down trousers tied up with rope. I could see the work they were doing was going to make them dirty, but their hair and skin looked greasy with long term neglect. All three of them were thin to the point of emaciation. No-one looked fat nowadays, but this seemed way beyond normal.

"Which one of you is Alan?" I asked.

The tallest boy raised his hand, still mute.

"I have just seen your sister; she sends her love to you."

The child's face lit up. "Is she alright, Miss? I told our mum I'd take care of her but they wouldn't let us go together."

I assured him she was fine, and the three of them relapsed into silence again.

"So which of you is John, and which Frank?" Having finally got them sorted, I asked, "Are you being well looked after?" A stupid question. I already knew they weren't. And I had worked as a teacher long enough to know when children are frightened. These boys were scared to speak to me. "Right," I said. "I am going down to the house to talk to Mr Rees. When are you due to have your lunch break?"

They looked at me blankly. "We have it here, Miss," said John. He turned and fetched a grey-looking cloth that was hanging from a fence post. "We bring it with us. Mr Rees doesn't like us to stop. He shouts at us if we do."

"Shh, John," said Alan.

"Show me what is in the cloth."

Carefully, John unwrapped their sustenance. Three very thin slices of obviously stale bread fell out. I stared in horror. "What did you have for breakfast?"

"It's a sort of porridgy soup the Mrs makes. It is not very nice, and there's not much of it, but she says beggars can't be choosers, and it costs a lot to keep us."

This was becoming more Dickensian by the minute and I was feeling more angry than I could ever remember being before in my whole life.

"Follow me."

Glancing at each other nervously, they followed me back across the field.

"Get in the car," I said.

I drove down to the farmhouse in silence. "Stay there until I call you," I ordered them.

The farmhouse door was open, and a large woman was sitting at the kitchen table opposite an even larger man. The kitchen smelled of cooking and I could see they were eating fried eggs with bacon and fried bread. They jumped to their feet as I pushed the door open.

"Who the devil are you?" he blustered, having obviously seen my uniform.

"I have been sent by the War Office to check on the wellbeing of your evacuees, Mr Rees," I lied, "and I should tell you that unless you have anything to say that will change my mind, I am accusing you of the wilful neglect of your charges and of defrauding the government of the money that is sent to you for their care. And I shall be removing these children to a safer place immediately."

Somewhat to my relief, there was no argument.

Mr Rees glared belligerently at me for a long moment, before transferring his attention to his wife. "Best get their stuff then, or she'll accuse us of stealing it."

Mrs Rees got to her feet and opened what appeared to be a cupboard under the stairs. She removed three cardboard attaché cases. "They came with these. We haven't touched them, except to take out the food that was going off."

And I'll bet you ate it, I thought. I took the cases, and saw they each had 2/6p scrawled on the side. "What is that about?" I demanded.

Mr Rees shrugged. "Was going to flog them at the market. Help feed the little buggers."

I couldn't resist it. "You pathetic, greedy pair of hypocrites! You will be hearing more about this." And I swept out, holding all three cases.

The boys were huddled together in the back of the car, but they all sat up when I started the engine. "Are we going home, Miss?" asked Frank, the first time I had heard him speak.

"No, I can't manage that, Frank, but I am taking you somewhere you will be looked after," and not used as slave labour, I added silently.

Heroically, Elaine was only slightly taken aback at receiving all three boys. As we watched Alan and his sister hugging each other, she turned to me with a grin. "Oh, well, the minister's house is too big for us anyway, they were always built for families. The village will help. In for a penny, in for a pound. We'll manage, Daisy. What about you? Will you be in trouble?"

"Probably. But I have a secret weapon." And I had. I had the photographs of the boys I had taken in the fields and of the suitcases with the price chalked on them. And of Alan reunited with his sister. In fact, of everything I needed.

There was a telephone at the inn where I was staying, and I phoned the Colonel's secretary to say that I needed to see him urgently. After some prevarication on her part, we agreed an appointment for the following week. That gave me time to track down the other child, the one who had been separated from her younger sister. That proved to be quite easy. The erstwhile invisible woman, who had been tasked with finding homes for the children, appeared at the inn the next day breathing metaphorical fire.

I was in the dining room, finishing my breakfast and looking at the photographs I had developed the day before, when she burst in.

Without any introduction she hissed "How dare you remove those children from where I had placed them. I have been informed of what happened, and I shall be reporting you to your superiors."

Controlling my anger, I replied, "I shall be the one doing the reporting, I think. You betrayed all the trust that was vested in you by not keeping these boys safe." And I pushed an especially graphic picture of Alan bowed over his heavy shovel, filthy with the grime of days, if not weeks, and with his thinness making it look as if he would fall if the shovel was removed from his hands.

She blustered for a bit, and then calmed down. After a while I began to feel a tiny bit sorry for her. It transpired that she had been volunteered to do the job with very little idea of how to do it. She was quite obviously poorly educated and not very bright. She looked after her elderly parents and had never done any kind of paid work. No-one else had wanted to do it, she told me with a mixture of self-pity and self-justification. I think that the post, briefly, and mistakenly, had given her some kind of self-worth. I thought it was a shame that no-one had cared enough to give her any advice or instruction.

Joan, the older sibling of the little girl Elaine was caring for, had apparently gone to the Big House. That wasn't my description, but what everyone called the large house where I found Joan. And apart from the fact that she was worried about her sister, she was being well looked after. The woman who owned the house had a small boy of her own, and her husband was a major in the army. She told me she had no idea that Joan even had a sister. I guessed that the child was so overawed by her new lifestyle that she hadn't dared mention it. But as soon as I told her the situation, she and Joan and the little boy were all bundled into my car and once again were back at Elaine's a couple of hours later.

There we reunited the two girls, and once we had reassured Elaine that she was losing a boarder, not gaining yet another one, we were on our way back to the Big House with two ecstatic little girls. Their foster mother sat with her little boy on her lap, obviously feeling both guilty but delighted at her new 'family'.

"I should have known. I should have talked more to her. I won't make that mistake again. I am sorry I was so distracted, too absorbed in my own worries," she confessed.

I really believe there are more good people than bad ones in the world. But sometimes it is good to have that demonstrated. Back to England tomorrow. I am going to get hauled over the coals. Ah, well.

My assumptions were spot on. Colonel Black was furious with me. Farmer Rees, apparently a 'good, honest tiller of the soil' (yes, he really said that!) had complained to the War Office. My actions had been high-handed in the extreme.

I sat in silence and let his tirade pour over me. He outlined my misdeeds, and my 'failure to do my duty', which appeared to be shorthand for not doing precisely what I had been told to do. He even said that I had 'betrayed my rank', which, given how easily it had been bestowed on me, I thought was a bit much.

However, I was much too sure of my ground to be intimidated, and I think that fact eventually filtered through to him. He finally lapsed into silence and, after a moment of sitting there glaring at me, said, "Well, Lieutenant, what have you got to say for yourself?"

I reached into my bag and took out two folders. One had the photographs that he wanted to see, cheery and well-kept children playing contentedly in the sun. The other held the pictures I had taken of the boys at the farm.

Dirty, malnourished, tired and obviously desperately unhappy. I spread them out in two piles on the desk in front of him.

I sat back and watched him. I did not think he was a bad man. Just a harassed and overworked man who would probably have settled into retirement by now in a more ordinary world.

After a long moment he looked up from the photos. "I assume these are the children you so summarily removed?" He gestured to the second pile.

I nodded.

"Well done, Lieutenant." He cleared his throat. "Are these chaps being properly looked after now?"

I nodded again. Another silence. He picked up the photographs and placed them back in the folders.

"I would like you to continue with the work you are doing, but part of your brief will be to check on the welfare of the evacuees. I would, however, prefer it if you could stay in touch with this office, especially if you find it necessary to remove any more children. I would also like you to work closely with Captain Hargreaves, and if you come across a similar situation to the Rees farm, which I hope you do not, the Captain will give priority to finding alternative accommodation for the evacuees."

He reached for the telephone on his desk, and spoke for several minutes. Replacing the receiver, he said, "Captain Hargreaves will meet with you on Wednesday to discuss how you should proceed. My secretary will arrange the details with you."

I rose to my feet, suddenly feeling quite exhausted. It made me realise how braced I had been to fight my corner at this meeting. The Colonel must have picked that up, as he looked up from his paperwork.

"What were you going to do if I did not back you?"

"Go to the newspapers."

He threw back his head and laughed. "I suspected as much. But, you see, we really do care, Lieutenant. And now, as it is Friday today, go home and see your family. Be back here on Wednesday, ready to continue your good work."

I thanked him, and left the office with an unexpected spring in my step. Home! For me, that was where Ruth was.

It seems that Dominic and I are to work together again. I must say, I enjoyed meeting up with him. Typical Dominic, never mind the shortages, he whisked me off to the Savoy for the kind of lunch I haven't had in a very long time. I sometimes wonder if I am unusually conscious of the class divide in this country. Everyone else seems to take it for granted. But how come all these rich toffs can still eat and drink as much as they always did?

Dominic took me down so that I could see the basement there, which is fitted out with beds made up with silk covers, just in case you are caught in an air raid. I could not help comparing it to the underground stations in the city and the people sleeping on the platforms there. I have taken photographs of many Londoners in their underground sanctuaries, and been so impressed with the attitude of the crowds who use them. Talk about stoical – my main problem was stopping them, especially the children, doing silly poses and pulling funny faces for the camera. Nobody cowering there, just a lot of laughing and considerable camaraderie, which I hope my camera reflected.

I tried to snap the Savoy shelter, but Dominic stopped me. "God, Daisy, if you put this in the paper they'd never let me eat here again."

And he was only half joking. But I decided to swallow my angst and enjoy the meal. Afterwards he explained that I am to report directly to him if there are any problems, and he will make sure that they are sorted. Also, where I think it is necessary to move evacuees, he will find the children new places. I asked if I could be informed when and where they ended up if they had to be taken from an unsuitable billet.

"You don't trust us, do you, Daisy?"

"Not altogether. Some of your lot are well meaning but inefficient. So I want to be able to check for myself."

"The same old Daisy. Only more so, I think. But yes, I will make sure that you have all the details of their new homes."

Later, I mused that he was right. I was 'more' nowadays. Stronger. The war, and especially Emma's death, had toughened me up. I didn't know whether that was good or bad, it was just what had happened.

I was a little bit crestfallen after my visit home, much as I had enjoyed it. Ruth had been pleased to see me, but not as ecstatic as I had hoped. I told myself that I should be grateful that she was so settled, but it still hurt a bit. I took her to see Mother and Arthur, and she seemed to enjoy the visit. Mother had actually dug out Percy, my pink rabbit, very tatty now, for Ruth. She loved him so we brought him home. But she dropped him onto the floor immediately we got back and I had to rescue him from the enthusiastic shaking of the puppy, now over a year old, and totally devoted to Ruth.

"PatsyMum!" Ruth threw herself at Patsy immediately on our return, and I couldn't quell a feeling of jealousy. Stupid, I know. Patsy is doing a wonderful job. And I reminded myself that I am not even Ruth's proper mother.

"Does that dog ever do any work?" I asked, as he and Ruth rolled together on the floor.

"Pickles? Not really," Patsy laughed. "Shep took on a new lease of life when he arrived, and Uncle Bert lets Pickles play with the children most of the time. Needless to say, Ruth and the boys picked his name! Daft name for a working dog, tells you everything really, doesn't it?"

It was hard to have to leave again so soon, but getting back home at all had felt like a bonus.

"Where are you off to next?" asked Alfie, over supper.

"Back to Wales, and then I am not quite sure. But I will let you know where I am. And, if you hear from Georgie, you will let me know straight away?" I had already given them the number for Dominic's office. Just in case.

They nodded in unison and a silence fell on us, broken by Uncle Bert exclaiming, "Tommy, will you not feed our good food to that dog!"

We all tried not to laugh as Pickles scurried off with a crust sticking out of his mouth.

The next morning I slipped away at dawn, having said my goodbyes the night before. It was nightfall before I arrived back in Wales, and my other life already felt like a dream.

The following months were so busy I hardly had time to think. Village after village, town after town, they all began to merge and retrospectively I couldn't tell one from another. But the important thing was the evacuees. Every one catalogued, assessed, photographed. The vast majority were fine. Even many of those who longed to go home were still, for the most part, being looked after well. Some lucky ones were having the time of their lives, breathing in the country air, meeting animals they had only seen in picture books, eating food that was an adventure to them, and even learning Welsh!

One couple, watching their two girls playing in the garden, confided in me that these were the children they had not been able to have.

"Sometimes," said their foster mother, "I find myself hoping that this war will go on forever, so we can keep them. But I know that is wicked and selfish of me."

"Perhaps they will stay in touch once they are back home," I suggested.

Her face lit up. "And they could come here for their holidays! Oh, that would be lovely, wouldn't it, Ivor?"

He nodded, smiling at me as he put his arm round her. I hoped the girls would indeed never forget this lovely couple.

They were not all like that, of course. But only a very small proportion were being treated badly. And I knew how to move very fast indeed with these, and so did Dominic. The one time I did not hear back from him with a new billet within hours, I packed the small boy in question into my car. I had discovered that his sleeping quarters were in an unheated shed in the garden, where he was expected to live and eat, as well. These were people, so poor that the seven shillings and sixpence was motive

191

enough to take a child, and so unprincipled they then ignored the poor kid. The poor, however, were not my problem, and the children were.

I took this lad straight to Dominic's office. Faced with having to take the child home himself, Dominic never dragged his feet again. We were a good team.

August, 1944

Our evacuee patrol, as Dominic called it, is finally being wound up. For the last few months we have spent most of our time checking on the children who can't go home, because there is no home there anymore and their parents are dead. Our task was making sure that their temporary carers were happy and able to give these war-orphaned youngsters a permanent home, or to make other arrangements for them. I always breathed a huge sigh of relief when they were able to stay with the host family because the alternatives were not good.

We had to place them in 'appropriate' Children's Homes, and some were obviously more appropriate than others. Where possible, we got them into the Dr Barnardo's Homes, which seemed to be less formal than some of the others. Their children seemed much the liveliest when we did our reconnoitring visits. But a lot depended on availability, and also geography, and it was with a heavy heart we deposited some children in homes that appeared so institutionalised it was depressing just viewing them from the outside.

In those cases, we had no choice but to cross our fingers and move on, telling ourselves that at least they would be warm and fed. I came to hate this part of our job, and would make a great show of taking very many photographs, both inside and outside the establishment. A sort of silent promise, or even threat, that we would be watching those in charge. Dominic promised that he would make sure someone kept an eye on the places that we were unsure of, and that he would instruct them to visit regularly, without warning. It was the best we could do.

So, I have finally been moved on, and I am now back in Paris, which feels rather weird. I am actually staying at the same *pension*, and Madame Bisset is still there. Thinner, and her hair has gone grey, but otherwise she hasn't changed a lot. We fell into each other's arms like long lost sisters, which, I suppose, in a way we are. Sisters in survival. She didn't know about Emma, and, in telling her what had happened, I tried to stay unemotional but we both ended up sobbing. I realised that it was the first time I had let myself cry for Emma, so perhaps it was cathartic.

"So many deaths, and for what?" asked Madame, between gulps.

"For the freedom of the world, I suppose," I answered, thinking not only of Emma but Georgie. Georgie will be home soon, we are told. Unlike Emma, my Georgie is still alive.

I am here to photograph the victory parade through the liberated Paris. And the following day, as I mingle with the cheering crowds, I reflect that their sacrifices, Emma's and Georgie's, along with millions of others, have not been in vain.

The procession down the Champs Élysées was more than triumphant; the crowd were ecstatic, nearly hysterical with joy. General de Gaulle made a speech exhorting the crowds not to rein back their emotions, and they certainly did not, they laughed and screamed and cried and danced. I found myself being whirled round wildly by a French soldier, and kissed as passionately as if we had known each other for years. Even though I was forced to hang on to my camera, and in doing so lost my hat, I thoroughly enjoyed the experience!

There is still fighting going on in other parts of France, but apparently de Gaulle felt it was important to restore the moral of the people of Paris. As I snapped the almost frenzied elation of the crowds, I could not but think that he had been right.

Seeing my camera, many of the revellers were helpfully pausing long enough for me to catch their image. I was just deciding that I had taken enough close-ups, and wondering if I could climb up to one of the balconies and get some crowd shots, when I heard a voice yelling my name. I turned, and found myself engulfed in a big hug and there was Dominic. He pulled me into a doorway, and we stood grinning at each other, infected by the unadulterated euphoria of those around us.

"What are you doing here?" I shouted above the clamour, "I thought I'd got rid of you."

"They sent me out to keep an eye on you," he grinned.

"Liar! Why are you here really?"

"Had to talk to some of the big bugs. Churchill is a bit worried this is all happening a bit too soon. Here," he grabbed my arm, "Let's go back to your place, it will be quieter there."

"Let me take some crowd shots first. Can you get us upstairs somewhere?"

He could, of course. Five minutes later we were on a balcony, and with the Arc de Triomphe framing my pictures I got exactly what I was hoping for. I went through film after film, handing the precious spent rolls to Dominic who stored them carefully in my bag. All those months of working together had not been wasted, I reflected with satisfaction. Eventually, he persuaded me that I had taken enough shots, and I reluctantly agreed that he was probably right. We braved the still-thronged street and began to walk to the outskirts of the city, just about the only place we had any chance of finding a taxi.

It took us about three hours to get back to my *pension*, we were more than half way there before we saw a taxi. We reeled through the front door, both of us exhausted with all the emotion as well as the physical effort. The staircase up to my apartment seemed to have elongated as we virtually crawled up it. Madame was nowhere to be seen, obviously joining in the gaiety somewhere. We were flat out, and I kicked off my shoes and sprawled out on my bed, while Dominic collapsed on Emma's. Except it was not Emma's any more, of course.

"Wine on the sideboard," I croaked.

He rose unsteadily and reached for the bottle. There was just one glass on the side. He filled it and offered it to me. I had a sip before handing it back. Then I closed my eyes. And immediately slept.

When I woke, it was to the smell of coffee. Proper coffee. Not ersatz. A smell from another time. Dominic was sitting on the end of my bed holding two steaming cups. I sat up and reached for one.

Pushing my hair out of my eyes, and relishing the first sip, I asked, "Where did you get that from?"

"Ah, wouldn't you like to know. Drink up and ask no questions."

"I'm amazed no-one shot you for it," I said sleepily. "Gosh, this is nectar. I'd forgotten what good French coffee tasted like."

Although it was dark now, the noise from the celebrations was still going on. Even here the streets were crowded. In fact, peering out of the window, it seemed that even more people were down there than earlier.

196

Someone was playing the accordion and a party was in full swing.

"I've got to develop the films," I said, rising shakily.

Dominic took my empty cup from me and placed it on the table. "Leave it. You won't be able to wire anything back until the morning, anyway." He pushed me gently back onto the bed and lay down beside me.

"Are you trying to seduce me?" I asked drowsily.

"I might be. Would you mind?"

He nuzzled my neck playfully. It felt good. Unthreatening. Tender, even.

I thought about it for a minute. "No strings attached?"

He laughed. "I think I am supposed to ask that. But no, no strings attached."

"Then I think I might like that."

A week on and back in England, I am feeling a bit disoriented. And it is not just the whole cultural thing. I am delighted not to be a virgin any more, and yes, I did enjoy the experience. Especially on the second time. And the third. And ... well, I should probably just admit that we did extend our stay in Paris a bit longer than was strictly necessary.

What I had not anticipated was that Dominic was not telling the truth. There were strings attached. He is not satisfied with us being just good friends and working colleagues who had a bit of a fling. He has asked me to marry him. And I don't know what to do about it.

My first reaction was to laugh. "Oh, yes, very funny. I can just see your parents' faces if you took me home."

To my surprise he did not laugh with me. "Daisy, the world has moved on. I don't believe they would give a

197

damn about all that stuff. And I think they would love you." He paused here. "As I do."

"But we have always been such good friends. We've worked together so well."

"And does that all have to stop? I think I have loved you for a long time, Daisy March. Do you remember our Christmas together in the mountains, before the war?"

"Of course I do."

"Well, if you remember, I tried to make a declaration of love then, but you sent me off with a flea in my ear."

"I remember you trying to kiss me with rather unnecessary passion under the mistletoe. I thought you were just the worse for wear. We had all drunk a great deal of wine."

He sighed. "I admit that there may be some truth in that, but we have done so much together since then, grown so close."

"But I don't think of you that way."

"Yes, you do. Not as a prospective husband, because you have made this stupid decision never to marry – no, don't look at me like that, I know you better than you think. We are lovers now, intimates. But I am not content just to become your lover, Daisy. It may surprise you, but I am not really that kind of chap. And Ruth will need a father, if you are going to adopt her."

Even with that inducement, I still needed time to think about all this, time to assess my own feelings. I could hardly say that I had merely wanted to lose my virginity, had not wanted to die not knowing what it would be like to be with a man. I asked him to give me until we were back in England, and I promised to meet him again in London, and give him an answer, when we had concluded our separate debriefings with the Colonel.

That gave me several days to think, which I needed badly. I wired home, and learnt that Ruth and everybody else were fine, and Georgie was due back in days. I was determined to be home for his arrival.

I recognised that I was hugely flattered by Dominic's proposal. Also that I liked him enormously, and that there was a sense in that I would be marrying my best friend, and perhaps that was the ideal basis for marriage. I did not think that I was in love with him, but I was not sure. How would I know anyway? How did one know? I wished Emma was here. She would have known what to advise me. Perhaps this enjoyment of Dominic's company – both in and out of bed – was love?

I was, of course, very well versed in many of the classic novels and I knew that all of Austen's heroines never actually realised they were in love until the moment of betrothal. But the reading of my favourite novels seemed a rather tenuous experience to be basing such a huge decision on. And I remembered that Jane herself had never actually married. So it was guesswork on her part, too.

I kept returning to one thought. How pleased Mother would be. She could be properly posh at last. It was in my power to give her the one thing I knew she had always craved.

My interview with the Colonel went well; he was pleased with the photographs I had wired to him. "I want you to stay in uniform a bit longer, Lieutenant March, I shall have another brief for you soon. But in the meantime, go home, see your family, and make the most of peacetime."

I asked him if he thought the end to the war in Japan was imminent. Thinking of Georgie being home soon had made me very conscious that a great many of our soldiers were still out there and I felt for their families.

The Colonel gave me one of his 'looks' which indicated quite clearly that it was none of my business, but then said, "We can only hope, Lieutenant."

I was to meet Dominic later in the day in Kew Gardens. It really is so beautiful here, a favourite spot for both of us. It was a warm afternoon, and I went and sat on the bench we had often shared, surprised he was not there already. Feeling something brush the top of my head, I glanced up into the tree that branched over the seat, and was startled to see a small parcel hanging there, with a large label dangling from it with DAISY written on it.

I reached up and disentangled it from the foliage. Opening it carefully, I realised it was a ring box. Wrapped round it was a note which said, "This is for you, with all my love. If the answer is 'No', put in on your right hand. If the answer is 'Yes', then ..."

I sat for a moment before carefully opening the box, revealing a dainty, but exquisite, diamond ring. I sat motionless for a minute, as I knew Dominic must be somewhere watching. Why are you waiting, was the question going through my mind. And I had no answer to it.

I placed the ring on my left hand. Which is how I came to arrive home the next day to welcome Georgie back, engaged to be married to the heir of the Earl of Flotenbury.

September, 1945

No matter how shattering or horrific world events are, unless you are actually there, they are just someone else's news. The Americans brought the Japanese war to a close last month by dropping two atom bombs on their country. And I know there is some controversy about whether it was justified or not, but I look at my poor Georgie and all I can think is that the war is over and the POW's will finally be coming home.

We had banners all over the front of the farmhouse. "Welcome home, Georgie". The children have no memory of their uncle at all, of course, but were very excited by all they had been told and had made all sorts of presents for him. Ruth had been teaching Pickles to do special tricks that he could perform for their Uncle Georgie.

Uncle Bert and Alfie fetched him from the station. None of us realised that he would be using a wheelchair. He was too weak to walk from the car. They helped him out and carefully lowered him into the chair, and wheeled him toward the house. I was standing outside, frozen with sorrow and anger at the sight of my big, strong brother reduced to this wraith. What the hell had those bastards done to him?

They wheeled the chair slowly over the always rutted path, and when they reached me, he motioned them to stop. I bent close to him to hear what he was saying.

His voice came out in a whisper, like everything about him it was a ghost of his former self. But the words were clear. "I have thought of you every day, Daisy. I will get better, I promise."

201

I touched his cheek gently and tried not to cry. I managed to smile through the tears that insisted on coming and he smiled back, and behind that smile I saw my own Georgie, my beloved brother, and I dared to believe that all would be well eventually.

Mother came over the next day, and, for the first time, I realised how much the war had changed her. Alfie had decided to bring a bed downstairs for Georgie, so he would not be isolated from the family while he was recovering, and Mother busied herself helping Patsy find sheets and pillows and making the bed up. Mother, voluntarily doing domestic chores, in someone else's house! Wonders would never cease.

I had not mentioned my engagement and had decided to take my ring off for now. Amid all the excitement of anticipating Georgie's return, no-one except Patsy had noticed it on my finger when I arrived the previous day. Before I had a chance to remove it, Patsy gave me a quizzical look and whispered, "Who?"

"Dominic." I whispered back.

She nodded, patted my arm in congratulation, and said, "Is it a secret?"

"Nobody knows yet, we haven't even told his parents. I wanted to come home and tell you all first. But I don't want to distract from all this." I gestured to the banners round the house, and added, "And, in any case, Georgie coming home is the big story. Dominic is coming to meet everyone next week, before I have to go away again, so that will be soon enough to explain."

Another nod. Dear Patsy, as always taking everything, including my Ruth, in her stride with no fuss, just concentrating on the task in hand. What a gem she is. Ruth was pleased to see me, but obviously has not missed me at all. She is much too busy, bless her, doing all the things that a five-year-old does. I feel sad that I have missed so much of her babyhood, but I am sure that I will eventually get the chance to be a proper mother to her. And it is not as if there has ever been any choice.

Three days on, Georgie is able to leave his wheelchair for short periods, and is already putting on weight. He hasn't told us much yet. I was curled up beside him on the sofa today; trying to fill him in on everything I have been doing, which he is very anxious to know.

Then I stopped, and said, "Your turn to talk as soon as you can, Georgie, darling."

He replied, "Soon, Daisy. I want to tell, and I think I need to tell you. But, notwithstanding all the bad stuff, I've still been luckier than a lot of the lads."

I left it there. I think he is haunted by his experiences, and still not quite believing that they are over. When he does speak about what happened, I think it might be cathartic. Or helpful, anyway.

The following evening, when our noisy, and thankfully happily robust, children are bedded, and we are all in the sitting room, Georgie looks over at me and pats the seat beside him on the sofa for me to join him. I sort of know, and I can see the others do, that he is ready to tell us about his last five, lost, years. Uncle Bert and Alfie have been discussing some farm business, and they fall quiet. We wait.

Georgie began: "We didn't even know that most of the men were rescued off the beaches. We heard rumours, some chaps said they had seen all the boats, but we had no way of knowing for sure. In hindsight, I think they sacrificed us deliberately, but knowing what I now do, I think it is a sacrifice most of us would have willingly collaborated with. Someone had to hold back the Germans while the beaches were being evacuated, and we were the chosen ones."

He fell silent. We did not interrupt. I found I could hardly breathe; the tension in the room was so great.

"We were captured just outside Calais. Don't know how many of us were there, I had no way of knowing. It was chaos, nobody knew where their units were, we barely knew which direction to go in. We had been ordered to try and destroy the equipment that was being left behind so the Huns couldn't use it. To get to some of the stuff, we had to pull the bodies of dead Brits out of the way before smashing it up. There were dead bodies everywhere."

I nodded, remembering the smell.

"Of course. I forget you were there, Daisy. You saw."

"Not as much as you did. And I got off the beach."

"But your friend did not. It was no place for women, even such brave ones. But then, it was no place for a man, either." He paused again. "Suddenly, the Huns were there, waving their guns about, shouting at us, rounding us up. And then we were forced to march. And march. And march. For three months. Our biggest problem was lack of food. Some days we were able to dig up a potato or a turnip from the fields, which we would eat raw, mud and peel and all. Other days there was nothing. We watched our mates fall by the wayside, too weak to go on. Sometimes the SS would draw up and shoot anyone who was fallen. They sometimes shot other chaps for the hell of it. A sort of lethal lottery. The ordinary soldiers weren't too bad; I don't think they were enjoying the marching any more than us. But the SS, they were evil bastards. Riding about in their open-top tourers looking to see who they could kill next."

He stopped again.

Uncle Bert said, "You don't have to tell us all at once, Georgie."

"I'm OK. I want to tell you. Get it off my chest. Our feet were a nightmare. Our boots were done for. We tore up what was left of our uniforms and wrapped bandages round our feet to try and protect them. No spare kit, of course. We had what we stood up in and that was that. We were all lousy, lice everywhere. It got so cold, sleeping in the fields at night you'd have thought it would have killed them off but they were hardy little buggers. Time blurred, merged. We made a big effort to keep count of the days. Knowing what day of the week it was, what the date was, sometimes felt like the only thing that made us different to the animals. One or two of the chaps prayed every night, and I used to think: 'your God is a bit deaf, isn't he?' But, five years on I'm not so sure. I'm back with you, aren't I? So perhaps he did hear."

A reflective silence this time. I squeezed his hand. He touched my hair.

"I promised myself that I was going to get through it. I was going to come back. Finally, we arrived at the Stalag. It was bloody awful, but it felt like paradise after the last three months. There wasn't much to eat, and they made us form working parties in the fields, but there were huts to sleep in and bath houses, and every now and again they distributed Red Cross parcels. I know now that we were the lucky ones. Some of the men in other camps, especially the French and Belgian prisoners, were used as slave labour. We got off lightly compared to them. But illness was rife, and largely untreated, and some of the chaps literally went off their heads. One of the blokes in my hut hanged himself. He was only twenty."

"Do you want to stop?" Alfie was looking very concerned. I knew what a struggle he had had with his conscience, after being persuaded to stay at home and work on the farm, when his brother was at war. But thank heavens he had, I reflected.

"No, I am tired, but I want to go on. Besides, Daisy won't be here tomorrow, will you?"

"I have promised Mother to take Ruth and stay a few days. Dominic is coming down."

Patsy glanced at me, but I gave her a slight shake of my head. This was absolutely not the time to intrude with talk of my engagement.

"So," Georgie continued, "we sort of reached a state of just surviving. Getting through each day as best we could. Most of us who were left were the tough ones, and we figured, wrongly as it turned out, that it couldn't get any worse. Bits of news filtered through to us, mainly from some of the guards who were as anxious for the war to end as we were. We guessed, more from what they didn't say than what they did, that we were winning. The food shortages got worse and worse. Many of us were only just this side of starvation. Then the blow fell.

'At the beginning of '45, when the weather was dire, we were evacuated from the camp. We were marched through the night, slept in an open field of snow, marched on again in the morning. This went on for over three months, well into March. Many of the chaps got frost bite. Occasionally we slept in a barn or a church, but most of the time we were in the open. Men were dying like flies. We were forced to leave them, alive or dead, if they couldn't walk. Sometimes we tried to carry them between us, but we were too weak to carry ourselves properly so that was a non-starter.

'The food was almost non-existent. One loaf of bread between six men for five days. And not always as much as that. No idea a lot of the time where we were or where we were going. I know now we walked over five hundred miles. Through the bombs and the air raids, the whole time, of course. Didn't know whether to cheer them on, or curse them. And then one morning, the guards, what was left of them, ran. And we saw the best sight in the whole bloody world! Yanks! Dozens and dozens of Yanks in jeeps. And we knew that it was over at last."

We were all in tears. Every one of us, Georgie included.

"And now," he concluded, "I am going to go to bed. Tomorrow I want my bed upstairs. OK? Time to get back to normal."

Alfie nodded, his face wet with tears. He put his arm round his brother.

"I hope they give every one of you a bloody great medal," he said.

I am picking Dominic up at the station, his petrol allowance has run out. It will be good when that is not a problem anymore. I make Ruth sit in the back when I am driving, as she likes to jump about in the car, which is still quite a novel experience for her. An occasional ride on Uncle Bert's tractor, which she loves, is normally as far as her experience of mechanised travel extends.

We get there much too early for Dominic's train, but Ruth is fascinated by everything, and I realise how rarely she leaves the farm. We have to say 'hallo' to Mr Western, the station master, who gives her a sweet. I

207

think she will love him forever. Sweets are still severely rationed and she savours the barley sugar with wide eyes, having promised 'not to scrunch'.

She is such a funny little thing. She packed her bag happily, with my help, and then decided she was not coming with me. I had to explain that it was a sort of holiday, like Mr Bear has in one of her picture books, and that she would be coming back.

"Back to PatsyMum? And Pickles?"

"Of course, darling. But Grandma Susan wants to see you now."

I sometimes feel that I spend my entire life leaving the people that I love. Ruth, Georgie, and probably Dominic again soon. I had a letter from Colonel Black this morning. I am to meet him next week to find out my new assignment. I am excited, because I love my work, love this unexpected career I have fallen into, but I know I shall hate saying goodbye to them all again. I found it especially hard to leave Georgie today, even for a few days, without having told him I am engaged, but I must tell Mother first, and then everyone else can know.

Ruth is torn between amazement and fear as the train comes clattering and steaming along the line. She buries her head in my skirt and I try to reassure her that all is well. As the noise abates, she finally looks up and asks, "Is it a dragon?"

I assure her that it is not, just as the carriage door swings open, and Dominic, the only passenger to alight, leaps out.

He strides down the platform, gives me a perfunctory hug and then, dropping his small bag, swings Ruth into the air. I mistakenly think she will be upset, but she screams with pleasure and grabs his hair.

"Ruth," he says, "I have been so looking forward to making your acquaintance."

She is laughing too much to respond, and I wonder if she has finished the barley sugar. Visions of her choking rush through my head, and I start to tell Dominic to put her down, but they are both having too much fun.

At last he does put her down and, squatting so that they are face to face, he says, "I am Dominic. Can you say that?"

"Dominic," she repeats, swallowing the last of the barley sugar and grinning at him.

I pick up his bag and trail behind them both to the car. It crosses my mind that everybody seems to bond with Ruth quicker than me. In the car, with Ruth settled back in her seat, I say, "I had no idea you were so good with children."

"Ah, you have a lot to learn about me, my girl. I have three older sisters and seven nephews and nieces. I am looking forward to introducing our little girl to them."

It takes me a split second to realise that he means Ruth. "Will your family be OK with her? And me? It's all a bit much for them to swallow, isn't it?"

Dominic laughs. "Sweetheart, they are going to love you. And Ruth. I am more worried about what you will make of them. Now, have you told your mother, or am I to ask formally for your hand in marriage?"

I explained that I had told nobody. Ruth had dropped off to sleep, so as I drove, I tried to fill him in on Georgie's story.

"But he is doing OK now?"

"Yes, he already hardly needs the wheel chair, is going upstairs to bed, and visibly putting on weight. But it was such a shock when we saw him. I expected him to

209

look different, but I am not sure that I would have recognised him."

"It's been five years, Daisy. We have all changed. And all the POWs I have spoken to seem to gloss over the years in the camp, which I think must have been awful, but are more or less blotted out from their minds by the final obscenity of the death marches."

I had never asked Dominic what his role in the war was. I only knew that he disappeared, sometimes for weeks on end, even when we were working together, and that I had absolutely no idea where he had been. 'Military intelligence' Colonel Black had once said, which I imagined might mean almost anything. And that I must not pry. But there was something in his tone that made me wonder, not for the first time, just how dangerous his war had been. I thought that I might never know.

Mother must have been looking out for us, as she appeared in the drive as soon as we drew up. Ruth stumbled sleepily out of the car, and Mother came and took her hand.

"Hello, Grandma Susan," said Ruth, smiling up at her.

Dominic stood back while I kissed Mother on the cheek, and then came forward as I introduced him. I still have to make an effort to remember that she is no longer Mrs Gosling.

"Mrs Carrington, I am delighted to meet you. Daisy has told me so much about you."

"And I have heard so much about you," Mother replied.

I wondered if she suspected. I had never brought a young man home before. We all went into the house together, Arthur appearing, slightly flustered, from the garden.

210

"So sorry, I didn't hear the car. Introduce me, Daisy."

Once all the introductions were over, Mother asked me to help her bring in a tray of tea, leaving the men chatting.

Once in the kitchen she hissed, "Well, have you anything to tell ..." and then she noticed the ring. "Oh, Daisy. And, is that, I mean, are you ..?"

"Dominic and I are engaged."

She was suffused with smiles. I had only seen Mother like this a couple of times in my life. She drew me into a warm embrace, the warmest she had ever bestowed on me. Then she held me at arm's length, looking at me as if she was seeing me for the first time.

"Dominic Hargreaves! My daughter is going to marry a Hargreaves! Oh, yes, my dear, I know who he is. Your father would be so pleased." I could hardly believe she had actually mentioned my father. "And Ruth? Is he happy to have Ruth? I know you want to adopt her."

"He is indeed." In fact, we had decided that we must try and trace her parents before formally adopting her, but I did not feel the need to go into that now.

She threw her arms around me again. I had finally made Mother ecstatically happy. It had taken long enough, I reflected. And I was only just beginning to understand how much her approval meant to me. I quelled the frisson of unease that was lurking somewhere in my subconscious.

Two days later, Dominic accompanied Ruth and I back to the farm. He had to get back that evening, but I wanted him to meet the rest of my family, and for us to tell them our news together.

Before the introductions had been properly made, Ruth announced, "Mummy Daisy is going to marry

Dominic." Only it came out 'to mawwy', and after the first startled pause, made everyone laugh. I guessed Mother had been coaching Ruth. She had already asked if she could be a 'bwidesmaid' and only Mother could have put that idea in her head.

Then everyone was congratulating us, and Uncle Bert fetched a bottle of homemade wine he had been hoarding and we found some glasses, and they all drunk our health. Tom and Bobby were marching up and down singing *Here comes the bride* and Ruth was trying to join in. And just to complete the melee, Pickles showed his approval by barking hysterically.

Patsy, with her prior knowledge of the engagement, had not only kept my secret, but now fetched a huge cake that she had baked for us.

"I would have liked to have iced it, but I couldn't get the sugar," she said.

I assured her truthfully that it was the best cake I had ever tasted. Dominic asked Patsy if she could teach me to cook, and I threw a cushion at him. My lack of domestic skills was legendary, but I had already fetched my camera and was snapping everyone for posterity. At least I had some skills!

"You will just have to take her as she is," said Georgie, smiling at us both.

He had been quieter than usual today and I thought he looked less well than he had. I was glad to see Patsy had her arm round him. She and Alfie are doing such a good job of nursing him back to health. I feel guilty because I haven't told them yet that I have to leave again. But I don't want to spoil this afternoon.

Alfie volunteers to drive Dominic to the station, and Dominic says he will ring me at the London hotel where I shall be staying, so I can bring him up to date on the Colonel's plans for me.

"And don't take that ring off again, I know about all those young blades at the War Office," he says as we kiss goodbye.

I am flattered. I am thirty-five years old, and although I know I don't look my age, I cannot believe that I would catch the attention of any of his 'young blades'. Later, in the garden, I say as much, with a chuckle, to Georgie. It is a beautiful, autumn evening and we are sitting on an old wooden bench watching the sun set over the trees.

"Daisy, any man worth his salt would notice you."

"Flatterer! But seriously, are you pleased? About me and Dominic?"

He takes my left hand, and looks at the ring on it. Then he slowly raises it to his cheek before placing it back in my lap. "If he makes you happy, then that is all that matters."

The moment is suddenly more serious and I don't know why. A blackbird trills over our heads and we both look up and laugh. We go back into the house. I shake off a slight unease. As if something has eluded me, and I cannot understand what.

Colonel Black was in a good mood today. He actually thanked me for helping to bring America into the war. I could not think what he was talking about at first, then I realised he was talking about the photographs of my dear, dead friend on the beach at Dunkirk. That seems so long ago now. I think he realised that it might be a difficult subject for me, and he changed tack quickly. But later I reflected that he might be right, and Emma would have been pleased by his comments.

It seems I am to go back to Germany. The trials of some of the Nazi murderers are to take place in Nuremberg, starting in November – yes, I did say murderers. Of course I have made up my mind already, how can anyone be neutral, and why should we even attempt it? But I do not confess this to Colonel Black in case he feels I am the wrong person to cover the trials.

He fixes me with one of his looks. "They will be tried under the law with impeccable justice, Daisy. Which is what we all want. Photograph what you see, as you always do."

"Who is coming with me to report on them?"

"Ex RAF chap. Splendid record. Wounded quite late on, invalided out, but one of the lucky ones, fully recovered. Law degree, but the balloon went up before he had a chance to practice. Done a bit of work for us recently, though. Very sound."

"I would like to go out before the trials start, and see if I can find out if any of the Klein family came through the war. And I just might find Ruth's real mother."

He knew about Ruth, of course, and his face softened. "Certainly. I wish you luck, my dear. Though you must have mixed feelings about the possibility of having to hand her back after all this time."

I had indeed, but I was surprised by his empathy.

"Take my chap out with you. Be good for him to see a bit of the place before the trials start, and might be a help to you. I'll arrange it. Can you be ready the day after tomorrow?"

I assured him that I could and thanked him, wondering if my new associate would be a help or a hindrance in what was essentially a private matter. As I got up to leave, I realised that I didn't know the name of my new colleague.

"Oh, sorry." The Colonel shuffled some papers. "Here we are. Squadron Leader James Carrington." He squinted at the note. "Says here you know him. Do you?"

"Oh, yes, Colonel. I certainly do." I knew I was grinning from ear to ear. "He's my step-brother." And I had to refrain from skipping out of the office.

Dominic rang me at the hotel and we agreed to go out for supper. He had found a Greek restaurant that had just re-opened in Soho, having been bombed out of business during the blitz. I had never tasted Greek food before, and loved it, even though the proprietor kept apologising for the shortages. Dominic had told them that we were just engaged, and arranged for us to be serenaded by a somewhat robust chap playing a mandolin. At least, I think it was a mandolin. And we had a bottle of champagne, which Dominic said had been sent up to London in my honour by his parents.

"You must come down and meet them, darling. They really are dying to welcome you into the bosom of the family. Especially now I have told them all about yours."

"Have you?" I was mildly surprised, though I don't know why I should have been.

"Of course I have." He sighed. "Daisy, I think you have a totally unrealistic picture of my lot. Admittedly, the house is biggish, but it's inherited and Pa spends all his time trying to make enough money to keep the roof from leaking. And he is not an idle aristocrat, he writes very academic books and stuff on historical military strategy, and Ma is a landscape gardener who designs gardens for people. We are quite well off, but neither idle nor especially rich."

215

"Oh," I replied, after a moment's contemplation, "and here I was, marrying you for your money. What shall I do now?"

After a split second, he threw back his head and bellowed with laughter. "Oh, Daisy, I do love you."

Such a lovely evening. And then we went back to my hotel, thanking heavens the hotel staff were both tactful and discreet.

The next day I met James at Croydon airport. We were both so delighted at having been teamed up, our reunion and his reassurances helped to allay my reservations about flying. It was my first time and I confess I was nervous. But James knew the pilot and introduced me to him, which was nice of them both and did help a fraction. I was one of only two women on board, as the plane was full of army lawyers going to Nuremberg to prepare for the trials.

"There are no civil flights from here yet, so it was jolly good of the Colonel to get us on board," explained James, "Especially as I gather we are coming out early to look for Ruth's family."

"And the Kleins," I added.

The plane took off before we had any more chance to chat, and I gripped my seat and closed my eyes as we took off. I have to admit the much vaunted romance of flying totally escapes me. I was never more pleased in my life than when we finally landed in Germany. To my step brother's amusement, I was a wreck. But a hot cup of ersatz coffee and a sticky bun revived me, and we picked up our army car and were soon on our way to Berlin.

We had no idea how difficult our search was to be. In Berlin, so devastated as to be nearly unrecognisable, we

216

were re-directed to Leipzig, where the records of the Jews who were in the camps were supposedly kept, and found nothing. Then we took the train to Brandenburg where again the existing documentation proved to be useless. None of the Kleins listed – and there were many, of course – were the ones that I was seeking. And as all I knew about Ruth's mother was her first name, my only chance of tracking her down was in finding Lotte.

"We are running out of time," I said on the third fruitless day, "I think we should go back to where the Kleins lived, and see if there are any neighbours who know what happened. Not all Germans were Nazis."

The house where Kurt and his parents lived was still standing. The doors and windows were boarded up. It was empty as were most of the houses in the street. Many of them had suffered bomb damage, but there were still signs of life in some of them. I heard a baby cry, and felt a surge of relief when I saw a young woman come out with the child in her arms. I crossed the silent street and approached her.

She backed away from me, covering the infant's head protectively. I summoned up my pathetic German, enough to make her understand that I was looking for the Kleins.

"Ja," she nodded her understanding. She looked hard at me, then she smiled. "*Sie arbeitete mit Kurt? Daisy?*"

This was our first stroke of luck. Bless her, she remembered me working here with Kurt. I nodded frantically, asking, "*Kurt? Kurt ist hier?*"

Then her face clouded. She shook her head. "*Sie nahmen ihn,*" she said. They took him.

My heart sank. "Frau Klein?" I asked.

She shook her head again and added something I did not understand. But I caught the names 'Hannah' and 'Lotte' and I saw her eyes fill with tears before she fled back indoors, and I knew there was no point in looking further. James put his arms round my shoulders and we walked back to the car. We drove in back in silence.

"We must check the names of the camp survivors with the Red Cross," said James.

"Yes." I knew he was trying to comfort me, but there was a hole in my heart where once there had been hope.

As we passed through the city, I thought of Hannah clutching Helga, her rag doll, Lotte rescuing and nurturing my Ruth while waiting for the husband who never returned. I remembered Mrs Klein's kindness to me, and Kurt's father patiently teaching Hannah because she was not allowed to attend any school. And most of all I remembered Kurt, my friend and colleague, who had guided me round this country which he loved, which eventually murdered him. And I wept.

The trials of the Nazi war criminals began today in Nuremberg. I was allowed into the court room as one of the official photographers. I used my camera extensively as the men (for today they are all men) filed in. My overwhelming thought was that they looked so ordinary. These monsters, for among the accused are Goering, Hess and Ribbentrop, looked so unbelievably nondescript. Their faces are, of course, instantly recognisable, plastered as they are in newspapers all over the world.

But I photograph them, and I watch them, and what I see is a group of apparently unremarkable, nervous, grey men. It is hard to believe these are the people who have presided over so much terror and ruin and death in

218

Europe for so long. I focus my camera on Ribbentrop, who I had snapped many times when he was living in London, before the war, as the German Ambassador.

Almost by accident, I was one of the few photographers who managed to snap Ribbentrop making the fascist salute to our monarch. King George looked as startled as you would expect, and I caught the moment when he nearly lost his balance as Ribbentrop's arm flew upwards. I was pleased with the picture, but it was not published and never appeared in the magazine. It may have been deliberately suppressed, but who knows? I was supposed to be doing a feature on the London Parks for the magazine at the time, so I guess it was simply that no-one thought it important. And it was probably too political for the National Photographic. Hindsight is, as they say, twenty-twenty vision.

The court is called to order, and Justice Jackson, the chief American prosecutor, rises to his feet. The trials have begun. The atmosphere in the court is electric. There has never been anything like this before, of course. The Allies have come together and established the procedures, so that both military personnel and civilians can be brought to justice for the unspeakable war crimes that have been committed. It is said that Mr Churchill would rather have simply executed the high ranking Nazis without delay, but was persuaded by the Americans that justice should be seen to be done.

James reckons there is a very fine line between the points of view. "They are going to be executed anyway, aren't they? Perhaps it would have saved a lot of time and money and agony simply to have lined them up and shot them."

I could see what he meant, but perhaps that would have made us as bad as them. I wasn't sure. But as we sat there, day after day, listening to the testimony of the survivors, it came to seem important that their voices should be heard. I do not believe anyone could have anticipated the sheer horror of the tales these people told. Witnesses who were still frail and wraith-like, in some cases hanging on to life just long enough to give their testimony.

This first trial is of the major war criminals. Most of the Nazi accused seemed to be pleading that the laws drawn up by the Allies were not in place when they had committed their crimes. I felt quite sorry for the people who were defending them, because it seemed to me that the undeniable murders and tortures committed were indefensible.

When I said this to James, he replied, "But that is precisely what I meant. The whole thing is a charade."

Charade or not, it was the most awful, the most gruelling, the most absolutely terrible series of stories that I have ever heard. By the end of the first three weeks, I was sick and unable to eat, and subject to a sort of palsy, fits of shaking that I could not control. I felt so guilty, because I was all too aware that if I felt like this merely sitting and listening to the survivors, I could not begin to imagine how they had borne their sufferings.

James and I decided that my presence in court all and every day was unnecessary as I was restricted as to the amount of pictures I was allowed to take there anyway. It was with a combination of shame and relief that I agreed to limit my pictorial records, and from then on I concentrated my efforts mainly on photographing the witnesses as they entered and exited the courts. By some strange and unexpected alchemy, these pictures starkly illustrated the positive power that giving their evidence had on these brave souls.

This first part of the trials is expected to go on for a year, but we were going home for Christmas, and were not due back until the end of January. I had promised Dominic that I would finally visit his family after Christmas. However, I wrote and told him how ill I was feeling and that I would like to spend longer recovering at home on the farm than I had previously anticipated. Dear Dominic came straight back to me, saying that I was to take all the time I needed, and he understood how dreadful it must be, and he wanted me to be back to my 'adorable, lively self' when I met his parents. I was delighted to learn he viewed me through such rose-coloured specs and it cheered me no end.

We flew back into London the week before Christmas and went straight to see Colonel Black. He is very pleased with us both and told us that we were doing 'splendid work'. Unusually high praise from him. I was quite worried that he might follow the remark with orders to go back immediately, but, in fact, he seemed quite concerned about my health. I was ordered to 'go home and rest', an order that I shall obey with gratitude.

It was arranged that James and I would go to Mother and Arthur for two days, and then I shall go on to the farm, where they will join us on Boxing Day.

I am longing to see Ruth again, but Mother has made such a fuss of us both that I find I relax into an unusually soporific state that first evening, dozing by the fire in a room lit only by the candles on the tree. I think James may have warned them not to ask about the Trials, or perhaps they are just being very sensitive, as they ask nothing. The resulting relief of being able to banish it all from my mind is huge. I even sleep dreamlessly that night, which has not happened for weeks.

"You are looking better already," says Mother, the following day.

"I feel it. And I have you and Arthur to thank for spoiling me like this."

She had appeared in my bedroom with a tray loaded with tea and toast, and, miracle of miracles, some marmalade. Heaven only knows where she acquired that, I haven't seen any since before the war.

Mother sits on the end of the bed. "I sometimes find it difficult to express my feelings, Daisy." She smiles. "I can only say it with marmalade."

We laugh together, and I know that it is probably the most intimate and loving moment we have ever shared.

I definitely am feeling restored by the time I get to the farm. It is a bright, crisp December day, and I am stupidly disappointed when I arrive that only Patsy is in, busy as always with some washing on the boiler in the scullery and something smelling very good indeed cooking on the range. I creep into the kitchen and surprise her, and am rewarded with a huge hug.

"Goodness, Daisy, you've lost weight. It's quite flattering but you don't want to end up looking like Wallis, do you?" She is laughing and cutting a large slice of home-made cake as she speaks, which she plonks in front of me. "Get your coat off, and eat that!" she orders.

So I obey on both counts, but not before pointing out that skinny Wallis snared a king. Our King, in fact.

"Well, we've done alright with his brother, haven't we? And, come to think of it, you've not done so badly yourself. How is Dominic?"

I explained that I was going to meet his parents before going back to Germany. "But how is everyone here? How are Georgie and Ruth and the boys?"

"Everyone is fine. I would have let you know if there were any problems. You will be amazed at Georgie. He is so much more himself again. He is helping Alfie on the farm, not heavy physical work yet, obviously, but he has taken over the ordering and balancing the books – all the stuff that Alfie hates, really."

"And Ruth?"

"Ruth is lovely. Very bright. Very happy. She will be going to school next term. Daisy, did you manage to find any of her family?"

I shook my head. "No. I could not find any trace of the Klein family, and all I knew about Ruth was that her mother's name was Myrna. We could not find anyone with that name, of about the right age, from the district she came from. To be honest, it was like looking for a needle in a haystack. I have nightmares worrying that the poor girl is somewhere, alive, looking for her child. But ..."

Patsy touched my arm. "You have done all you could. Perhaps it might be possible when things have settled down more to search again. But, you know, we have to remember how traumatic that might be for Ruth. To be wrenched from the only life she knows and the people she loves."

I did indeed think about that constantly, and not only in the context of Ruth's German mother. I did, after all, have some relevant personal experience. Soon after this

223

conversation, the children came rushing in, having been helping Daddy gather the hens' eggs. I realised that Alfie had become 'Daddy' to Ruth as well as Bobby and Tom. Which was natural, I supposed. She rushed past me to show Patsy the egg that Daddy had given her for her tea.

"PatsyMum – look! To cook for my tea! With sojers?"

Patsy took the egg from her carefully, along with those from the boys, and assured them all that they could have 'soldiers' with their boiled eggs at tea time.

"But you haven't said hello to Mummy Daisy," she gently reminded Ruth.

The boys turned and chorused, "Hello, Aunty Daisy," and then turned back to the business of removing their wellingtons. Ruth galloped over and planted a kiss on my cheek, and then with a "Hello, Mummy Daisy," she danced off after the boys, who have rushed upstairs to pursue some mysterious game.

My arms were already half out-stretched for a cuddle and I quickly withdrew them, feeling foolish and, well, a bit rejected.

Patsy was watching and she came to sit beside me. "Daisy, I know it is a bit hard, but when she sees more of you it will be different. All of us here, we are the people she knows. For better or worse, we are her family. With the best will in the world, you are an occasional visitor in her life."

"And I am off again soon."

"You have a choice. You could tell the people that you work for that you wish to resign now the war is over. And, looking at you, you could even plead ill-health. I hear about these Trials on the wireless. And I know how edited, or censored, what we hear is. You do not need to be part of that nightmare, Daisy. You could walk away."

I know she is right. I could indeed walk away, take Ruth, and marry Dominic and settle into peaceful domesticity. Why don't I do just that?

I am interrupted by a familiar voice. "Where is she? I saw the car outside."

And in strides my Georgie, looking a million times better than two months ago. I fling myself at him in a bear hug, which he laughingly returns.

"Well, now there's a welcome," he says, disentangling me from round his neck and holding my hands together before raising them to his lips. "Oh, my God, Daisy, it is so good to have you back."

And we fall together on the sofa, as always our mutual delight in each other's company totally unabated by our time apart..

"I missed you so much, having to leave again when I have only just got you back." I say, acknowledging the truth of this even as I say the words, "I think we must be soul-mates." I add, and I am only half-joking.

"Indeed we are," says my brother, with his arm affectionately round my shoulders.

"Indeed you are," says Patsy, watching us from across the room with an expression I cannot quite interpret.

Christmas was everything Christmas should be. The evening before, the children were helping to decorate the sitting room with the paper chains they had been making for days from discarded newspapers. Alfie and Georgie hauled in a tree and we hung it with pine cones and ribbons and some very sparkly stars that Uncle Bert had brought out every Christmas for years.

225

On the day, the house rang with children's laughter from about five o'clock in the morning, but we grownups forgave them and joined in the tradition of stocking emptying with gusto. Patsy had managed to conjure up an orange for the toe of each stocking, and she had hoarded sugar and made sweet mice and sugared almonds and a toffee apple for each stocking. Her *piece de resistance* was a fat barley sugar stick that poked out of the top of the stockings and which they were allowed to start licking straight away.

Ruth's attempts to make poor Pickles wear a paper hat that morning were finally halted when he ate the hat, much to everyone's amusement Then, breakfast over, we all walked down to the village church. The small congregation surpassed itself with the carol singing, as did the vicar's wife on the organ. The children go to the Sunday school so it was a chance for them to give their friends the cards they had made from cutting down old exercise books and using the covers. There was much shouting and hugging and kissing and considerable good will to and from everyone.

We had a huge Christmas dinner, which I had insisted on preparing and cooking (with Georgie's considerable help!), and it turned out to be surprisingly good, given my infamous ineptness in the kitchen. Patsy had to be almost forcibly made to sit and rest by Alfie, but I had persuaded her that, for once, she must let me spoil her. I finally collapsed on the sofa with Georgie when we had finished clearing up and let all the special magic of a family Christmas engulf me.

The King's Christmas broadcast was in the afternoon, so we gathered up the children and filled our glasses with homemade wine for the toast and sat round the wireless to listen. A lot of what he had to say was about 'the family of the Commonwealth', but he also stressed that his vision of peace, which he talked about last year, had become a reality at last. And that we had paid a terrible price, but that it was a price worth paying.

I couldn't resist thinking, glancing at Georgie, my soldier brother, that a choice would have been nice, but I knew he was right. When they played the National Anthem at the end, we all stood up and raised our glasses 'to the King'.

And Uncle Bert muttered, "Worth ten of his traitor brother."

Amen to that, I thought, remembering the Duke strutting around Berlin before the war. Nasty little man.

Following the broadcast the children erupted with excitement again, as now there were even more presents to be handed out. We had made Christmas easy for ourselves this year by banning gifts for grownups in view of the austerity drive.

Mother had sent over some of the books that I had owned as a child and Ruth fell on these with cries of delight. I had bought her a doll, made of the new plastic stuff, which boasted several sets of clothes, and, for the boys, board games – Snakes and Ladders, and Ludo. Georgie gave them each an intricately carved, quite stunning, wooden box which he had made himself, filled with playing cards. There was Snap for Ruth, Happy Families for Tom, and proper ones for Bobby, along with a crib board.

And, finally, the crowning moment. Uncle Bert and Alfie had made a wooden tractor for the boys, who were stunned into rapt silence for all of ten seconds when he produced it from its hiding place in the shed, and a doll's pram for Ruth. So, of course, it was outdoor clothes on again, and off they went to play with those in the garden, giving us a blissful few minutes of peace. But not before I had followed them round and taken some photographs, of course.

I nodded off to sleep in front of the fire, and woke to the strains of *Silent Night* on the wireless. I could hear the others moving around in the kitchen, except for Georgie who was beside me. I sat there without moving, listening, mulling over Patsy's question from the day before. She was right. I could resign, come home, marry Dominic, adopt Ruth. Get my life back. So why didn't I?

I thought of the horror of Nuremberg, I thought of Emma, I thought of Myrna, Ruth's mother. And I knew in my heart that if I walked away now it would be wrong. I needed to follow this through, however hard that might seem. It was as if fate had taken me back to Nuremberg deliberately.

"What are you thinking?" asked Georgie, and I realised that I still had my head on his shoulder.

I tell him. "Am I right?"

He sits, Georgie-like, thinking. "I am not sure there is any right or wrong answer, except what is in your heart. And you have already decided what that is. So you must do that. But, Daisy, come back safely."

I hold his gaze. "What about you? Now you are out of the army, what are you going to do next? Will you stay on the farm?"

"Yes and no. Uncle Bert is helping me to set up a workshop in one of the old barns. I am going to make furniture. I have always enjoyed making stuff as you know, and I have my gratuity to help get me going. I have invested in a warehouse full of imported wood in the docks which somehow survived the blitz. There is a demand for basic furniture now, because folks have lost so much in the war, and I believe people will want to buy beautiful things for their homes when the country is prosperous again. So I intend to make both. The basic and the beautiful. I already have a few commissions through some army friends."

"Georgie, I think that is a wonderful idea. How clever of you." I picked up one of the card boxes he had given the boys. "These are exquisite. May I photograph them?" I put one in his hand and snapped it, to give an idea of the size. Then I raised my camera and took one of him before he had a chance to duck.

"Are you trying to break the camera?" he laughed. "Put that thing away and come and sit back down with me."

So I did, and we sat companionably listening to the carols.

"Do you remember the concert Alfie and I did for you?"

"You read my mind. Of course I remember. That was one of the worst days of my life, you know."

"And mine, Daisy. And mine."

James drove Mother and Arthur over on Boxing Day, but did not stop. He is off to see his girlfriend, Jill, who lives in Canterbury. Mother and Arthur have already met her and say she is charming, so I shall probably have another sister soon. Talking of which, I asked Mother if she ever saw Aunty Hannah nowadays. I remembered she had refused to come to Mother's wedding.

"I think she has had a job forgiving me for being happy," said Mother. "But I see her very occasionally.

229

She was so unpleasant to Arthur on the one occasion they met; I have not asked her to the house again. I don't know what gets into her sometimes."

I think it may be jealousy. Mother is still extremely attractive, always 'the pretty one', I suspect. But Aunt Hannah's determined discontent with life in general is etched unbecomingly on her face. One can only hope that she derives some happiness from being so unhappy.

We had a comparatively quiet day, with the children showing off their new toys. Arthur went out with the boys and was spotted squatting on their tractor while the boys pushed him round with gales of mirth. Mother spent some time on her knees helping Ruth dress and undress her new doll. She had brought Ruth a jigsaw, and later in the day the two of them sat up at the table with heads bent together over it. I was both delighted and envious of the way Mother interacted with Ruth. She seemed to have a bond with her which eluded me.

Georgie saw me watching, and as so often, read my mind. "Perhaps you try too hard?" he commented gently.

Perhaps I did. But I did not know how to behave differently.

James came to pick up Mother and Arthur in the evening, bringing Jill with him. They had tea with us before all departing and I agree, Jill is very nice and exactly right for James. I shall enjoy getting to know her better.

The next day was my last at the farm before going to meet Dominic's family, and the weather had turned wet and nasty. The outdoor toys were out of bounds in the shed, and we played the various games the children had been given. Ruth proved to be a demon at Snap, and later astonished everyone by correcting Bobby's arithmetic as Georgie attempted to teach him the rudiments of Crib.

"We've got a bright one there," commented an amused Uncle Bert, and I was quite puffed up with pride.

Off to meet Dominic's family today. It was hard saying goodbye to everyone. I assured Ruth that I would be back in a couple of weeks, and went to give her a big cuddle, but she gave me a perfunctory kiss before getting back to her doll and her puzzle.

"Well, do you want her to be devastated? In floods of tears?" asked my pragmatic brother Georgie, who was taking me to the station.

"No, of course I don't. I would just like to think she cared a bit more."

"Hmmm," was his answer. He is annoyingly right, of course.

Unsurprisingly, there is no sign of any activity at the station. Timetables are a bit of a joke as far as the railways are concerned.

"Do you need to get back?" I ask. "I can sit in the station waiting room."

"No, Alfie is coping OK. But if we have to wait too long, it might be warmer in there."

We sat in unusual silence for a few minutes, both watching the horizon as if expecting to conjure up the train.

Then I asked the question that had been hovering on the edge of my mind all over Christmas. "Georgie. Do you think I am right to be marrying Dominic?"

He turned slowly to face me. "You really can't ask me that, Daisy. How can I possibly know what is going on in your head, or your heart, for that matter?"

I was startled at how cross with me he sounded. "Sorry. Didn't mean ... oh, Georgie it is just that you have always been there in my life. I felt as if my heart had been torn out when we thought you were gone forever. All through the war, there were so many times when I wanted to talk to you, to discuss things with you. You've always been the perfect big brother, constantly there to advise me."

"But you had to make up your own mind about a lot of things, Daisy. Without your 'big brother' advising you. And you must take that responsibility now. Do you love Dominic?"

The question came out abruptly, taking me by surprise. "I think so. Oh, Georgie, I don't know. I think I do, but how are you supposed to know?"

Georgie grabbed my hands and pulled me toward him. Our faces were very close. "Listen to me. There is something that I should ..."

At that moment the thunderous noise of the train erupted around us, blotting out all other sounds, as it came charging in to the station, engulfing the car and everything else in a white cloud.

"What were you ...?" I began to ask as the noise gradually subsided.

"Never mind." Georgie let go of my hands and pushed open the car door. Within moments my suitcase and I were out on to the platform and being bundled into a carriage.

The guard was already waving his flag, as I was the only passenger either coming or going. Over the clatter and roar of the train firing up again, I shouted out of the window, "What were you going to tell me?"

As the train began to draw out away, Georgie yelled, "Have a good time and be careful."

I screamed back again, "What were you going to say?"

But he was striding out of the station. At the exit he turned and waved, already receding into the distance.

Dominic's parents are very nice, just as he described them. I didn't realise that his father had served in the army, but as soon as we met I was reminded of Colonel Black. His erect posture, and his clipped way of speaking, shouted 'army service' and, as I soon found out he did indeed hold the same rank, which was a bit intimidating.

"Should I call you Colonel?" I asked, sounding bold but in reality just not wanting to get it wrong.

He and Dominic both roared with laughter as if I had made a very funny joke. "No, my dear. I think that might be a bit formal for my future daughter-in-law! Harry will do very nicely."

I knew immediately that I would never be able to call him by his Christian name, so I am plunged into that never-never land of not calling him anything. I was hoping Dominic might help me out but he didn't see that I was a bit flummoxed. Anyway, I am sure, in time, it will resolve itself. Perhaps when Ruth meets him he could become 'Granpa' to us all? I catch myself smiling at this.

I am more at ease with Dominic's mother, Deborah, who greeted me with a hug after she had wrenched off her gardening gloves.

"I cannot tell you how much we have been looking forward to meeting you, Daisy. Dominic has been a most determined bachelor. His father and his sisters have quite despaired of him."

She is a small, pretty woman with longish white hair which somehow makes her look very young, and within minutes she has insisted that I accompany her down the garden to see her latest project. The garden is huge, and although I have not been in the house yet, Dominic's description of it as biggish seems less than accurate. It also looks huge to me.

I have remembered that Dominic's mother is quite a well-known garden designer, but I am unprepared for the beauty of this garden. I am bowled over by the variety of colour and shapes everywhere, and also the way we keep coming across statues, and fountains, and dove cotes peering from totally unexpected places but looking absolutely right. She leads me through a tunnel of willow, bending delicately over us, to an arbour where a construction of some kind is obviously happening. We sit on a stone bench together, and I am glad I have my thick coat on and plunge my icy hands into the pockets.

"Oh, Daisy, I am sorry, I wanted to have you to myself for a while, but are you freezing?"

"I might be if we sit here for long, but not yet," I smile. "How do you get so much colour in the garden in December?"

"Well, it is mostly grasses and trees, but even in this country we have some plants that will bloom in December as long as they are sheltered. But this is what I wanted to show you." She points to the half-constructed building which I have assumed is a summer-house. "It will be a Japanese tea-house," she exclaims triumphantly, "and this, in front, will be where the lake will go for my Japanese garden."

"Goodness," I say weakly, overwhelmed by her enthusiasm and her sheer energy.

"It will be the focal point for your wedding reception. I plan to have it finished by then, and ... Daisy, dear, you look a bit stunned. You will want your reception here, won't you?"

I am torn between laughter and tears. How to tell this amazing woman I only met minutes ago that we haven't even thought about the wedding yet, let alone anything else. If I don't look out she will have me up the aisle next week, I think. Before I have time to wonder why that idea is so alien, she grabs my hand.

"Harry says I am like a blunderbuss, and he is right. Sorry, Daisy. I am going too fast for you. I will slow down, and we can get to know each other. But you see, I feel as if I have always known you."

My confusion must have shown in the look I gave her.

"My dear, we knew that Jacob adored you."

I froze. Mother would have a fit if she could hear this conversation. Deborah was still holding my hand, and I did not like to remove it. She was obviously completely unaware of my discomfort as she continued.

"I mean, we knew he thought the world of Susan, as well. We never met your mother, of course, but if things had been different Jacob would have married your mother like a shot.

In spite of my unease, because after all, this subject had been forbidden in our house all my life, my curiosity was piqued. "Why didn't he, then?" I ventured, thinking, 'Mother would kill me if she was here', but suddenly desperately wanting to know what Deborah was about to tell me.

"I thought you would know?"

I shook my head. "Mother has never even actually admitted that Sir, I mean Jacob, was my father."

"Oh, my dear. Well, then, let me elaborate. The reason was his wife, Violet. She was ten years older than him, and had been an invalid since shortly after they were married. But the thing you must understand is that Jacob, your father, grew up in the East End of London, the child of poor immigrants. He had a brilliant brain, and managed to get himself a job clerking in a much respected law firm. They quickly realised what they had in him, and sponsored his education. He got a first at Cambridge, you know."

I didn't, of course. I didn't know any of this, and now I was riveted and wanted to know everything. I waited.

"His rise to the top was dazzling. He quickly made a name for himself as a prosecutor, and became one the youngest chaps ever to take silk. And the first Jew in this country to do so. But Violet was able to give him the one thing he lacked. She came from a very old and very moneyed family, the Stanburies, and she fell for your father hook, line and sinker. Rumour had it that she courted him, not the other way round. But whatever the truth of that, they were married within the year and Jacob was suddenly sociably acceptable as well as everything else."

"Did he love her?"

"Who knows? They seemed to jog along happily enough. She went on living in the country and he travelled back there regularly, when not involved in a case. But then she became ill. They said it was consumption. I imagine we would call it tuberculosis nowadays. He was assiduous in making sure she was well looked after and comfortable. But about a year after her illness took hold, we heard rumours about him and this beautiful young actress."

"Actress?!"

"Didn't you know? Oh, Daisy, you have been kept in the dark. Susan was the toast of London. Beautiful, accomplished – Ivor Novello was supposed to be interested in using her in one of his plays. Then she disappeared from the public view. And from Jacob's life. Gone. Just like that. Jacob was distraught. It took him over four years to track her down, and then came the revelation that she had hidden herself away because she was having Jacob's baby. You, my dear. She erroneously thought that he would abandon you both. I don't know any details of where your mother was, or how she managed during that period, only that there was an ecstatic reunion between her and your father.

'We knew what was happening because Jacob confided in Harry, but he was desperate not to hurt Violet. And he told us that Susan understood that there could be no question of divorce. They found a house together and were both models of discretion. The really cruel part is that Violet died six months after Jacob, so he and your mother would have been able to finally marry."

I did not know how to respond to this avalanche of information and she was perceptive enough to realise that. "Come along, let's go back indoors and get warm. They must be wondering where we have got to. And mum's the word – we'll keep this conversation under the *chapeau*, I think?"

I nodded fervently. Deborah chattered happily as we walked back up to the house, but my mind was in a whirl. So many revelations to digest at once. I realised with slight amusement, that the only one that had truly shocked me was that Mother had once been an actress. But I also realised how well she had played the part of 'The Very Posh Lady' and I began to understand how much she had given up both for Jacob, and for me, her daughter. And that she must have felt great love for us both.

"So," asked Dominic, "what do you think? Do we pass muster?

I have been here for several days and today we drove into the nearby town, still bright with Christmas decorations in the shop windows. There were definitely more goods for sale in this part of the world, I reflected. Even though austerity was widespread, the affluent still maintained a considerable edge. I said as much to Dominic when we returned to the house.

"Is that so bad?" he asked teasingly.

I didn't know how to answer. One of my many Christmas presents from him was a box of chocolates! I had no idea you could still get such things, especially as sweets, along with just about everything else, were still on the ration. How difficult to explain to these delightful and caring people, that they were being protected from the everyday hardships of life by just being able to buy their way out.

My present to Georgie this year was a scarf which I had knitted from an old jumper that I had laboriously unpicked. His to me had been a carved wooden bangle. Dominic had given me a gorgeous gold necklace dotted with sapphires. Knowing that this was a family heirloom didn't make me feel any better about the hand knitted socks (from the remains of the same jumper!) that were my gift to him.

238

Struggling to answer truthfully, I said, "I can't really get to grips with all this affluence, Dominic. I had no idea you were so rich, and it has thrown me rather."

"I don't know that we actually are that rich ..."

"But, in a way, that's the point. You all take it for granted. I am sure your parents could point to sacrifices they have made during the war, but they have no idea how luxurious their life would seem to most people. Harry was telling me again today about how he bathed in five inches of bath water every night for the duration. I mentioned to him that the vast majority of people in this country, even those who have not been bombed out, still don't live in houses with bathrooms, and guess what he said?"

Dominic grinned, "I can't imagine. But why do I think you are going to say something like 'let them eat cake'?

"You are not far off. He said, 'but dear girl, how do they keep clean?'"

Dominic roared with laughter, but stopped when he saw my face. "Well, then. When you are Lady Flotenbury, you can help to install bathrooms for the poor."

I stared at him. "Dominic, I do love you, but I am really not at all sure that this is going to work out." I took off my ring and handed it to him.

"Daisy, don't be stupid." Something between shock and amusement was making his voice shake. "You can't refuse to marry me because some people don't have bathrooms. That's absurd."

"Please take the ring." I pushed it into his jacket pocket. "I really am sorry. It's not just the bathrooms, Dominic. Truly." I allowed myself a small smile. "I don't fit here. I never will. It is not just your wealth; it is the whole way of life. A whole attitude. I can't explain. I just know I can't marry you. I am not blaming anybody for that, it is just the way things are. I'm not right for you and you are not right for me. I think, somewhere, deep down, you know that, too. We are good friends. I'd like us to be able to keep it that way."

"I do love you. You know that."

"But not, I think, enough for a lifetime." I kissed him on the cheek. "I would have to go tomorrow, anyway, so I think I will slip away now. I can just catch the late afternoon connection. Will you explain to Deborah and Harry?" Both his parents were out, visiting friends.

"I don't understand myself, so how can I explain to them?"

"I think you might find that they are not too surprised." And, in spite of their generosity toward me, not altogether unhappy, I suspected.

I arrived back at the farm in the station taxi, very late that evening, having had the usual battle with late running trains. Only Alfie and Patsy were still up, going through the farm accounts.

"What are you doing back so soon?" asked Patsy, taking my small suitcase from me.

"It's a long story," I said through a loud yawn. "I'll fill you all in tomorrow when Georgie is here."

"He's away for a few days. Won't be back before you have to go to Germany. He said to tell you that he hoped all went well with the parents." Alfie looked at me quizzically.

I sat down with a thump, suddenly quite tearful. I had really wanted to discuss everything with Georgie. "Where is he?"

"He's gone up to London for a few days, to meet someone from an American firm. Apparently he sent them some of his drawings and they are interested to see more of his designs. It could be a big deal for him."

I squashed my selfish disappointment at his absence. "That's good."

Patsy had gone into the kitchen and was back with a pot of tea. She poured three cups for us, and then said, "Well?" and sat back expectantly.

"I broke off the engagement. No," I could see the question forming on her lips, "the parents were lovely. And nice to me. But right from the first moment, it didn't feel right. Not for me. I don't know how to explain. I took loads of photos and perhaps when they are developed it will be easier to explain. I am so fond of Dominic, but when I looked at his life, it sort of defined him, and I could see it would come to define me, and that was not what I wanted to be."

"You've lost me," said Alfie. "You mean you couldn't bear to be rich?"

"Strangely, in a stupid sort of way, you may be right. I was thinking, on the train this evening, about going back to Nuremberg next week, and how the Colonel said that Dominic was not the right person to send with me. And perhaps that is it. Dominic is protected, his family are protected, I would say from real life, but their life is as real as anyone else's, but different. They feel things, but somehow they are always one step removed, as if they are looking at a film or a play. Deborah talked to me about Mother and Sir, without any idea of the misery and the difficulties and the sheer awfulness of it all. It was just a story to her."

I stopped to draw breath, and to try and make my feelings clearer. "She knew I was due to go back to Nuremberg, but to her that was just a nuisance because it would delay the wedding. She knows that I am a photographer and actually asked whatever did they need me there for? Who ever needed to see photos of those poor wretches? Her words, not mine. She was not being disparaging – well, not deliberately, but she thinks that I should just take pretty pictures of flowers."

I paused again, thinking. "And, you see, however much he said otherwise, I knew that deep down, that is what Dominic thinks as well. There is a sort of brittleness about them. As if there is a wall between them and the rest of the world. 'Those poor wretches' are to be pitied, but from an emotional distance."

Patsy said, "To be honest, Daisy, I never did think it felt quite right, so though I am sorry, I am not sorry, if you see what I mean."

I did, of course, and wickedly, couldn't resist adding, not quite accurately, "And they wanted me to get married in a bloody Japanese tea house!"

It broke the atmosphere and we all began to laugh.

"So how long are you back for?" asked Alfie.

"A couple of days, if that's OK. Then I'll meet James at Mother's as we arranged and it is back to Germany with the pair of us. But I'd like a bit of time with Ruth first."

And, I thought somewhat grimly, how was I going to explain this to Mother?

"Here we go again," said James, as we climbed aboard the plane. "Just keep your head down, Daisy, and think beautiful thoughts. You will get used to this flying business."

"I doubt that. I am going to close my eyes and try to sleep."

"Best of luck," grinned my Squadron Leader stepbrother, still highly amused at my fear of flying.

He was off into the cabin to talk to the pilot, who was an old chum, so I snuggled into the rather uncomfortable seat, closed my eyes, and re-ran the events of the last few days. To my surprise, Mother had been comparatively philosophical on receipt of my news. Disappointed that I was not to be elevated to the aristocracy, but not devastated. I was mightily relieved.

I expressed my thankfulness to Arthur, who confided, *sotto voce*, and glancing over his shoulder to make sure the coast was clear, that as Dominic's family were related, however distantly, to Sir's wife Violet, he felt that Mother had harboured some reservations about the match. So that was the major hurdle cleared.

I was still dying to talk to Georgie, but that would have to wait. I had some leave due at Easter, and hoped he would be at home then. I had enjoyed my short time with Ruth, who had started at the village school earlier in the week, and I had been able to go and meet her teacher. Ruth introduced me with a flourish as Mummy Daisy, which did not seem to faze Miss Winton at all.

"I know all about how Ruth has two mummies," she assured me. "She is a very well-adjusted little girl, as I told Mrs March the other day."

Mrs March? It took me a moment to realise that she meant Patsy. Talk about *déjà vu*!

This is the hardest thing I have ever done. Sitting here day after day, listening to witness after witness describe almost indescribable evil. It is impossible to go back to the barracks and just switch off. Every evening is spent developing the photos that I have taken during the day, and wiring them back to England.

I am aware that I have developed a kind of fanaticism, compulsively snapping and snapping and then snapping some more, in case I miss something crucial, an image that might help future generations to ... to what? To believe this all happened? Surely that will never be in doubt. And yet, and yet, the sheer awfulness, the horror of these stories makes it necessary to underline the truth of them, in case in fifty, or a hundred, or two hundred years from now it is decided that they are too exaggerated to be true. If these trials do nothing else, surely they will etch these crimes forever in history, and make their repetition impossible.

Today Marie Claude Vaillant Couturier was in the witness box. One of my heroines from before the war, she was among the very first women to make a name for herself as a photographer and a journalist. They used to call her 'the lady of the Rollieflex' and I met her briefly when Emma and I went to see Edith Piaf that night in Paris. She spotted my camera and came over to say hallo and I was so in awe of her that I could not think of anything intelligent to say.

And here she is, much thinner, much older looking, but still recognisable. She was a member of the Resistance, and was captured and sent to Auschwitz. She tells the court, calmly but succinctly, of how couples were tricked into thinking they were going to work in labour camps as they processed to the gas chambers. She goes on to tell of the other prisoners, pretty young girls dressed in blue skirts and white blouses, who formed the orchestra that was forced to play cheerful tunes from The Merry Widow outside the gas chambers while their fellow countrymen were escorted to their death.

She tells of the young woman, only survivor of a family of nine, whose job was to undress the babies before they were sent to the gas chamber. She tells of the furnaces, stoked daily to cremate the dead, of the internees who were made to fetch the corpses and carry them to fires. She tells of the day when the *Gas Kommando* ran out of gas capsules and they threw live children into the fiery pit. And, as she tells, she places her hands over her ears and you know that she is still trying to shut out the screams.

The attorney, Dr Marx, tries to discredit her story. He suggests that as she is a journalist, and has told her story so well, she must have made it up. She tells him that of the convoy of two hundred and thirty people with whom she was captured, only forty nine are still alive.

Dr Marx decided to rest his case at this point and Marie-Claude is allowed to leave the box. Later, I ask one of the officials if I may speak with her, and he returns to say she will see me that evening.

She is staying in the town and I borrow a car and drive in. She looks exhausted, but is obviously pleased to see me. To my amazement, she remembers me.

"The little English girl with the camera! And you had a friend? How is your friend?"

But she sees my face, and touches my shoulder briefly before saying, "Ah. I am so sorry."

Thankfully, no questions as to how or when. But death has become a way of life to this woman. I know her young husband, also a resistance fighter, disappeared at the beginning of the war, and only God knows how many of her friends and family have been shot or massacred.

She pours us both a glass of wine. I tell her I still marvel at the ability of the French to conjure up a decent bottle of wine and this makes her laugh. I ask if I can photograph her, and feature the tattoo on her arm, the number that she was stamped with in the camp. I would not dare ask this in normal circumstances, but somehow being two professionals together makes it alright. She rolls back her sleeve, fluffs out her hair, smiles, and gives me the sort of once in a lifetime picture that photographers dream of. I stammer my thanks, but she laughs and makes me take the photo again 'to be on the safe side'.

"Besides, this might be the one that will make you famous, and immortalise me, and thereby help to defeat those bastards and their creed forever."

We raise our glasses to that and I leave. She is going back to Paris tomorrow and I know I shall never see her again. Today, the trial, and tonight, with me, was a kind of exorcism for her and I understood that instinctively. I fall asleep that night praying that she will find the peace she has earned so dearly. And that I will find a fraction of her strength to get me through the next few months.

This is like standing on the edge of hell. Day after day, they come. Witnesses to what is surely the most graphic execution of evil in the history of humanity. Story after story of unbelievable depravity. Cruelty beyond words. Beyond images, though I photograph with a furious determination. And still they sit, these twenty-two men accused of being the surviving 'top men' of the

Nazi regime, seemingly unmoved. Thank God Hitler, along with Himmler and Goebbels, committed suicide before the trials began. The thought of them sitting there, with a sneer on their faces, is unbearable.

Many of the witnesses are still physically weak, and will quite obviously always bear the scars, often all too literally, of what was done to them. But their spirits are the great shining beacon here, proof that there is decency and bravery in the world. Their courage, their stoicism, their grief, combine to demonstrate that there is still hope for humankind. This reassurance is badly needed as we reel into the third month of the trials.

But these people, from all walks of life and cultures, also validate the whole procedure that is taking place here. They do, I now realise, need to be heard. And we need to listen and remember.

Today we were told of how the Jewesses from Salonika, on being welcomed with smiles and music to the camp, were given picture postcards of a fictitious resort, Waldsee, printed with the message: 'We are doing well, we have work here, we are well treated, we await your arrival.' Having signed these, they were then immediately stripped of everything they owned, including the clothes on their backs, and marched to the gas chambers. The camp secretaries then posted the cards to their families, many of whom packed up their belongings and travelled to join them, delighted to hear of this idyllic refuge.

The horror does not abate. In fact it intensifies. James and I have both lost weight, because how can you keep an appetite amidst all this recollected brutality? Next week is Easter and we are flying home to England. I have never wanted anything so much in my life as I want to get back to the farm and recoup. Hear about normal things and hear the children's laughter. I want to believe in goodness again.

I did not even mind flying as much as usual, so desperate was I to get out of Nuremberg. It makes me ashamed to be so weak in the face of so many people's strengths. I have developed this stupid, irritable cough which I can't seem to shake off. But I will once I am back at the farm – home, sweet home!

Mother didn't want me to leave their house, which was actually quite touching. I had gone back with James, of course, and planned to stay a couple of nights with them but Mother was really concerned about me.

"Daisy, you are skin and bone and that hacking cough sounds dangerous to me. You must see Dr Wilson. I insist."

And before I had a chance to demur James had been sent to get the poor doctor and both he and I were hostages to Mother's worries. I had been persuaded to go and lie down, and the next thing I knew there was this stranger bending over me. I jumped off the bed and yelled loudly, by which idiocy I am now totally embarrassed. Mother rushed in and explained.

"My goodness, Daisy, you are so jumpy," she exclaimed.

Dr Wilson smiled at me. "Just back from Nuremberg, I hear? I think I might be a bit 'jumpy' after what you have been hearing." He turned to mother. "Mrs Carrington, why don't you make this young lady a warm milky drink – it will help to calm her nerves."

I expected Mother to argue, but I underestimated the influence of the country doctor – second only in status to

248

the country vicar, I remembered now. Mother trotted off meekly.

"Powerful woman, your Mother."

I nodded agreement.

"Worries about you. Tells everyone about your pictures. Very proud of you."

Astonishing what you learn about your nearest and dearest from other people. I was at a loss as to how to reply.

He listened to my chest and felt my pulse. He shook the thermometer before taking my temperature and then he stood over by the window and held it up to the light to read it. "Highish, but not terrible. I shall leave you some M&B tablets, take one in the morning and another at night. That will deal with the cough. Some good food, lots of rest, and get yourself out into our fine country air. But wrap up warm and don't overdo it."

"I need to get back to my other family, to my daughter and my brother, and I am sure Mother will object. Will you tell her that I am well enough to travel?"

He looked a bit worried. "Will you have far to go?"

"We live on a farm in East Kent."

"Sounds a perfect way to convalesce to me. Not too far away, either. But try to avoid the train until you have lost the cough. All that nasty steam, enough to make anyone chesty."

"I am sure James will drive me."

At that moment Mother entered with a cup of warm milk, as prescribed. "Where will James be driving you?"

Dr Wilson intervened and explained how good it would be for me to be on the farm. Then he turned to bid me goodbye, and out of sight of Mother, gave me a huge wink. "And, Lieutenant March, how soon are you due back in Germany?"

"We have six weeks over here before we have to go back."

"If you have any doubts about your health before you leave, please let your doctor know. Now, if the Squadron Leader will take me back to my surgery, I will get your tablets. Goodbye, my dear. And may God go with you."

Fortunately Mother went downstairs with him to find James, as the doctor's kindness and understanding had made me a bit weepy. I washed my face and went downstairs, to find Arthur unloading a wooden trug full of vegetables on to the kitchen table. He glanced up and tactfully ignored my slightly red eyes.

"Doing my bit for austerity," he grinned. "I've grown so many turnips and potatoes I am surprised we don't look like them. And wait until you taste my parsnips."

He gave a wonderfully lascivious grin and we both burst out laughing.

"What are you two laughing at?" asked Mother, just returning from seeing the doctor off.

"Just vegetables, my darling," he said, "just vegetables."

I do love my stepfather. And I am so glad that he wanted to marry Mother, not me.

And the day after tomorrow, I can go to the farm. To Ruth, and to Georgie. Home. At last.

It was afternoon before we arrived at the farm, and this time, just about everybody was there to greet us. Mother told me that she had written to tell them that I had not been well. Even before I had a chance to open the car door, Georgie was there, flinging it back, helping me out and engulfing me in his lovely, warm arms.

"Do you need me to carry you?" he asked anxiously.

"I most certainly do not!" But I let him keep his arm round me as we went up the path into the house. "Oh, Georgie, I have missed you so much."

"Possibly almost as much as I have missed you?" His eyes were dancing, and all the reserve between us that I had felt the last time I was home had melted.

I stopped and looked full into his face. For a brief moment, it was as if time stood still, there was just a slow revolving of the air around us, and then, without warning, a body catapulted out of nowhere, knocking me back out of Georgie's grasp.

"Hey there, be careful, you mind your Mummy Daisy, she's a bit too fragile for human cannon balls, young Ruth."

But I knelt down and put my arms around my daughter, and pressed my cheek against her chubby one. Georgie and Ruth. Home. At last. My cup runneth over.

James was already taking my case in and kissing Patsy and the boys and shaking Alfie's hand. But I stayed where I was for a few seconds longer, holding Ruth close, and smiling up at Georgie. Then he reached for my hand and pulled me to my feet, and we went into the house together.

Two weeks later I was feeling like myself again. The doctor's M&B pills had done their work and the cough had totally disappeared. I had begun to go for short walks, firstly just round the farm with Alfie and Uncle Bert, admiring everything from the burgeoning harvest, to the two cows kept for milking, one of which was, of course, called Daisy.

"Couldn't resist it," grinned Alfie when I remonstrated with him.

The children insisted on showing me their three pigs, which I loved, but I will never make a farmer as I could not bring myself to dwell on their eventual fate. Uncle Bert finds my reluctance to eat meat very funny, but forgives me because he says, in his rolling Kentish burr, "Well, you are certainly not a softy, so I suppose I must be tolerant of your London ideas."

I have tried to explain that my ideas seem even stranger to many Londoners, and that I think the closest companion of my childhood, my lovely spaniel Sooty, may have coloured my feelings about eating, or rather, not eating, animals.

Uncle Bert just fixes me with his twinkling eyes and replies, "Like I said. Very odd."

I don't know how old he is now, but he must be getting on a bit, though he never appears to be much older. Apart from letting Alfie do the heavy stuff, he is as active on the farm as ever. He always treats me as if I am a blood relation, as he does Ruth. I think as far as he is concerned, we are just as much his family as the others. I sometimes reflect that MumMarch would be so happy to know we are all together still.

Georgie is making the most brilliant furniture. Some of it is theoretically quite mundane, tables, chairs, dressers, but all of it is imbued with grace and a love and understanding of wood. He already has more private commissions than he can really cope with, as well as an offer to supply a shop in Piccadilly, so he is thinking of taking an apprentice.

He spends a lot of time working in the barn, and has provided me with a special armchair so I can sit comfortably watching him. He has just finished a beautiful walnut sideboard, and I am intrigued to see him carving something on the back of it.

"What are you doing?"

"Carving my trademark. It's on all my stuff."

"I had no idea. What is it?"

"Come and see. I've just finished this one." He sat back on his haunches and beckoned me over.

I crouched down beside him and gasped in surprise. I ran my fingers over the small and delicate piece of filigree etched into the wood, and felt the petals of the flower. I turned to him, and knew my eyes were glistening with tears of sheer delight.

I whispered, "Oh, Georgie ..."

"What else could it be but a daisy?"

And then we were in each other's arms, and Georgie was no longer my big brother but the man I suddenly knew I had loved all my life. I finally understood why I had not been able to marry Dominic. In those few blissful minutes I understood a lot of things, and they were all good.

"Marry me, Daisy. Before someone else comes along again."

"Yes. Yes, please. Oh, Georgie, I don't think there has ever been anyone but you, really."

"You made a good job of pretending then."

"Let me show you how sorry I am about that ..."

After some considerable time we pulled apart and went back to the house to tell the others our news. Patsy had just returned from fetching the children from school. She took one look at us and a broad smile lit up her face.

"Is it possible you to have something to tell us?"

It was and we did. Then I said, "You guessed, didn't you? You've known all the time."

She laughed and hugged me tightly. "I think everyone did but you, Daisy. We were beginning to get quite worried about the pair of you mooning around being all lovelorn."

We protested that we had not been, but Alfie and Uncle Bert came in and insisted that we had, so we gave up trying to convince them because who cared anyway? Even the children were hugging and kissing us without really knowing what was going on, and we eventually all collapsed over Uncle Bert's homemade wine, produced for every celebration. We had never uncovered the whereabouts of his secret, but seemingly unending, store. We gave the children some lemonade in wine glasses.

Uncle Bert raised his glass and said, "To Daisy and Georgie – look at the pair of them, glowing bright enough to light the room up!"

"So," said Patsy, "when will you do the deed?"

"When I get back from Germany?"

Georgie nodded. "Better to wait till that's over. No need to rush. We'll do it all properly. And we don't want to be apart before we've even had time to get fed up with each other, do we?"

I assured him, as he intended, that I would never get 'fed up' with him, and everyone made 'aah' noises, and Tom put his fingers down his throat and made the age-old sick noise that kids do at the first sign of sentimentality, and Patsy told him off. I looked at them all with love. And realised that I was really going to be part of this family at last.

I raised my glass. "To MumMarch."

"To Mum," said the boys and Patsy.

254

"To Mum," echoed Ruth, over her lemonade, looking wonderfully confused.

"You know," said Patsy, "we could have a Christmas wedding."

"I love the idea," I said slowly, "but we must go and speak to Mother and Arthur before we make any plans."

"Ah," said Georgie. "That should be interesting."

My thoughts precisely. But Mother, as so often, managed to surprise me. But, apparently, I had not surprised her.

"Oh, Daisy, I have seen this coming for a long time. I must confess to some disappointment that you are not to be a countess after all, but I have got used to that now. And I am happy for you. We are all happy for you."

In fact, Arthur and James were absolutely delighted and there was much masculine shaking of hands and patting on the back with Georgie. I don't know why men can't just give each other proper hugs.

Later, when the three of us were on our own, Mother asked us both if I had chosen a ring yet, and we shook our heads. We hadn't had time, and in any case, I hadn't really thought about it. Mother went upstairs and came down holding a ring box.

"Your father gave me this, and I was never able to wear it. It is such a relief to me that neither you nor I will ever have to explain anything to your husband, Daisy, as you have always known the truth about us, haven't you Georgie?"

I could see Georgie was slightly embarrassed but also pleased at Mother's confidence in him. He nodded. "It has never been important," he said simply.

"Not to you, but it has to others. If you will not be offended, I would dearly love Daisy to have this ring. Your father's ring."

She handed me the box, and, opening it, I saw it contained the most gorgeous sapphire and diamond ring. "I should be proud to wear it, Mother," I said.

She looked at Georgie. "You don't object?"

"How could I? I know how much it will mean to Daisy to wear her father's ring." He was right, of course. He knew me so well. My heart felt full to bursting as he slipped it on my finger himself.

Back at the farm, a letter from the Colonel. I was due back in two weeks and he wanted to brief me. James had already heard from him and mentioned us going up together, so I was expecting the summons. But it did not stop my heart sinking at the thought of going back to Germany.

Georgie and I had already talked about our need to stay near the farm when we were married, as Georgie was unlikely to find anywhere better than the barn to work in, and I could work anywhere. Georgie was going to see if he could find a house for us in the village while I was away.

"Ruth could stay at the school, then. And about Ruth – will you be happy for us to adopt her?"

"If that seems to be the best thing for her, of course."

It was not quite the rousing affirmation I had expected, but I put it to the back of my mind.

"I am going to have to leave so much to you," I wailed.

"Darling Daisy, you have an important job to do. Go and do it. I will be here when you get back. And the only

256

important thing is that we are going to be together. All the rest of this stuff is trivialities, and I refuse to allow either of us to be bogged down by them."

"Sorry. I am sublimating my fears about Nuremberg, aren't I?"

He put his arms round me. "Yes. And so would I be. You are brave, Daisy. And you need to be brave a bit longer. Carry on showing the world the truth of what happened. And I absolutely forbid you to get ill again."

I planned to resign my commission when I returned in October. So there was an end in sight. And then perhaps we could both manage to put the war behind us at last.

Colonel Black was his usual brusque self.

"Doing a grand job, the pair of you. Very impressive. Want you to carry on concentrating on the witnesses, Daisy, though obviously we need a record of the fascist monsters as well. We like the shots you have taken in the court. Not just the lawyers, but the faces of the onlookers. Very impressive. Might have some more work for you when this is over. That photograph you took of the French resistance woman, brilliant. Pretty woman. Dreadful tattoo. Clever of you to get that contrast. Yes, a lot of people are very impressed. Any questions? No? Off you go then, I'll see you both in October."

As James commented later, how would we dare pose any questions? It was like a royal audience. We meekly uttered our thanks for the compliments and slipped away.

"He gets more and more eccentric," muttered James.

"And intimidating," I replied.

Just a few more days, then back to Nuremberg. I must make every one of those days count.

I am trying to remove myself emotionally from what I am hearing. I do not believe I will be able to do my job here unless I can manage that. Georgie told me that erecting a kind of glass wall between himself and the camp when he was a prisoner helped him to get through it. I have been practising this, and he is right, it enables me to almost become someone else. It does not stop the nightmares, however.

Witness after witness, telling their stories. I have come to feel sorry for the lawyers defending these Nazi monsters, a thankless task, but I suppose justice has to be seen to be done. I notice they are nearly all German, perhaps they hope to redeem a little honour for their country. Who knows? Some of the witnesses for the defence are the accused themselves, such as Rudolf Hess. James says they are hoping for a more lenient sentence by doing this. I am not sure if that makes them less or more evil. But sometimes I am not sure of anything in this weird half-world we are living in here.

But today something extraordinary happened. I was in position, camera at the ready, for a new witness, and had just snapped the woman, another haunted face for my gallery of ghosts, when she gave her name. Myrna Huber. Now obviously Myrna is not an unusual German name, but as she introduced herself, I realised that the address she gave as her last before the camps was the *strasse* where Lotte and Hannah had lived. And she gave her age as twenty-six, which I thought lined up with the little information Lotte had about her. I was almost certain that, against all odds, I had finally found Ruth's mother.

Myrna appeared to be at least a decade older than her given age. She spoke in a whisper, as if afraid to be heard, in contrast to her obvious bravery in testifying.

Several times she was asked to speak up, but prompted to do so gently. The whole court held its breath each time; as if we knew that the least suggestion of wrong-doing might finally crush the fragile spirit of this woman. I waited for her to tell the court about her abandoned baby. My heart was breaking at the thought of parting with Ruth even while I knew I should be rejoicing. There would be no question as to the right thing to do.

Myrna described how she had escaped when her family and many of their neighbours were rounded up and abducted by the Nazis one evening on their way home from the synagogue. How she had hidden in a cellar below the building and eventually escaped. She told how she had managed to find the room in the same house as Lotte, where she thought she would be safe for a time. Then she related how the landlord of this room, who agreed to rent it to her when she gave him all the money in her possession, betrayed her to the Nazis. And this was where her real defiance showed through. She stood upright and spat out, 'I hope he received his thirty pieces of silver,' and a murmur of approval ran round the court, to be quickly quashed by the judge.

I was more and more confused. She went on to relate how she was sent to the camp, and, once there, how she was used in a series of horrendous medical experiments before being sterilised. But no mention of her baby, even after that. The defence counsel had little to say to her, apart from mentioning to the court that there had been experiments with genetics in America earlier in the century. However, even he seemed to understand the futility of that argument as an acceptable precedent for these inhuman deeds. Myrna Huber was finally thanked for her evidence and stood down from the witness box.

I decided I must speak to her. I left the court hurriedly and bumped into James. I realised immediately he had also put two and two together and that we were on the same errand.

"She is staying in the hostel. The Red Cross are caring for her. We must be careful not to upset her any more than she is already."

We crossed the road together, James leading the way. Myrna was with an older woman and together they entered the cafe next door to the hostel. We waited on the other side of the road until we saw through the window that they were seated.

Then James said, "Come on, then. You do the talking, Daisy, she might feel threatened by me."

We walked straight over to them, and I asked softly, "Fraulien Huber, may I speak with you, please?"

Myrna literally backed away from me, shrinking into her chair, and her companion said, with a strong German accent, "I think the Fraulein has had enough speaking for one day. Are you from the press?"

"No, indeed. I am Lieutenant March here to record the Trials and this is Squadron Leader Carrington. I am here as a friend of the Kleins. I wish to ask Fraulein Huber if she remembers Lotte and Hannah? I never knew their surname, but Lotte's maiden name was Klein? "

Myrna's English was better than my German, or perhaps she recognised the names, as her face lit up and she nodded and asked her friend something. I wished we had the automatic translation that was used in the courts.

Her companion, whose name was Silvia, asked Myrna's question, "Are they alive?"

I shrugged and raised my open palms to indicate that I did not know, but replied, "Would you show her this?"

'This' was the picture of Ruth I always carried with me. A six-year-old Ruth now but I was looking for a way in to the conversation we needed to have. Myrna looked at the picture and smiled.

"*Ya*?" as she handed it back to me.

"Will you please tell her that is a recent photograph of baby Ruth?"

Silvia looked puzzled but conveyed the message.

Myrna's hand flew to her mouth and her eyes filled with tears. She threw her arms round my neck in an unexpectedly strong embrace, and all the while a torrent of words issued from her. Finally, she sat back, still tearful, but smiling, and still holding my hand.

Silvia spoke, "She says the baby belonged to a young couple who lived next door to her family. On the night they were all rounded up as they left the synagogue, the mother, Esther, had the pram with her and she pushed it behind some bushes. Her husband made some distraction to enable her to do that, and he was beaten to death on the spot for it. When Myrna came up from the cellar, she went to see if the baby had survived the Nazis. Relieved to find her unharmed, she pushed the pram through the streets, asking the few people she met if they knew of anywhere she could board. Everyone assumed the baby, Ruth, was hers and she let them, as there was no time to explain and who else would take her, anyway? Finally, a man who was on his way to the station gave her the address of his room, as he said he was leaving Berlin before it was too late."

"But why did she let Lotte think it was her baby?"

We waited while the question was posed and the answer given.

Silvia continued, "Myrna says she had no-one. Everyone had gone. She thought she and the baby could comfort each other. She would not be alone if she had Ruth. She was going to tell Lotte the truth when she got to know her better but, of course, that never happened. She had thought that Ruth must be long dead, as her mother, Esther was. Myrna was sent to the same camp as Esther and was with her when she died. She says Esther always believed her daughter would survive, that God was watching over her when she hid her child. Myrna is asking, 'where is Ruth now?'"

Myrna's joy on being told that Ruth was safely in England, was quite beyond adequate description, she was crying and laughing at the same time, and rapidly relaying the story to others in the cafe. A large gentleman came and shook my hand, and several women came over and kissed me. I was trying to explain that it was Myrna who had saved Ruth's life, and then Lotte, but no-one cared about that.

Silvia said, "Myrna has just told me that she believes there might be hope for the world, after all."

And then I cried, too. I told Myrna about the farm, and the boys, and the village school, and how loved Ruth was. And I gave her our address in case she ever came to England, though nobody thought that very likely. But we parted with real affection and gratitude on both sides. And, at last, I knew Ruth's story.

I wrote to Georgie that evening, and to Patsy, and to Mother, and finally to Dominic, who had been so instrumental in getting Ruth back to England. I also told him of my engagement to Georgie, and apologised once more for ending our relationship so abruptly. Then I went to bed and slept a dreamless sleep for once.

The verdicts were handed down today, October 1st. The first twelve of the Nazi monsters to be tried were found guilty. Eleven will hang. Martin Bormann was tried in his absence, believed to be dead. I hope he is. I was afraid that I would be asked to photograph the executions, but I am being spared that, thank God. Some other poor soul has been given that task. So, finally, I can go home. I should be excited, and I know I will be eventually, but for now, I am just drained. Emptied. Tired beyond words. And I feel dirty, as if the evil has rubbed off on me. Like Lady Macbeth, 'will all the perfumes of Arabia ...? Shakespeare knew a thing or two about the effects of evil, even at one stage removed. But I am being allowed to go home. To England. My green and pleasant land. Home. At last.

I have decided that, by some dubious magic, the journey home from Nuremberg actually takes twice as long as it does to go out there. James tells me that he is inclined to agree. But eventually we arrive at Mother and Arthur's house. It has never become home for me and, for the first time, it occurs to me that I am going to have a proper home of my own soon. Georgie has found a small cottage a few miles away from the farm on the outskirts of the village. We are both familiar with it, as Mrs Jempson, the previous tenant, was a friend of MumMarch's for many years, and used to hold the Sunday School there while the adults were in church.

When he wrote to tell me about it, Georgie reminded me that Mrs Jempson used to make rock cakes for us children, and one of my milk teeth had once got embedded in one and was instantly extracted. I remembered it well, of course, and also MumMarch giving me a silver three-penny piece for it that night. We are both delighted to be living somewhere that has links back to our shared childhood. And it is convenient in that Georgie will be able to drop Ruth off to school on his way to work in his barn.

"All sounds perfect," comments Arthur, when I tell him and Mother the details.

"So you are still set on adopting Ruth?" asks Mother.

"Yes, of course. Why wouldn't we be?"

"I just thought that perhaps ..." Mother fades off. "I am sure you will do whatever is right for everyone, Daisy."

"Let's get you two travellers off to bed. You both look exhausted." That was Arthur, sensing, quite rightly, that Mother's question had cast a slight shadow over the homecoming. And he was right on both counts.

The next morning Georgie was due to fetch me. I had slept more soundly than for months, and was up with the dawn, making plans for not only the day, but the rest of my life. How wonderful, I thought lazily.

I had received a letter from the Colonel, accepting my resignation, but asking me to go and see him the following week. Apparently he had someone who wanted to meet me.

"How mysterious," said Georgie, after we had hugged and kissed and laughed and done all the silly things that lovers who have been apart do. "But first, off to the farm, where everyone is so excited about you being back. It's been a long time."

It had indeed. Nearly five months. But it felt even longer. We hugged Mother and Arthur goodbye, and waved James off to visit his Jill.

"Wedding bells for you soon, as well?" I asked him.

"Might be. If I ever pluck up enough courage to ask her," he laughed.

We were barely in sight of the farm before we were greeted by a small convoy consisting of Ruth, Tom, Bobby and Pickles. We slowed the car so they could run along beside us, whooping and cheering. And barking, in Pickles' case, of course. The children were waving small Union Jacks which Georgie explained they had used for the VE celebrations in the village, and decided to keep to welcome me home. And when we arrived at the farmhouse, I saw that it was hung with a banner proclaiming 'Welcome Home' and decorated with daisies. I was quite aching with laughter by the time we climbed out of the car to be greeted by the grown-ups.

"What a welcome," I exclaimed between hugs. "I cannot begin to tell you how wonderful it feels to be back with you all."

"Aye to that," said Georgie. "And here's hoping you won't be gallivanting off again. Ever."

"I object to the word, but share the sentiment," I replied, smiling at him.

"I was only joking, Daisy. I know it was a desperately inappropriate word, I am just trying to help both of us forget where you have been."

"I know that." And I squeezed his hand to show that I did.

Patsy had laid out lunch, and we all squashed round the kitchen table and chattered, catching up and barely pausing for breath. Ruth was the biggest surprise, jumping down to fetch one of her books and returning with my old copy of *The Secret Garden*.

"Who is your favourite person in it?" I asked.

"Dickon," replied my precocious daughter without hesitation.

"What do you like best about Dickon?"

She thought for a moment, fingering the book cover gently. Then, "He is a good boy," she said.

"That is an excellent thing for one so young to recognise, Ruth," said Uncle Bert affectionately.

I was staggered that her reading was so far ahead of my expectations, until Alfie reminded me that I had read some of that same book to them when I was only five.

"Mum used to say that it was a good job we had some brains in the family," he grinned.

"But I am showing Ruth how to milk the cows, said Tom, "and Bobby is teaching her about looking after the sheep and the hens."

"And I could not manage without either of you," said Alfie proudly.

"And PatsyMum is teaching us all to cook, but I am the best at it," added Ruth, making us all laugh.

Later that day Georgie and I drove over to see Mrs Jempson's cottage, appropriately called Sunday School Cottage. I didn't remember it having any name at all, and Georgie said it had sort of happened over the years until eventually one of the villagers made the stone name plate and put it over the door for her. I thought that was a charming story.

The cottage is delightful. Even though it has been empty for some time, it didn't have that abandoned feeling some places acquire. We walked round the small rooms, planning what we should get and where it would go. Georgie has already made us a dresser and table and chairs, and Mother says I can have the bed from my old room for Ruth. So we do not have a huge amount of things to find. Mrs Jempson's ancient bed, with its brass bed head, was still in place. A large double with a sparkling clean white cover on it.

"I don't remember a Mr Jempson, do you?"

"No, but I guess there must have been once," Georgie replied.

"It looks quite inviting, doesn't it? Do you think perhaps we should try it out?"

And we did, dear reader, we did.

On the way home, Georgie drove and I read him the Colonel's letter.

"I've got to go up to Piccadilly next week to sign this contract, and talk to them about what precisely they want. Why don't we go up together?"

I agreed that was a brilliant idea and we stopped at the Post Office to phone the Colonel, who said he would meet us both for tea at the Ritz and bring his mysterious friend with him.

"And bring some photos with you."

"What sort?"

"People ones. War ones. Any ones. Oh, I don't know, choose some of the ones you are most proud of."

"Tea at the Ritz. How could I possibly not agree?" I asked, getting back into the car.

"Not possibly," said Georgie, nuzzling my hair before we started back to the farm. "You know, Lieutenant, you should try and subdue this glow. It is a trifle too unbecoming for an unmarried lady."

"Have you seen your own face?" I retorted. "Smug doesn't begin to describe it."

I do love being in love.

Over the next couple of days, I developed and catalogued the photos that had not been wired straight through to the War Office. The photo that I was proudest of, as she had predicted, was the one of Marie-Claude, but the Colonel had already seen that. But there were others. I had snapped the people in the cafe, caught the spontaneous outburst of joy when they realised a child that none of them had known existed minutes before, was safe and happy. I had also recorded for posterity Myrna's delight at the news.

Then there were the other witnesses. Faces triumphing over the horror of their experiences, determined to be heard, to see justice done. Long shots of the bent and maimed, the young made old before their time.

And the evacuees. Small ones, big ones, children growing up in my lens as I revisited them. The camera catching burgeoning relationships, often achieved with reluctance, harassed foster parents, worried actual parents. Children holding animals – cats, dogs, rabbits, the occasional reptile or budgerigar. They were almost always smiling in those. Was there a message there? I thought so. I grouped them together.

And my friends. Lotte, Hannah, Karl. Mr and Mrs Klein. Still unaccounted for. Still hope they may yet be survivors. But not much hope left any more. But at least my photos will prove they were once there. They were real. They were loved.

The Hitler Youth movement, the Windsors shaking hands with the Fuerher. And the beaches. Dunkirk, the dead and the dying. Emma. My friend Emma. Dead on the beach but my photo making her death count. Paris on the brink of war, the Little Sparrow singing her heart out. Click, click, click. It was all there.

"How are you doing?" asked Georgie, when I eventually emerged from my dark cupboard the night before we were to go to London.

"OK," I said. "I think I am doing OK."

We went to see the owner of the Piccadilly shop first. Georgie had been a bit apprehensive but he needn't have been. They had some of his smaller pieces and my photos of the larger ones. They offered him everything he was going to ask for and then threw some more in besides. Such as being responsible for transporting the larger pieces up to London, and giving him a down payment toward the cost of materials. They were so enthusiastic that he signed on the dotted line then and there and we came out walking on air.

"I shall have to practice saying, 'my famous husband, the furniture designer', I teased.

"Quite right. Teach you a bit of respect."

Then off to the Ritz. Though we did walk in Green Park for a while first as we were earlier than we had expected and this is an especially lovely autumn. Or perhaps we are viewing it through rose-coloured specs? Just possibly, I suppose.

Mr Morgan, the chap who is so anxious to meet me, is one of those people you wouldn't notice in a crowd. Quite small of stature, a soft voice, it is only when you notice the warmth in his brown eyes behind the horn-rimmed glasses that you start to feel a certain impact emanating from him. Certainly the Colonel is more deferential than I have ever seen him before.

They are already there when we arrive and the waitress shows us to our table. I had tea at the Ritz several times with Dominic and the very phrase seems to have delightful connotations, though I am not sure why. I introduce Georgie to the Colonel and they shake hands, the Colonel actually saying how pleased he is to meet my fiancé, 'one of the heroic soldiers who made the Dunkirk evacuation possible'. I feel myself grinning with pride. Colonel Black is obviously more verbose when not in his office.

Then he introduces us to Mr Morgan who, without appearing to at all, takes over the conversation. It appears that Mr Edward Morgan has been given some authority, and a certain amount of leeway, by the newly founded (and funded) Arts Council, to follow his particular passion. And this takes the form of endeavouring to expand people's perception of what constitutes art.

"You see," he explains, his glasses slipping down his nose as he speaks, "many folk, even those who should know better, think art is classical music, ballet, formal theatre and painting. They refuse to take seriously any modern form of music, especially anything popular, any new forms of dance or theatre, and, most especially in our case, they deny that films and photography are valid art forms. And it is up to people like us, you with your photography, and also perhaps, you, Sir, with your exquisite furniture, to change the snobbish perceptions of the hidebound." He sits back and smiles at us.

We were both a trifle stunned by his intensity and it took me a moment for my ingrained prejudices to shift and to see exactly what he meant. And absolutely agree. I remembered years ago, at school, Miss Turner looking at my photographs and saying, 'art is in the eye of the

270

beholder, Daisy.' I had never realised until now how widely that phrase could be applied.

"How can I help?" I asked.

"I want to hold an exhibition of your work. I want it to be gritty. I want to see the story of your war in pictures, Daisy. The Colonel showed me your picture of Marie-Claude, who was an acquaintance of mine from before the war. I thought that one single photograph of yours said more about France and the resistance than several thousand words. And the picture of your colleague who was killed at Dunkirk, that must be included. And whatever else you think should be there."

"That's quite a tall order. I love the idea and I am immensely flattered. But I do have two reservations."

"Name them."

"Well, firstly much of my work is not in my own portfolio; it belongs to the War Office."

The Colonel interrupted. "You will be allowed total access, Daisy. Use whatever you want. Edward has the agreement of the War Office for this. In fact, I would go so far as to say that one or two of them are even quite enthusiastic." He smiled at Mr Morgan, and I realised that the two men knew each other well. I was slightly surprised at this as it seemed an unlikely bonding, and this must have shown on my face.

"Edward is my nephew, Daisy. My sister's boy. And what was your second reservation?"

I hesitated. This was more difficult to explain. I was aware of three pairs of eyes on me while I struggled for words.

"My photographs are specifically my vision. I was never ordered, or given more than the loosest of guidelines, as to what to photograph. They are what I

271

saw. As you said, my war. They will be a very narrow view of an enormous canvas. Will anyone find them relevant? Find my work even remotely significant? I mean, some of it is very personal. My pictures of the Klein family, for instance. They will mean nothing to anyone but me."

"Yes, they will, Daisy. If, for instance, you were to group the family together with a few words saying who, and where, they are now."

"But I don't know ..." I stopped abruptly, light dawning. "Oh, yes, I see. Yes. The personal turned into the iconic. Yes, I see. I think Karl would have approved of that." I thought for a minute. "What should we call it? Where will we hold it, and when?"

Edward visibly relaxed as he leant across the table, nearly knocking a tier of cakes over. Our waitress reappeared and discreetly placed them on a nearby trolley, smiling all the time. After all, this was the Ritz, I reflected.

"We shall call it *One Woman's War*, we hope to hold it in the crypt of St Paul's Cathedral, and we are looking at next April for a grand opening." He sat back in his seat and regarded me. "Well, Daisy March, are you up for it?"

I glanced at Georgie, who was squeezing my hand under the table. "Oh, yes, Edward," I said, "I think I am most definitely up for it. And thank you. I am thrilled and honoured. I will try not to let you down."

"I am quite sure you will not," said Colonel Black.

And Edward rose to shake my hand. "I will be in touch in a few days."

We left them and walked slowly back to the station. I was thinking hard.

"Georgie."

"Yes, Daisy?"

"Would you mind if we had a very quiet wedding? Just the family. In the village church. No fuss, no white dress, no huge reception. Because I think it is going to take every minute of the next six months to get this off the ground, and I don't want to wait until it is over before we get married."

He stopped walking and turned my face up to his. "Daisy, I think that would be wonderful I am so proud of you. I could see how much those two valued you today, almost as much as I do! This is incredibly important, a chance in a lifetime And as far as you and me are concerned, *being* married is the important thing. The wedding will be great however we do it. And you are absolutely right. No fuss, no frills, just us and the family in the church. That suits me fine. Oh, and I suppose we had better have the Vicar along, too!"

I knew I was marrying the perfect man.

Mother is insisting on making me a white dress anyway. She says she has got hold of some parachute silk, which has greatly intrigued Tom and Bobby who seem to think that I will take off like a balloon from the church. I have asked if she could make it slightly shorter than a normal wedding dress so perhaps I might be able to wear it again, with a few alterations. It has occurred to me that I will need something posh for the opening of the exhibition, and Mother says she will keep that in mind.

We are going to be married on Boxing Day. The vicar is happy to do it and, as his wife pointed out, the church will still be decked with holly and mistletoe. And it seems that the bell-ringers are determined to come out and ring for us, so, of course, we have had to say how

273

welcome their families will be. As they most certainly are, but, as Georgie says, "There goes our quiet wedding!"

However, we are touched and delighted, of course. There is much scurrying around and whispering in corners at the farm, and several visits by Mother and Arthur, so I gather our reception is growing by the hour as well. But I am keeping my head well down and pretending not to notice. The exhibition is going to mean many trips to London for me, so Georgie and I have decided to concentrate on getting our cottage habitable before plunging into our other commitments in the New Year. I can't believe it is nearly 1947.

Dominic is sorting out the legalities of Ruth's adoption, and I have been trying to explain to her that she will be living with Georgie and me in Sunday School Cottage. We have taken them all over to see it, and Alfie and Uncle Bert have been helping Georgie sort out the plumbing which was almost non-existent. With the help of one of the farm workers, they have built a lean-to accessed by a door from the kitchen, so we shall not only have running water in the house, but the lavatory will be part of the cottage instead of down the bottom of the garden where it was previously.

Patsy has suggested that we collect Ruth from school on her first day back after the holidays, and take her back to the cottage with us then. She thinks that will make the transition easier and I think it is a good idea. It will give us a few days 'honeymoon' alone in our new home, and make it less of an upheaval for Ruth. I have spoken to her so often about how she is now going to live with me, her 'other' mummy, that I think she will settle down with us very quickly.

Christmas is upon us in a flash this year. Patsy and I made an excursion into town for presents for the children but there is very little to be had. However, we have done a fair amount of swapping with some of the villagers. We have acquired various things, including an army of wooden soldiers, for our children, and have quietly passed on, in return, some of their abandoned toys. This was Patsy's idea, greeted with considerable relief all round, she really is such a clever, practical girl. And Mother and I have both been knitting like mad, which brought back some memories of our early days together. We have knitted not only hats and socks and gloves and sweaters from unravelled old jumpers, but made a new set of clothes for Ruth's doll.

"I had no idea that I was marrying such a talented woman," says Georgie.

"You haven't seen anything yet," I reply with a grin.

Patsy is wisely keeping me well away from the kitchen; my talents do not extend that far. In fact, increasingly everything I touch seems to either refuse to cook or burns to a cinder. I think living with me might be more of a shock than Georgie is yet prepared for, though I have warned him.

Christmas is such a happy affair this year. No bombs, nobody disappearing abroad, even if it is a bit make do and mend, who cares? Certainly not us. It is a wonderful day, and we are joined by Mother and Arthur, who are staying over for our wedding tomorrow. James is with Jill's family today, which is probably just as well or we would be packed in like sardines. But he is coming back tomorrow for our big day.

Came the great day, Georgie and his best man, Alfie, are banished down to the vicarage, where Mrs Vicar is making sure they are smart and ready. Ruth is dancing around wearing a long blue dress that Patsy has made from an old frock of hers, and is indeed my 'bwidesmaid'. She looks gorgeous.

"Good enough to eat," says Uncle Bert, giving her a hug, and causing her to rush off and straighten the tiara of paper flowers that Patsy has pinned to her hair. Tom and Bobby are wearing long grey trousers (very grown up and a first for them both) and white shirts with blue ties under splendid Fair Isle pullovers. And Patsy has put her hair up and is wearing the coat and skirt she was married in, though she tells me that today she has two vests underneath.

I am too exhilarated to be cold. Mother has made me a beautiful ankle-length dress and has conjured up a green velvet cloak to go over it. I have a vague feeling that it may once have been my bedspread! The family go on ahead, and Arthur and I follow in his car.

I feel as if I am floating down the aisle on my step-father's arm, only conscious of Georgie, standing in front of the altar, turning to smile at me. The service passes in a blur. It seems only seconds until I am coming back down on Georgie's arm. No longer brother and sister, but husband and wife! The bells ring out proclaiming our happiness.

Almost the entire village is squashed into the farmhouse, talking, laughing and congratulating us, and it is dark before we leave for Sunday School Cottage. We don't have electric light here yet, so we carefully light the oil lamps and then stand looking at each other.

"I love you, Georgie March."

"And I you, Daisy March."
A perfect day.

January, 1947

A week after the wedding, the winter term begins and the school goes back. Patsy drops the children off and then comes over with a case full of Ruth's things.

"I'll take them up to her room, shall I?" she asks, as I am sorting through piles and piles of photographs and negatives at the kitchen table.

"Oh, thank you. I'll just get this lot straight and then I will be with you."

A few minutes later I go up to find her clutching Ruth's favourite doll.

"I'd better put her on the bed. She likes to sleep with her." I had heard Patsy blowing her nose, and now she sounded a bit choked.

"Oh, Patsy, are you getting a cold?"

"No, no. I am fine. I've put her things in the chest of drawers. And her books are on the window sill. Must be getting back. Alfie and Uncle Bert will be wanting their dinner." She turned, and placed the doll on the bed. "Daisy, I ..."

I waited for her to finish. It was not like Patsy to be so unsure of herself, I thought.

"You have to say goodnight to Peggy," (she motioned to the doll) "as well as to Ruth. OK?"

"Yes, right, of course. Patsy, don't worry, she'll be fine."

"Yes. Yes, of course she will. Sorry, Daisy, must rush."

And Patsy was down the stairs and rattling away in Uncle Bert's ancient Ford. It was so out of character for her not to stop and chat, especially as Arthur had just sent me all the photographs he had taken of the wedding on

278

Boxing Day. In spite of her denials, I hoped she was not going down with a cold.

At three o'clock I drove to the school. I knew I would have to wait a while before the children came out but I was so excited I wanted to be there. Georgie was going to come home from the barn early so we could both have tea with Ruth. Eventually, the afternoon bell went and she trotted out of school, swinging her shoe-bag and talking to another little girl. When she saw me she came running up.

"Mummy Daisy! Am going home with you today."

I bent to give her a hug, but she was jumping into the car before I could envelop her. "Is Uncle Georgie going to be there?"

I assured her that he was. Patsy had told me that the after school 'tea' was usually a slice of toast and a cup of milk and it would be better to stick with that. The children usually had a hot meal about six o'clock, so Georgie and I were organising our routine around Ruth's existing one.

As soon as we were home, Ruth extracted from her coat pocket some drawings which she had done at school that day. She told me they were of Pickles and of Bobby, and I went to pin them up on the cupboard.

"No, Mummy Daisy," she said, reaching to take them back and putting them in her pocket again, "want to take them home."

I opened my mouth to explain, but then thought better of it. Of course she would want to show everyone her pictures. Ten minutes later, we were crouching by the fire toasting bread on a long fork, and chatting about Ruth's day, when I heard Georgie's rattle-trap of a car coming up the road.

"That's Uncle Georgie," said Ruth, also recognising the car's guttural gasps, and she scrambled up to go and greet him.

"Hallo there, Ruthie. What have you been up to today?" He was swinging her in the air and making her giggle as she hung on to his hair.

"Put down!" she ordered, and when he obeyed, she ran across and fetched the drawings to show him.

"My goodness, an artist in the family. Well done, Ruth. Shall we pin them up somewhere?"

She snatched them back. "No, take home."

He looked across at me and I shrugged. We watched as she replaced them carefully in her coat pocket. Then we all settled down to the business of making toast. Later, Georgie played *Snap* with Ruth while I managed to produce a meal of corned beef with a jacket potato each and a poached egg. Flushed with triumph, I called them to the table.

"Mummy Daisy is getting to be a good cook, isn't she?" Georgie asked Ruth, grinning widely at me. In truth, until today he had cooked more of our meals than me, and was much better at it. My lack of culinary skills was becoming legendary. Uncle Bert said that when it came to cooking, I lacked concentration. And sadly, I knew that was fair comment, my mind was always running on other things. But I did want to be a good mother to Ruth, and being a good cook seemed to be an expected part of that job. So I was trying hard.

Daisy, having eaten every last scrap, nodded enthusiastically. She put her head on one side and looked at me questioningly. I was not sure what she was asking me.

Georgie said, "Yes, Ruth, you may get down."

And she jumped off her chair and ran across the kitchen. Standing on tiptoe, she reached for her coat, and before we could stop her, had pulled it on.

"Thank you for having me. Go home now?" she asked.

My heart sank. "Ruth, darling, this is your home now. You are going to live with Mummy Daisy and Uncle Georgie, don't you remember all our talks about it? Come upstairs with me and I will show you your bedroom. It is all ready for you. Peggy is waiting on your bed." I held out my hand to her.

Still clutching her coat tightly round her, she took my hand and we went up our narrow wooden staircase. She stood in the doorway just looking at the room. "Is very nice." She crossed to the bed, and picked up Peggy, holding her close. "Peggy and Ruth go home now," she said firmly.

Georgie came in behind and went and sat on the bed. "I think you should try out this bed," he said, bouncing up and down. He reached out his arms to her and she went in to them. Pulling her on to his lap, he jiggled her up and down until she began to laugh.

Getting into the spirit of it, I joined them bouncing on the bed until we were all laughing. Then Ruth's laughter grew less until it finally died, when she jumped down and looked at us solemnly, holding her doll close to her chest with both hands.

"Ruth not go home? PatsyMum not love Ruth anymore? Ruth has tried to be a good girl. Didn't mean to tease Pickles." Her little voice cracked and, although she was obviously trying not to cry, a tear escaped and ran down her face. "Pickles will miss Ruth." The tears came even though she put her hands over her eyes to stop them.

I was frozen with shock and with shame. And was catapulted back thirty years to another little girl trying not to cry as her world was shattered. I remembered MumMarch and her tears, and Patsy's sniffles – or her weeping, as I now realised – this morning. How could I have been so insensitive, so unfeeling? I had blindly gone ahead with my plans to adopt Ruth, ignoring what I might be doing to everyone else. Including Ruth.

I looked at Georgie. "I think we must take Ruth home. She is right. Pickles and her mummy will be missing her."

Without argument, he nodded, and picked up Ruth and her doll and took them downstairs. He knew all along, I thought, but he loved me so much he wanted it to work. In fact, they all did. That was why no-one had pointed out my pig-headed stupidity. They had put me before either Patsy or Ruth. I needed to put things right, and quickly.

I pulled my old carpet bag from the top of the wardrobe, brushed the cobwebs off it and packed Ruth's so recently unpacked possessions into it. Then I followed them down the stairs. Georgie had his coat on and the car keys in his hand.

"We'll take my car," I said. "Yours isn't really up to two journeys in one day."

He nodded, understanding that tonight, driving would be easier for me than sitting with Ruth. "Ruth and I have been agreeing that she will come and stay with us sometimes when she is bigger, and we will keep her bedroom all ready for her. Isn't that right, Ruth?"

She nodded, but it was obvious she was anxious to leave. We piled into my car, and Georgie and Ruth sang nursery rhymes all the way back to the farm. And it was me who was trying not to cry now. They heard our car as we drew alongside the cottage and Patsy flew out, her face worried, closely followed by Pickles and the boys.

"Daisy? Is Ruth alright? Oh ..."

Ruth catapulted from Georgie's arms into Patsy's. Patsy looked over her head at Georgie and I, caught in the car headlights, and I smiled at her.

"I think we have a tired little girl here. Give me a kiss, Ruth, and I'll put the kettle on while PatsyMum puts you to bed."

Still clutching her doll, Ruth came and kissed us both. As they went upstairs we could hear her talking about her precious drawings and asking Patsy if she could pin them up in the morning. I suddenly felt incredibly tired.

We went into the kitchen, where Alfie and Uncle Bert were sitting by the range. I filled the large kettle and we sat in silence as it murmured away on the hob. Tom and Bobby stood in the doorway watching us, unusually silent.

Then Tom said, "Is Ruth going to live with us after all?"

I nodded.

"Good," he said, and he and Bobby, who seemed to communicate without words, went up to their room and could be heard thumping around.

Patsy reappeared and before she had a chance to speak, I said, "Patsy, I have been so selfish. I went ahead without any thought of your feelings, or how hard it would be on Ruth to uproot her."

She tried to interrupt, but I wouldn't let her. "Of all the people in the world, I should have known better. Can you forgive me?"

283

"Oh, Daisy, there is nothing to forgive. You've been doing stuff all over the place, good stuff, so if you lost track a bit of what it was like here, well then, that's life. And it all might have worked out. But, oh," and her eyes filled with tears that she made no attempt to hide, "we are so glad to have her back, aren't we?"

Her two men made grunts of assent, obviously also feeling an emotion they felt it would be less than manly to indulge in. Patsy and I were in each other's arms and both crying now.

Alfie said, "Daisy, will it be OK if we change the adoption thing? If Patsy and I adopt her? Because, well, to be honest, she feels as much our daughter as the boys are our sons."

"I will call Dominic tomorrow and arrange it," I promised.

On the way home, Georgie, driving this time, said, "I am proud of you, Daisy."

Startled, I thought he was joking for a moment. "For making such a mess of everything? For nearly doing to Ruth what was done to me?"

"No, idiot." He reached across and touched my hand affectionately. "For knowing when to say 'sorry' and for not making everyone even more miserable by letting it drag on."

I supposed that accolade might help my battered ego eventually. My sense of loss is not as enormous as I might have expected. I know that I will always be Mummy Daisy to Ruth, and that is a massive consolation. I will be in her life and she in mine. Perhaps, after all, I am not cut out for motherhood.

The next day I immersed myself in the photographs. It is all very well for Mr Morgan to say 'we want a picture of your war' but where to start is the problem? Where did 'my war' begin? Every surface in our small sitting room is covered in photographs, including the floor and I cannot seem to get a perspective on them. After a couple of weeks of this, Georgie has a brainwave.

"Come and work in the barn, with me. I can put sheets of hardwood over some trestles and you can really spread things out and see what you have got."

My husband is a genius. It certainly makes a huge difference, and it is good to have someone else to discuss things with, as well. I think we are both delighted with this idea. I have all my photos from my first exhibition, indeed my only exhibition, in a big folder marked 'Medway Towns'. What a long time ago that seems, now. 1935 was another world. Those pictures could have been taken a hundred years in the past instead of not much more than a decade before.

In the past few days, getting our cottage straight and making it our own, I hung up that very first photograph of Emma's. The one of me and Sooty in the chair in Mother's garden. Taken in 1919. The one that began it all. Reflecting on that as I repeatedly sorted through my pictures, I suddenly realised that was where my exhibition should begin. With that photograph. In peacetime. In the aftermath of another war.

I found the ones I had taken of a happy, laughing Emma in Paris. The shadow of the next war was already hanging over us, which became more and more obvious as I began to lay out the photos in chronological order. And there was that picture. Emma, laying lifeless on the beach at Dunkirk. And, as I looked at them, I knew absolutely what my theme was going to be, the glue that would hold all my experiences together.

It was going to be women. The brave women I had met and had the privilege of knowing and photographing during this horrendous and tumultuous decade. Not only Emma, and Marie-Claude and Myrna, but the women who put their lives on hold to take in evacuees in this country, and the women in uniform who I had photographed endlessly on the streets of Britain. And the women with hair scrunched into turbans because they were just coming home from the factories, the tired faces of women striving to 'do their bit'.

And the other side of the coin. The privileged women I had met in the London hotels, who barely knew there was a war on. The Duchess of Windsor who seemed to think Hitler was her pathway to the monarchy.

The faces of women who had lost everything. Husbands, sons, fathers. I had shared their anguish when we thought Georgie was dead. Tormented, distressed women everywhere, triumphant, laughing women, bemused and confused women. I had photographed them all. Some pictures more personal than others, some that I had known and mourned. Some that I celebrated.

And the women witnesses at Nuremberg. Women who had survived the camps. Who would never, could never, be the same again. I had heard their stories. Many people had not. And the women on trial, who had guarded and goaded them. I had their faces, as well.

The Colonel was right. My photographs had a story to tell, and I was going to make sure that it was shouted from the rooftops.

The exhibition opened last week, and I was frankly terrified. All the months of work, of hanging and then re-hanging because something didn't look quite right and finally this was it. Judgement day. Georgie and I have been staying in Hampstead with Edward Morgan these last few days, so as to be on the spot if anything went wrong. It seemed to me that just about everything was going wrong when we began to mount the photos but Edward was invariably sure that I was panicking over things that merely required minor adjustments, and he was almost always right.

He has been a tower of strength and, between them, he and Georgie have boosted my confidence no end. I would never have managed this on my own. I decided to do the annotation myself, as so much of it was very personal, and he helped me to keep it all short and to the point.

We had the private view the night before the official opening, when all the big names and the press came. A lot of the more well-known were people whose photos figured in the exhibition, so I was anxious for their approval. I need not have worried. One of the first people in was the wonderful pianist Myra Hess, who had held many lunchtime concerts in the National Gallery during the war, which was where I had photographed her. She had come over from New York especially to see the exhibition! And I had a congratulatory telegram from Edith Piaf, who had been wrongly, but fortunately only briefly, dubbed a collaborator after the war. We pinned that up on a special board, along with ones from both President Truman and General de Gaulle.

Both Mr Churchill and Mr Atlee came to the private view, and Mr Churchill shook my hand and said, "Well done, Mrs March, well done," in that distinctive voice of his. But one of the best moments came when Marie-Claude appeared. I had not been sure she would make it.

Her photo has attracted a lot of attention. As we stood side by side, smiling for the press cameras, she whispered to me with a smile, "There, just as I said. Now you are famous, Daisy."

Barbara Castle, the new Labour MP, who is making quite a name for herself already, came and congratulated me and said how nice it was to see women being lauded by another woman. "All too rare," she added. And to add to my list of famous people, there was Vera Lynn, who I actually thought Mother was going to curtsey to!

Our family were there, of course, Alfie and Uncle Bert both looking rather uncomfortable in their 'wedding' suits, but beaming with pride. After much discussion, we had decided that the children were too young to come, and Patsy had left them with the Vicar's wife.

And we had invited two of the chaps, with their wives, who were captured with Georgie, fighting the rearguard action at Dunkirk. They stood quietly together examining the pictures of Emma, and I saw that one of the wives was crying. I noticed Mr Churchill go up to speak to them. Afterwards, Georgie told me that he had remarked to them that it might have all ended very differently without their sacrifice. I think that meant a lot to all of them. It was nothing but the truth, of course.

One of the most personal pictures for me was Ruth's face, blown up large with her name, Ruth March, under it. My picture of Myrna, rejoicing on hearing that Ruth was alive, was beside it. And underneath were photographs of Lotte, and of Hannah holding her rag doll. And underneath those, my lovely friend Kurt, and his parents. Many people stood reading the pieces that I had written beside those pictures and I saw some of them cross themselves before moving on. Many people were in tears.

The section devoted to Nuremberg was viewed in silence, except for the occasional gasp, or sob. Overall, the tone of the evening was unique. So much to celebrate, but so much to mourn. I hope we have done justice to both. Edward said that I had no need to be at the exhibition every day, but as a lot of people are coming in and asking questions that only I can answer, I am spending a great deal of time in London.

I asked Georgie if he minded, and he said, "Daisy, this kind of thing was always part of who you are, and what I love about you. So I am not going to moan about it, am I?"

One Woman's War is due to end today, but I have been asked to take it to New York. I said 'no' first of all, as I did not want to leave Georgie, but now a film studio out there wants to talk to him about a project they have for a period film. Apparently, they want him to make some furniture. I asked why they couldn't just buy some antique stuff, and he said because the period is 23,000AD! I can tell how excited he quite rightly is. And the money they are offering him is enormous. So it looks as if we will go.

I was feeling a bit sad at the thought of clearing everything out of the Cathedral, when Edward came in. That in itself was not surprising, and my first thought was that he had come to cheer me up and cheer me on, so to speak. But there was something about him that brought me up short.

"Edward? Is anything wrong?"

289

"No. No, Daisy. But I have a lady I should like you to meet."

"Of course," I said, following him out of the crypt and into the passageway. A lady of about my age stood up, looking a trifle nervous, and held out her hand to me.

Edward said, "Daisy, this is Rosemary Jones."

"Hallo," I said, shaking her hand. "But we have met before. Surely you were here the other day?" I remembered seeing her standing in front of the photos of the Klein family.

Mrs Jones nodded. "I came back to be sure. May I call you Daisy?"

"Yes, of course. But sure of what?"

She glanced over at Edward, who went and beckoned someone in from one of the side rooms. A man, leading a girl who appeared to be in her early teens, came up to us. She was, rather incongruously, holding a doll. She was smiling at me.

"I thought you might not recognise me, Daisy."

Her voice was familiar. Accented. My jaw dropped. "You are ... are you ...?" I did not dare say her name in case I was wrong.

She held up the doll. "I thought you might remember Helga. She has not grown up like me."

"Oh, my God! Hannah! You are alive. Oh, my dear, I have thought of you so often ..."

And then I was hugging her for all I was worth until I broke down and sobbed my heart out.

Later, when we had all calmed down a fraction and Hannah's new father was showing her round the cathedral, Rosemary explained, "Hannah's mother put her on the train to come here. Mr Winton's kinder transport. It undoubtedly saved her life. I guess, that you, like us, have tried to track the family down?"

I nodded. "Nothing."

"No. The same with us. So we have formally adopted Hannah. She is the child we could not have, and she makes us very happy. We live in Wales, but I saw your photos of the Klein family in the paper and I thought I recognised the doll. Hannah's beloved Helga that she was clutching when we first saw her. And she had told us that she thought the lady her Uncle Kurt had brought to see them was called Daisy. We already knew that her mother's name was Lotte, so it all hung together. But I wanted to come and meet you, and also see the pictures for myself, before bringing her down to London."

"I cannot tell you how much it means to me to know that she is alive and well, and has such a happy life." At this point, to my shame, I broke down again.

Rosemary put her arms round me and passed me a handkerchief. "Here, it is one of life's mysteries why we women cry at good news, isn't it? But now you must stop, or I will start, and that would upset my daughter."

Gently reprimanded, I dried my tears.

Rosemary continued, "We shall take her back to Wales this evening. It is good for her to have met you, to have this link with her past, but I don't want her to remember too much. I am sure you will understand that."

"May I take a picture of her and add it into the ones of her family? It would be good for people to know that she survived. And that she thrives."

Rosemary smiled, "Of course. How could I refuse?"

"So," said Georgie, the following day, when I was back home. "Have you developed the photo so that I can see it?"

I beckoned him into my dark cupboard, where the print was hanging to dry. Mr and Mrs. Jones, with Hannah between them. All smiling. And another one of Hannah holding Helga up for the camera with a miniature Union Jack wedged into her hand.

"Hannah's idea. She wanted people to know that she is British, now."

"Those photos are the crowning touch. They'll love them in the States, I reckon."

"So do I," I replied.

And you know what? They did.

The End

The Ides of Daisy March

was inspired by the photograph which forms the cover of my book. The little girl in it is my mother, and the early part of Daisy's story was indeed hers. But I am a writer of fiction, so Daisy's story, set in what are possibly the most tumultuous three decades of the 20th century, quickly became all her own.

There is another character in my novel who is inspired by my own history. Like Georgie, my father was one of 40, 000 men who stayed behind at Dunkirk to hold the enemy back so that the boats could take our army to safety. Unlike Georgie, he was repatriated riddled with tuberculosis, for which there was then no cure. My mother was pregnant with me when he left to fight for our country. He died without ever being able to give me a cuddle.

All these years on, I am mystified that those men, many of them who made the ultimate sacrifice, have barely been recognised. It is a received truth that without their bravery, we would probably have lost the war. Where is their medal? Surely it is more than time to honour and thank them.

So this is the background to the fictional life of the fictional Daisy March. But like all invented characters, she has grown from truth. I hope you will love her as much as I do.

My other novels are:

Lillian's Story, One Woman's Journey

through the 20th Century,

The Sweetest Empire

Painting by Numbers

Finding Cordelia

A Part of Having

They are all available in paperback and on Amazon Kindle, and you can access them with one click from my web site:

www.sallypatriciagardner.co.uk

Made in the USA
Charleston, SC
02 January 2017